PART WOLF

Written By:

A.D. GALLO

Part Wolf

TABLE OF CONTENTS

PROLOGUE

Below the ridge, men in dark coats stand where the trees have been cut back. The clearing is too clean. Too deliberate. Fresh earth lies open beneath their polished boots, black and wet and turned over like something dug up against its will.

These men are in human form tonight. Suits, gloves, lanterns. Civility worn the way other men wear armor.

Lanterns burn along the temporary road. Workers move between them with lowered heads, hauling stone, iron, timber, all the beautiful bones of the academy that will rise here by spring.

Saint William Academy, the brass plaque will read. A noble name. A clean name.

A name parents will repeat in drawing rooms and board meetings and private clubs. A name that will make mothers straighten their daughters' collars and fathers write checks large enough to purchase silence. A name that will sound like opportunity to anyone standing far enough away.

But the wolves know better.

The wolves know what men build when they are afraid.

At the center of the clearing stands the Bradford patriarch. His great-grandson, born a century from now, will carry his name: Rowan.

He is the reason the others keep their voices low.

The Bradfords have led this pack since before the pack remembered why it had chosen a leader at all. Generations of Bradford men have stood exactly like this one, hands folded, jaw set, waiting for a room to recognize them. They have buried sons and burned letters and chosen between mercy and continuity more times than the ledger will ever account for. They have also, every generation, produced one wolf large enough to be feared by the others. This one is that wolf.

He does not need to raise his hand for quiet.

Quiet comes to him.

Beside him stands Ashcroft.

The Ashcrofts are the line of pen and protocol. Where Bradford speaks and the room obeys, Ashcroft writes and the world is bound. Two generations ago an Ashcroft drafted the pack's first written constitution, replacing the old oral law with something that could be cited, amended, and weaponized. Tonight's Ashcroft is the grandson of that man, and he has been preparing for this clearing since he could read. He carries the ledger as if it weighs more than him.

To Ashcroft's left, Forrester.

The Forresters have always watched. In the old days they tracked threats at the edges of pack territory. When the territory became a town, then a county, then an industrial corridor running up the coast, the Forresters adapted. They watch differently now. They have informants in newspaper offices and clerks in courthouses and one cousin who attends every charity benefit in Boston with a glass of bourbon and excellent hearing. The current Forrester is forty-two and has not slept a full night in nineteen years. He believes vigilance is love.

Harlan stands further down the table, the only one with a coat that fits him properly.

The Harlans are the voice the pack uses when it wants the world to listen. They marry well, host beautifully, and travel with letters of introduction signed by the right names in the right cities. They have spent a century turning the Bradford name and the Bradford town into something the human world can comprehend without panicking: an old family in a quiet New England town, with land and money and patience and discreet manners. Harlans do not lie. They simply describe truths in a language the listener already wants to believe.

And at the end of the line, the only human in the clearing: Montgomery.

The Montgomery man knows it.

So do they.

He is a financier in his middle fifties, the head of a banking house that has been pleasant to three generations of Bradfords without ever asking what their land was for. Six months ago he was told. He has not slept well since, but he has also not declined. The deal is unrepeatable: access to a power structure his world will never know exists, in exchange for laundering its public face. The Harlans will tell him which doors to knock on. He will open them.

He is not at this table because they trust him.

He is at this table because the academy cannot exist without a human signature.

Bradford rules. Ashcroft writes. Forrester watches. Harlan softens. Montgomery signs.

Old names.

Older hunger.

A bargain none of them will name out loud.

They stand in a half circle around a table brought out from the compound and set directly on the raw ground. On it lies a ledger bound in black leather, a map of the property, and a narrow wooden box containing the first bands.

Silver for the ordinary.

Red for the loyal.

Black for the blood that inherits.

Beneath the three rows, there is a fourth groove in the velvet. Empty. Deliberate. Not oversight. Removal.

Montgomery looks at it too long. "There was another?" he asks.

No one answers him.

Ashcroft closes the box.

"The bands are not a courtesy," Ashcroft says, opening the ledger without looking up. "They are a record. Anything outside them does not exist."

His voice is mild. Educated. The kind of voice that can make violence sound administrative.

"Then we make certain nothing exists outside them," Bradford says.

A worker stumbles at the edge of the clearing. The iron gatepost he is hauling slips an inch in his grip. Forrester turns his head. Just his head. The man does not lift his eyes again for the rest of the night.

Harlan watches the exchange and does not smile. He does not need to.

"The school will sort what the forest used to," he says. "Cleaner. Quieter."

A beat.

"And the lines we do not want carried," Harlan continues, "we do not carry."

He says it without inflection, a sentence Harlans have spent a hundred years refining: one meaning in this clearing, another in any drawing room in Boston.

Bradford allows it. Ashcroft writes it down.

Montgomery looks at the words on the page and looks away.

The Ashcroft man dips his pen and writes the institutional language across the top of the ledger's first page. The words come from somewhere older than him, somewhere none of them will ever name out loud. He says them once, as if testing the weight, before committing them to paper.

"*Fera sub regula.*"

Bradford repeats it without looking up. "The wild under rule."

Harlan's mouth lifts. "Outsiders will hear discipline."

"And insiders will hear order," Forrester says.

Ashcroft writes the motto into the ledger. Three words on the page. Then, beside it, he sketches the crest: a shield divided in black and red, crossed by a gold cinch, a small gold cross set in the upper field. The kind of insignia that will be engraved on uniforms and stitched onto blazers and pressed in wax onto envelopes carrying tuition offers. The kind of insignia parents will frame.

The motto and the crest together. Two halves of the same lock.

A motto that sounds, to the right ears, like a school philosophy.

To the wrong ears, like a sentence already passed.

The pen lifts. The ink shines black in the lantern light.

Then the eyes appear. One pair. Then another. Then dozens.

Low between trunks. High along the ridge. Watching from the black spaces where lantern light refuses to go.

The wolves have come to witness the founding.

Or the warning.

Bradford lifts his chin.

He does not flinch. He does not look away. He has done this before, in smaller rooms, with smaller animals, and he has learned that the trick is to be the thing in the clearing that does not move.

"*Fera sub regula*," he says, this time to the dark.

No answer comes.

Only the eyes.

Some catch the lantern light and burn gold. Some hold silver back, deeper in the cover. Some stay black until they choose to be seen.

Montgomery makes a small sound at the back of his throat. He has been told about them. He has been shown documents, photographs, even one pelt laid across a desk in a private library on the night the partnership was offered to him. None of that prepared him for the eyes. None of that prepared him for the way the air changes when forty or fifty of them are watching at once.

He does not run.

A Montgomery does not run.

But his hand finds the edge of the table, and Harlan's hand finds his wrist, and Harlan's grip is the kind a man uses when he has done this before with men weaker than himself.

"Steady," Harlan murmurs. "They are not here for you."

Bradford turns back to the table without lowering his chin. "Continue."

The Ashcroft man dips his pen again.

Forrester is still watching the woods.

Inside the clearing, the first black band is lifted from the box and held up to the lantern light.

It gleams like a promise.

It gleams like a threat.

"This will be the order," Bradford says. "From this night forward."

The workers resume. Stone rises. Iron sinks into earth.

A gate begins to take shape where no gate belongs.

CHAPTER I

SAINT WILLIAM ACADEMY

Winter

I stopped waiting for my mother to come back when I was nine. I started wanting her again the morning the scholarship email arrived.

California sunshine never meant much to me. It was traffic, sirens, heat rising off the pavement.

So when an exclusive academy somehow finds and summons me, I leave.

Now gray clouds hide the sky as I stare out the Greyhound window, New England unfolding ahead of me on the way to my new life.

Running has always been the cleanest thing about me. Which is its own kind of indictment, if you think about it. I need it to stay that way here, because if I lose my spot on the team, I lose the only reason anyone opened this gate for me. Even now, with my backpack under my knees, my body reads the air the way it does before a race.

The pressure sits low. Clouds hang heavy. The kind of weather that makes your lungs work harder.

Early September doesn't feel cold yet. It feels alive.

The road twists through countryside that looks untouched, carrying me farther from the last hard edges of the city, toward Bradford, Massachusetts, into something quieter, more deliberate. Trees crowd the horizon, dense and unbroken, branches knitting together above narrow roads as if they're closing ranks. The forest

1

presses in from both sides, dark and endless, and my body registers the shift before I name it. Not fear, exactly. Alertness. The kind that comes from being told all your life that the woods are where bad things happen, then arriving to find the woods looking back.

A feeling you get in new places with unspoken rules you can sense. Saint William Academy doesn't appear, it announces itself. Not with buildings, but with a gate.

Stone pillars. Ironwork. A tiny guardhouse with glass too clean and too exact, built to see everything.

The bus hisses to a stop at the entrance. This is as far as the world may go. No main road runs through the campus. No traffic, no casual shortcuts, no town spilling into the school like it belongs there. Everything funnels into this one point, this narrow mouth of iron and stone.

If you want in, you come through the teeth.

People unload in clusters, then start the walk in. Suitcases bump over uneven ground. Parents in expensive coats and practiced restraint, trying not to look inconvenienced because the academy doesn't bend for anyone.

A sign hangs beside the guardhouse. The font is clean and the tone is friendly. It's the type of rule that masquerades as a suggestion:

WELCOME TO SAINT WILLIAM ACADEMY
PEDESTRIAN ACCESS BEYOND THIS POINT
VEHICLE ENTRY BY AUTHORIZATION ONLY

A man in uniform stands beside the barrier arm, posture loose but not relaxed. A clipboard. A tablet. A glance that doesn't linger, but doesn't miss either. He doesn't look like campus security. He looks like the kind of man who knows where you're allowed to stand.

The bus driver doesn't even pretend he might pull forward. He pops the luggage compartment and starts unloading as if this is routine. As if the gate always wins.

I step down with my backpack slung over one shoulder and my life compressed into a rolling suitcase that clicks and chatters on the gravel.

I haven't left home.

Just the last place I slept.

Twenty-four hours ago I packed everything I owned into that suitcase, shoved what mattered into my torn backpack, and boarded a plane out of LAX.

Two flights, one bus, and now I stand at a gate that doesn't look like it opens for most people.

A folding table sits beside the guardhouse, tucked under the eaves like an afterthought that isn't optional. Staff move with brisk efficiency, clipboards, tablets, plastic sleeves, processing arrivals the way airports process permission.

I step forward in the line. Ahead of me, a woman slips a red wristband onto a boy's wrist without asking.

Quick and familiar, like ritual. The band is glossy, embossed with the academy crest, made to be seen.

He doesn't thank her. He keeps moving. The band is part of the entry.

When my turn comes, she doesn't reach for the wristbands at all.

The woman behind the table doesn't look up when I reach the front. She glances at my papers, then smiles, already turning back to her screen.

"You'll want the other desk," she says. "This one's for families."

She gestures toward a long table near the only window of the guardhouse, where parents lean in close and staff keep things moving. Thick card stock passes from hand to hand, cream colored, official. Parents exchange names. Smiles flicker, brief and practiced.

I follow her hand in the opposite direction, to a smaller table tucked against the wall. No sign. No line. Just a man flipping through a stack of folders, as if he isn't in a hurry to find anything.

The main desk keeps moving. When the man looks up, he smiles like this is routine. Like it is kind.

"Scholarship students take longer," he says.

Take longer means there is a way I am expected to move through this place.

He takes my papers and sets them in a separate pile without asking.

"Wait there," he says, nodding toward a strip of wall beside the guardhouse, a space that isn't a line but functions like one.

I step into it anyway.

The family desk keeps moving. No one looks at me while they pass.

Past the pillars, the academy path isn't a road. It is stone and gravel and intention. A walkway that forces your pace to match theirs. Students move as if they've done this before. Parents follow with practiced expressions, as if even their discomfort knows it has to stay quiet.

Cars only come through for people important enough to be on a list. A black SUV rolls up to the barrier arm while we stand there adjusting straps and wheels. It doesn't slow the way normal cars slow at gates. It approaches as if it has already been waved through.

The guard glances at his tablet, lifts the barrier arm without stepping closer, and the SUV slides past with tinted windows and no eye contact. The guard lifts his radio.

"Legacy vehicle cleared."

No questions, no pause, no acknowledgment. The rest of us keep walking, like we agreed to walk before we got here.

The path forks once, a thinner gravel line that angles closer to the trees. Quieter. Less watched. My feet drift toward it blindly.

"Stay on the main walk," the guard calls, voice mild, like he is giving directions to a tourist. "Until you're cleared."

I stop. Look back.

He doesn't meet my eyes. He lifts his chin toward the wide path.

I move where I'm told, and don't try that angle again.

By the time the buildings come into view, my legs have warmed the way they do before a race. My lungs have settled into a steady rhythm. The air smells clean in a way I don't trust, damp earth and stone and something mineral under it, like rain waiting its turn.

Saint William Academy is careful in a way that feels expensive. Controlled. Intentional. Towers rise beyond the trees like something built to last through weather and war and whatever else people survive when they have the money that makes surviving easier.

Nobody here needs to know the places I come from.

Or what it takes to leave them.

Nobody needs to know anything.

My dorm sits at the far edge of campus, closer to the forest than the main quad. I notice it immediately, the way the paths thin and the buildings space out as I drag my suitcase toward it. Blackwood Hall rises ahead, gothic stone and narrow windows, iron lanterns already lit despite the daylight. It's closer to the woods than anything else. I keep walking anyway.

The reader beside the door blinks green for the student ahead of me. One smooth motion. He is inside before I reach the steps.

When I press my wristband to the glass, nothing happens. No light. No sound. The reader stays dark.

I stand there with my suitcase handle in my hand and pretend I am adjusting my grip.

One beat.

Two.

Then a soft click, deliberate, from inside, like someone has been watching.

The door eases open.

"Winter?"

A woman stands at the check-in desk. Mid-twenties, dark curls, a Saint William hoodie softened by too many washes.

Warm smile, practiced.

"I'm Laura. We've been expecting you."

She presses a key into my palm and slides an envelope across the counter.

"Room key and athletics intake card," she says. "Baseline evaluation this week at the Field House."

Not if you want to come.

Not a question.

She looks at me as if I should know where to go. I walk to the first set of stairs I see.

I figure it out. I always do. It's the one transferable skill of growing up in places where no one explains anything.

My room is bigger than I expect it to be.

An arched window. Heavy beams. One wall of uneven stone, with plaster covering its charm. A radiator hums, but the cold still finds its way in through the glass. And silence, wide and unfamiliar, the kind I'm not used to having to myself.

I cross to the window.

The forest fills the view, not framed, not softened by distance. Dense and gray green, branches swaying like something breathing. From this angle, it feels too close. Less like a view and more like a boundary someone dresses up as scenery.

My reflection hovers in the glass. I look at her the way I always do. Hair half braided from the trip, bronze and unruly, the platinum streak at my left temple catching the light in a way that makes it look almost silver.

I tried to dye over it twice.

It came back both times, refusing to be dimmed.

I look like I don't belong here. But I am here, and that has always had to be enough.

I unpack. Clothes into drawers. Running shoes lined up. The envelope from Laura sits on the desk, unopened.

I already know what it says.

I sit on the edge of the bed.

Thirty seconds. That is what I allow myself. Enough to acknowledge. Not enough to fall into it.

The silence presses in anyway. From the walls. The window. The empty bed across the room.

And for one unguarded moment, before I can stop it, I feel it.

The kind of ache that comes from absence that never changes.

I stand up before it can finish arriving.

A card slides under the door while I am unpacking.

WELCOME ASSEMBLY.
GREAT HALL AT FIVE O'CLOCK.
ATTENDANCE REQUIRED.

No signature. No please.

It is still Saturday. I haven't even found the Great Hall. I go because the card doesn't ask.

The Great Hall seems older than everything else, with high ceilings that swallow sound, floors worn smooth in the places people have always walked.

I find a seat near the aisle. The back is hiding. The front is trying.

I watch the wristbands. Red ones scattered through the room, their wearers occupying space the way territory gets claimed, assumed rather than aggressive. The room was already divided before anyone entered, and they are simply standing in their allocated portion of it.

Then the room changes.

Not loudly.

The way rooms change when something enters that the air already knows.

She comes from the side door, not the main entrance, not the stage stairs. A door that opens without anyone holding it. She moves through the faculty row without looking down, finds her position at the podium with the unhurried certainty of someone who has stood there a hundred times and intends to stand there a hundred more.

Silver hair. Straight posture. A dark blazer that is chosen rather than worn.

She sets her hands on the edges of the podium and lets the quiet finish before she uses it.

"Welcome to Saint William Academy."

Her voice fills the hall without effort. Warm in a way that comes from practice so complete it no longer feels like practice.

"For some of you, this is a return. For others, it is a beginning."

She pauses.

"Both are harder than they look."

I watch her the way I watch things I don't understand yet. Not with suspicion. With attention.

Headmistress Evelyn Ashcroft-Forrester talks about the school the way people talk about things they build, with an ownership that doesn't need to announce itself. But beneath the warmth and precise welcome, calculation runs like a current.

The kind that decides what a room needs to hear and delivers it without letting on that a decision is made.

I recognize that quality. The most effective authority is the kind people don't think to question because it never gives them a reason to.

Near the end, a moment so brief I almost miss it. Her gaze moves across the room the way practiced speakers do, never landing too long.

It lands on me.

And it doesn't move on.

A beat. Maybe two. Long enough to be a choice.

Her expression doesn't change. The warmth stays where it is. But her eyes sharpen, the way a predator's attention sharpens when it identifies something worth tracking.

And the moment her gaze finds mine, something happens in my chest.

A pull, directional and specific.

There is another pull I've been carrying since the bus crossed into Bradford, low in my chest, oriented somewhere out past the trees. It hasn't moved all afternoon. It doesn't move now.

This pull is different. This one is here, in the room, threaded between her gaze and mine. And unlike the other one, it answers.

Two pulls. Two directions. Two recognitions, and I'm standing between them.

I don't have the language for it. Like something on the far side of this campus feels the attention land on me and leans toward it. Like I am being located.

My hands go still in my lap.

The headmistress moves on. The room remains unaware.

I keep my face neutral and think about what it means that my body just responds to being looked at by reaching toward something that isn't in this room.

The assembly closes with the school's motto, Latin, not translated, not explained. Students murmur it from muscle memory.

FERA SUB REGULA.

I don't know the words. I feel them anyway. Low in my chest. In the same place the pull lives.

The hall empties. I let the current carry me toward the door, then stop and look back.

She is already in conversation with a faculty member. Silver head tilted, listening. Her back to me.

She knows I stop.

I don't know how I know that.

Later, I am on my bed in my room, thinking about how foreign it feels. Then the click of a key in the lock.

Not a knock.

Just the decisive sound of someone who already knows the space will accommodate them.

She steps in as if the room has been waiting.

Dark hair cut blunt to her chin. Beautiful in the way rare things are beautiful, without trying. I notice her bright gold watch and soft cashmere, effortlessly expensive. A monogrammed bag drops onto the empty bed with the casual ease of someone who has never once checked a price tag.

She takes in the room in one glance: stone wall, warped window, radiator, me.

Then her eyes find mine and stay.

Not curiosity, assessment.

"You must be Winter," she says.

"That's me."

"Catherine Montgomery." She gives me a warm smile I'm not prepared for in this chilly place. "Blackwood Hall."

Her eyes sweep the room like she's stepping back into a place that already knows her.

"They don't put just anyone out here."

A beat.

"Unless you're a Legacy," she adds, like it explains everything and nothing.

Her phone chimes twice. She glances at the screen, then flips it face down on the mattress.

Her gaze shifts to the athletics envelope on my desk. Not my face. The envelope.

A beat. Quick.

Her mouth tightens, then smooths into something careful.

She knows something.

Not about the school. About this. About that envelope sitting on my desk on the first day, already printed, already waiting. She chooses not to tell me.

"What do you run?" she asks instead, as if she is making conversation.

"Cross-country. 5K mostly. Sometimes the longer stuff if the course calls for it."

Outside, branches scrape the glass.

Catherine Montgomery, I will learn, does nothing without a reason. But tonight she just sits on her bed and talks about the school, about the social geometry, about which teachers matter and which don't, in the easy way of someone who has never once had to earn a room.

I listen.

I file.

I give back exactly enough to keep her talking.

It is the most human evening I've had in longer than I can remember, which is its own kind of warning.

Later, when Catherine is asleep and the room has gone quiet, I lie in the dark and look at the ceiling and think about the pull I feel at the thinner path. The pull I feel in my chest when the Headmistress looks at me. The way the forest presses against my awareness since the moment the bus crossed into Bradford.

Like something here already knows my name.

Like it has been waiting.

I tell myself that the scholarship is luck. Lying here in the dark, in this room that sits too close to the trees, in this school that sorts people before they've unpacked, I'm not sure I believe that anymore.

I think about my mother.

I think about how she never once mentioned Bradford, Massachusetts.

Not once.

My fingers find the pendant at my throat.

Cold metal.

Familiar shape.

The stamped symbol presses into my skin, a mark I never asked her to explain.

I hold it anyway. I close my eyes.

The forest breathes outside the window, and I pretend I can't hear it.

CHAPTER 2

BRADFORD COMPOUND

Lochan

I read a room before I enter it. Every wolf does. Not sight. Scent. It's the first thing we're taught and the last thing we unlearn.

Scent is not a mood. Scent is not atmosphere. Scent is information: identity, history, intention, fear. You can lie with your face. You can lie with your voice. You cannot lie with your body's chemistry, and every wolf in a room knows this, which is why the most dangerous conversations in this world happen in silence.

The compound at dinner smells like cedar and iron and the sharp note of men who have been running perimeters all day. Pack scent, layered and specific, the accumulated chemistry of wolves who have spent centuries on this land and pressed their claim into every stone and root and corridor of it. It smells like Barry at my heel, ancient, certain, mine. It smells like Alpha Rowan at the head of the table, which is its own category entirely. A scent so dense with authority that younger wolves instinctively give it more space than the physical body requires.

Barry is Bartholomew Bradford, an old name, an older thing. This is what my world calls a familiar. He came to me the day I was named heir, walking out of the forest as if he had been waiting for the appointment to be made official, and he has not left my side since.

12

He presents as a large dog to anyone who does not know better. Anyone who does know better understands that the animal beside me is a wolf and that a wolf who has chosen to stay is a different thing entirely from one who is told to.

How old he is, nobody knows. Old enough that the compound treats him the way it treats certain pieces of furniture, with the specific respect you give something that has outlasted everyone who could explain it.

None of the wolves at this table are in the form that tells the truth about what they are.

That is the discipline. That is what it means to hold a compound, to sit in a room full of wolves in human skin and feel the current of what moves beneath and keep your face exactly where it belongs.

I have been doing this since I was old enough to sit at this table. I have never once encountered a scent I can't place. Until a week ago.

But that isn't tonight's problem.

Tonight's problem is standing at the far end of the table with his chin up and his shoulders back and the specific stillness of a man who has confused preparation with readiness. His name is Callum. He is about to learn that they are not the same thing.

I feel it before he speaks, a pressure drop in the room, subtle as weather, the kind of shift that moves through a pack the way current moves through deep water. Heads don't turn. Eyes don't lift. But every wolf at this table feels it and does the same thing I do.

Nothing. We wait.

Here is what you need to understand about public correction at this compound: it almost never happens. Not because challenges don't arise. They do, quietly, in the way ambitious men always measure themselves against the men above them, testing the edges of what they're permitted to want.

But Alpha Rowan's authority doesn't require demonstration. It simply is, the way gravity simply is, and men who understand this world feel it without needing it explained to them.

The fact that Callum is standing here, in front of everyone, making this declaration out loud. That is the real problem. Not the challenge itself. The fact that he believes it is necessary.

Which means somewhere, somehow, the compound's certainty has developed a hairline crack. And every wolf at this table is now wondering where it is and whether they caused it and whether Rowan knows and what Rowan knowing will mean for them.

Callum speaks. Territory. Patrol assignments. Rank. What he deserves and the gap between what he's been given and what he believes he's owed.

The words are almost reasonable. Almost. If you don't hear the thing underneath them, which every wolf in this room hears with perfect clarity. I want more than you've given me. I will take it if I have to.

My father sets down his fork. The sound is small. The room understands it as the end of something.

Rowan doesn't stand immediately. He gives Callum's words their full weight and their full rope, and I watch Callum's certainty curdle in real time as the silence stretches, the specific silence of a man who has said the prepared thing and is now understanding that preparation is entirely the wrong problem to solve.

Then my father stands.

And I feel my wolf surge, not toward Callum, not in dominance or anger. Toward the door. Out.

My wolf, who has never once shied from a fight, who has spent nineteen years leaning into every hard thing this world has put in front of us, cannot watch what is about to happen without every instinct screaming to be somewhere else.

I don't move. I press my hands flat on the table. I feel my nails want to lengthen at the edges, the smallest involuntary shift, the body's first language, and I press my palms harder into the wood and breathe through my nose and hold every single thing inside the line of my skin.

What happens is not loud. That's what I will remember. Not volume, but the absence of it. The particular quality of a silence that has weight and texture and temperature.

And one sound. Just one. The sound of Callum's knees hitting the stone floor.

Not a fall, a placement.

His body choosing it. His body understanding what his mind refuses to, that it is never going to win this. That it is always going to end here, on this floor, in front of these men, in the only language that leaves no room for misinterpretation.

When it's over, Callum is still breathing.

That's the mercy.

My father returns to his seat. Picks up his fork. Someone two seats down resumes a conversation that was quietly set aside, and the room follows, voices returning in careful increments, cutlery resuming, the compound's surface sealing back over the moment the way water seals over a stone.

Thirty seconds. The table sounds as if nothing happened. Because in this world, for the purposes of this world, nothing did. Order was tested. Order held. The mechanism functioned exactly as designed.

I excuse myself before dessert. Barry is at my heel before I clear the doorway.

The corridor is colder than the dining room, and I walk it the way I always walk this compound: measured pace, neutral face, both hands loose at my sides.

I get all the way to the base of the stairs before it hits me. I stop. Press my back against the wall.

The corridor smells like dinner still. Cedar, iron, the accumulated weight of men who have spent their lives in this building. And underneath it, faint but unmistakable, the absence.

Grayson used to stand at the far end of this hallway. Not often. But enough that I know the shape his presence left. The way the air moved differently around him. The way junior wolves tracked him without meaning to, bodies turning toward authority the way plants turn toward light.

He isn't here. He hasn't been here in three years. The compound speaks of it the way it speaks of everything uncomfortable: in past tense, with clean language, without looking directly at the fact. Removal. Necessity. The land's decision, not ours.

The land's decision. As if the forest reached up and plucked him out, and the rest of us just watched.

I know what happened. I was there. My father knows what I know, and neither of us has spoken of it since. That is its own kind of weight. The kind that lives in the chest instead of the mind. The kind that gets heavier, not lighter, with years.

Grayson is the one I am allowed to remember. There are others I am not. A girl, a long time before Grayson, before my father held the chair. The compound used a different set of words for her. Quieter words, framed in care, as if the language could decide what the act had been. I was not there. I do not know her name. I only know that the woods on the northwest edge are not patrolled the way the other edges are, and when I ask why, the older wolves tell me there is nothing of value out there. They say it the same way every time, like a recitation, like they have all been told to give the same answer.

I press my palms flat against the wall.

My hands are shaking.

Not from fear. Not from violence. I have seen worse, been part of worse, grown up in a world where worse is the lower register of normal. Not from the anger of watching it, which I am also not permitted.

From the effort of remaining seated. From nineteen years of keeping everything inside the line of my skin and the accumulated weight of what that costs.

And tonight, for reasons I don't have clean language for yet, the weight is different. Tonight the cost feels personal. Like I am not just watching Callum learn what happens to wolves who want more than they're given. Like I am watching a warning meant for me.

I think about want. Not hers, I don't have her yet. Not with my waking mind, not with anything I can locate or name. But something has been building in my sleep for a week. Some awareness of a direction. Some pull that arrives when my defenses are down and stays long after they rebuild.

A scent I have no log of, in a world where I have an entry for everything. Sweet, warm, alive, out of season. Like something that blooms in a place where nothing should bloom. It has no business existing in the compound's cold, controlled air, that sits in my lungs every morning as if it belongs there.

I have not told anyone. I understand, watching Callum's knees on that floor, exactly why there is already an answer prepared for what I am supposed to want. Her name is Maris Harlan. The arrangement has existed since before either of us was old enough to understand it. The compound doesn't call it a cage. It calls it a future.

Barry presses his shoulder into my leg. The tether pulls steadily. This is how it works. You don't want, and in return, nothing is taken from you. You stay inside what's permitted, and the rest is decided for you before you ever have to ask.

I breathe until my hands stop. Then I take the stairs. I close my door. I sit on the edge of the bed in the dark and think about what this world does with want it hasn't authorized.

One thing. One response. I'll watch it tonight.

Barry lies across the threshold, guarding. His breathing slows. His eyes stay open, amber, steady, ancient in a way that has nothing to do with the years he's been alive and everything to do with what he is.

My familiar. My anchor. The tether that has kept my wolf on the right side of the line since I was old enough to understand there is a line.

He watches me the way he watches me when he knows something I haven't admitted yet.

I look away first.

I stare at the ceiling until the compound goes quiet in the way it only goes quiet after the order of things has been reset, a cleaner quiet, a more certain quiet, the quiet of a world that has reminded itself what it is.

And then, because my body stops asking my permission, my eyes close.

The dream comes the way it always comes now. Not gradual. Immediate. Like a door I have been pressing against has finally given way.

In the dream, I run. The forest opens for me the way it only opens for wolves who belong to it, not clearing a path but receiving me into one, roots and dark and the cold smell of pine, the ground rushing under my feet with the specific generosity of terrain that has known my family for two centuries. Every root. Every dip. Every place the soil turns soft.

Tonight it feels like it has been waiting.

I don't question the direction. I stop questioning it on the third night. Left at the lightning split, down where the pine needles thicken. Through the narrow cut where the branches close overhead and the sky disappears, and it is only forest and dark and the sound of my own breathing and hers.

Her scent.

It arrives before anything else. Before I see her. Before I'm close enough to justify it. And it does what it always does.

Clears everything out. Not fades. Clears.

Like a room swept before something important.

Every thought I arrive with, Callum, my father, the sound of knees on stone, the fork going back to the plate, gone. Displaced. Made irrelevant by something that has decided it is the only relevant thing.

Sweet. Warm. Alive. The scent of something that has nothing to hide and doesn't know it should. And beneath it, something deeper, a weight that lands into my chest like a second heartbeat arriving to correct the first one.

My wolf does not fight me. He runs with me. One thing, one direction, no negotiation, no cost.

I didn't know it could feel like this. I didn't know I had been in pieces my entire life until the dream showed me what whole feels like.

Barry runs at my flank, silent, exact. He doesn't try to stop me. He decides before I do and waits for the rest of me to arrive at the same conclusion.

The path tightens. Her scent deepens. Something in my chest pulls toward it with a force that has nothing to do with decision and everything to do with the specific gravity of two things that belong together finally getting close enough to feel each other.

Barry stops. Clean. Final. Hackles up. Weight forward.

Every line of him saying: here. The line is here. This is where I stop. This is where you should stop.

I feel the boundary in the air, a pressure shift, the forest floor giving way to something older. My body crosses before my mind decides to.

The air changes immediately. Her sweetness sharpens, electric, alive, the scent of something that has been waiting without knowing it was waiting.

Barry doesn't follow.

The trees break. The clearing opens like an exhale.

And she is there.

She stands at the edge of the moonlight as if she belongs to it. Still. Hair loose. Face turned just enough away that I can see the line of her jaw, the curve of her throat, the way she holds herself, contained, careful, smaller than she needs to be. Like the world asks her early to take up less space, and she obliges.

Heat moves through my chest, not want, but want hums beneath it. Low and constant, no longer something I try to deny.

Something older.

Something that looks at the way she's standing and wants to give her room to stand differently. Wants to put itself between her and whatever taught her that less is safer.

Her scent reaches me at full force.

I lose a step.

Not weakness. Collision.

She turns. Her eyes find mine.

No searching. No hesitation. Like she already knows the shape of my face in the dark and is simply waiting for it to arrive.

The breath goes out of me.

She is not afraid. That's the thing. Not her face, which the dream light keeps just out of focus. Not the way she looks in the moonlight. The fact that she is looking at something that should frighten her and she is not frightened.

She is looking at me like she recognizes me. Like she has been waiting.

My hand lifts.

Not reaching. Arriving.

A motion that begins somewhere before this dream and only now completes itself. I feel the warmth of her before I get there, her body answering mine before contact, the space between us already charged, the bond announcing itself in the inch between our skin like it has been here the whole time and we have only just arrived at it.

Close enough to hear her breath. Close enough to feel my wolf go absolutely still.

Not suppressed. Not managed. Done.

Like he carries something for nineteen years and finally, in this clearing, in this inch, sets it down.

The dream tightens.

I wake.

Hand off the sheet. Heart loud. Ceiling exactly where it always is.

Barry is already beside me.

The scent is still here.

That's the first thing I check. Every morning for a week. And every morning the same answer, present, threaded through the compound's cold controlled air, sitting in my lungs like it belongs there.

I press my wrist to my nose. It deepens. On me, in this room.

A scent that has no source in this building. Nothing here blooms. Nothing here smells like this. I have catalogued every scent in these walls since I was old enough to read them, and this one has no entry, no origin, no name.

It is on my skin like a claim.

And I don't know whose.

I run the problem the way my father taught me: systematic, unemotional, consequence chain.

If the scent is on me it reaches the corridor, and from the corridor it gets logged, and once logged it gets interpreted. Interpretation in a pack runs fast and assumes the worst, and mate-claim talk attached to the heir's name is not a rumor. It is a verdict.

My jaw tightens.

That's the first problem.

The second problem is that I don't care about the first one the way I should.

The second problem is one inch. The warmth that arrives before contact. A girl who looks at something that should frighten her and is not frightened.

My wolf is not clawing or demanding. He is standing in a direction. Patient, absolute, done.

I go to the window. Press my forehead to the glass.

Outside the compound runs its rotations, guards, perimeter, the iron certainty of a world that corrects what steps outside its order without hesitation and without apology.

I watch what that looks like tonight.

I know exactly what this world does with desire it hasn't authorized.

And I stand at a window in the dark with an impossible scent on my skin and a wolf inside who has stopped negotiating.

The only thought I can finish is that I don't have her name or her face. I have one inch of her, and my wolf, who has never once in nineteen years been wrong about anything that matters, is certain.

It is enough.

CHAPTER 3
SYSTEM

Winter

Monday morning, I stop pretending I can delay the inevitable.

Catherine is still asleep when I leave, one arm over the edge of the bed, dark hair fanned across the pillow, the particular stillness of someone who has never once gone to sleep wondering if she'll still be safe in the morning. I watch her for a moment from the doorway, not with envy, with something closer to relief. At least one of us gets to sleep like that. Better odds than I'm used to.

Main Hall is already busy: families, transfers, scholarship processing. The school running before classes even start.

The building runs warm, radiator heat trapped behind old stone, and the moment I step inside, my skin registers it. Floor polish. Paper. A metallic undertone, like keys handled too often.

A line snakes beneath the vaulted ceiling toward a long table with laptops and stacks of plastic ID badges. No banners. No balloons. It's a sorting system. Everyone stands a little straighter than necessary, paperwork clutched like proof.

Some of them are already marked, red ribbons from yesterday's arrival still looped at their wrists. Legacy arrivals. I clock it automatically. They don't look like they're waiting to be approved. They look like they're confirming the system sees them.

Two girls near the front glance back at me, take in my sneakers, oversized coat, the travel bruise under my eye, and decide quickly what I am.

Then I take off my coat.

Heat creeps up my scalp, wrong for September. Not embarrassment, not nerves. An internal sensation. I smooth my hair back, expression neutral. People stop smiling when I hold their gaze too long.

A boy ahead of me turns mid-laugh and falters. His eyes catch on my face and linger a beat too long. Surprised.

He recalibrates when he notices I don't have a badge clipped to my jacket. His mouth tightens. He faces forward.

A student in a blazer walks the line with a clipboard. Not staff, but treated like it. People step aside without being asked.

"Prefect," the boy mutters.

Her blazer doesn't wrinkle when she moves. She doesn't hurry. She doesn't need to.

When it's my turn, the woman behind the table slides a laminated form toward me without looking up.

"Name."

"Winter," I say. Then, because precision matters here: "Winter Cates."

Her fingers move across the keyboard. My reflection ghosts faintly in her glasses. Too sharp for this hour. The heat sharpens with it. Paper. Floor polish. The separate cadence of heartbeats I shouldn't be able to isolate, but I can. I don't react. I let the line carry me forward.

She pauses mid-type. Half a second. Not a glitch. A catalog.

Then she reaches into the stack and pulls a badge without searching. It was already set aside.

She slides it toward me. Her eyes lift.

"Keep it visible," she says. "If you don't scan, you don't exist."

A staffer gestures toward the reader.

"Scan to activate."

I press the badge to the glass. It blips oddly. Not loud. Not an alarm. A second tone that doesn't belong.

The staffer's hand stills. The line compresses. The Prefect's head lifts.

"Secondary activation," the woman says.

Too smooth.

She flips my badge, checks the strip, rescans it herself, slow enough that it feels instructional.

Green.

"No issue."

She makes a small mark beside my name, then slides the form into a different stack. Procedural, not personal. Which is worse, in my experience. Personal you can argue with.

The Prefect watches the stack, not me. She catches the mark. Then she looks back down.

I step aside.

The badge is heavier than it should be. Clear plastic. My photo already printed. Taken when? Taken where? I haven't been here long enough for anyone to have taken a photo of me, which means someone took it before I knew I was coming.

Beneath my name: BLACKWOOD HALL ATHLETE. Not prospect, not conditional. Declared.

I've been labeled before. Foster. Transfer. Problem. Potential. Those labels came with social workers and waiting rooms. This one comes with gates.

I clip the badge to my jacket and walk out of Main Hall without looking back.

My phone buzzes as I'm cutting across the quad, the lanyard rubbing the back of my neck like a leash.

Unknown Number: XC intake. Report to Field House, Office B, in 15 minutes. Bring badge + student ID. No hello, no signature, no please. A command dressed up as information, which is the most expensive kind of information.

I stop for a beat, staring at the screen like it might change under pressure. Around me, campus keeps moving, students laughing, doors opening, somebody calling a name I don't recognize. The normal world.

My thumb hovers over ignore.

Then I feel the weight of the badge against my chest. Proof I've already been recorded. Ignoring it won't make me free. It will make me late.

I turn toward the Field House.

The building sits at the edge of campus like it was designed for utility, not beauty. Bright lights, clean glass, banners that say CHAMPIONSHIP in fonts that assume you're already proud.

Inside, it smells like rubber flooring and disinfectant, sharp enough to sting the back of my throat.

A desk sits near the entrance with a sign-in tablet and a small camera angled down like it's bored.

I type my name.

WINTER CATES flashes green.

APPOINTMENT CONFIRMED.

So they didn't text the wrong person.

A door opens before I can decide whether that comforts me or makes me sick.

Coach Klein steps out. He's not old, not young, built from routine. He looks at me once and I have the immediate sense he's already seen a file.

"Winter," he says, like my name is a data point that checked out.

"Coach," I answer. Because that's what you do here.

"Baseline eval," he says. "Twenty-minute tempo, then a 5K time trial. I need to see your gait, your recovery, your ceiling."

He looks down at his clipboard, then back up.

"Any injuries I should know about?"

"No."

"Good. We'll start on the track for the tempo, then move to the trail loop for the 5K. Senior's already out there finishing his own session. Don't let it throw you."

I don't let things throw me. That's the first rule. Everything else is built on top of it.

By twelve I had been running five miles to school every morning. Not because I had to. Because I arrived calmer. Because the distance between that house and that building was the only part of the day that was entirely mine. Coach Freeman saw me once, unlocking the gym as I came in off the street. She asked where I lived. When I told her, she went quiet, then said, "Be here Saturday. Six a.m."

Her name was Tonya Freeman. She looked at me like I was worth showing up for, and that was the rarest thing anyone had ever given me.

I showed up.

And I kept showing up.

The track wraps around the back of the Field House, asphalt edged with painted lines, the forest sitting just beyond the far curve like it's been waiting for the right moment to mention itself.

I feel it the moment I step outside, that low pull, the same one I've felt since the bus crossed into Bradford, sitting at the back of my throat like a taste I can't place. Today it is louder and more insistent. As if something on the other side of the tree line has noticed I'm here and moved closer to the fence.

I breathe through it. File it. Focus.

The senior is already running when I come around the corner. I clock him the way I clock everything, automatically, without meaning to. Tall. Long stride. Dark hair. Moving with the easy authority of someone who has owned these miles for two years and doesn't need to think about it anymore. He doesn't look up when I step onto the surface. He's in his own rhythm, his own world, his own morning. He is not thinking about me at all, and I file that as the closest thing I'll get to a welcome at this place.

I set my watch. Coach Klein marks something on his clipboard.

I start to run.

The first lap is clean. My body finds the rhythm it always finds, lungs calibrating, stride lengthening, the metronome clicking in behind my sternum. The cold air works through me. My arms drop into their natural carry. This is the part of running I trust, the part that has nothing to do with anything except the body doing what it was built to do.

The senior passes me on my left going the other direction. Close, four feet, maybe five. The inside of the track.

The heat arrives without warning.

Not exertion heat. Not the burn in the quads or the flush across the chest that comes from pace. Something else. Deeper. Internal. Starting at the base of my spine and spreading outward with a speed that has nothing to do with effort. As if something underneath my skin has been asleep my entire life and something just walked close enough to wake it up.

I miss a stride. Catch it. Keep moving.

The forest pulls harder. I've felt the pull before, on the walk in, in the dark before I sleep, in the quiet moments when my defenses drop enough to let it through. But this is different. This isn't a low hum. This is a demand. Directional and absolute, as if a hand at the back of my neck is actively turning me toward the tree line with a force I have to resist.

I keep running.

The senior passes again on the next lap. Closer this time, the track geometry, the inside lane, nothing intentional. He still isn't looking at me. He is just running his session, just existing in his own morning, just a person moving through space with no awareness of what his proximity is doing to mine.

My vision sharpens. Wrong. Too far. Too clear. Like my eyes have adjusted to something I didn't ask them to, the tree line snapping into focus with a precision that has no business existing at this distance, individual branches resolving from blur into specific shapes, the shadows between the trunks becoming readable in a way that makes no sense for this light, for this hour, for eyes that have always been ordinary.

My hands. Something at my fingertips. A pressure. A heat.

I shove them into fists without breaking stride and feel my nails, short, always short, cut short because long nails catch on things, press hard into my palms.

The pain grounds me, for about four seconds.

The nausea arrives on the back straight. Not from pace. Not from effort. From the pressure of holding something enormous inside a body that has never had to hold it before, like a door straining against something on the other side that has decided it is done waiting.

My stomach seizes. My stride shortens. I feel my gait change beneath me and I cannot stop it, cannot correct it, something fluid and animal entering the way I move that is not mine, that I did not put there, that has come from somewhere underneath the seventeen years of being just a girl who runs.

I am not just a girl who runs.

I don't know what that means yet.

My body is starting to.

The forest screams. Not sound. Sensation, the pull becoming something that has no patience left, that has been waiting since I stepped off that bus and has decided that waiting is over, that whatever is on the other side of those trees is where I need to be and my legs are already agreeing before my mind catches up.

I leave the track.

Not a decision. A direction.

My body moves toward the tree line with a speed I have never once produced in competition, a speed that does not feel like effort. It feels like a release. Like finally. Like something that has been coiled inside me my entire life unwinding all at once.

I hit the grass at the edge of the field. The trees rise in front of me.

And something in me, the part that has survived seventeen beds and seventeen schools and seventeen versions of starting over, the part that has always known that drawing attention is the most dangerous thing a girl in my position can do, slams into the pull like a wall.

I stop.

Six feet from the tree line. My hands on my knees. My lungs working. The heat under my skin so intense I can feel my own pulse in my teeth.

I stop.

And I fight.

It is the hardest thing I have ever done. Harder than the group home at thirteen where I learned that being invisible was the only currency that kept you safe. Harder than the Saturdays Coach Freeman made me earn before the sun came up, when showing up was the only promise adults ever broke. Harder than the morning I ran five miles to school in October rain because the alternative was getting in a car with someone I didn't trust. Harder than every race I've ever run, every finish line I've ever crossed, every moment I've chosen to keep going when stopping would have been easier.

This is different because I don't know what I'm fighting.

I just know I cannot lose.

I get myself into the tree line, just barely, just far enough that the field is out of sight, and I put my back against the nearest trunk and press my palms flat against the bark and breathe.

Counted breaths. The only tool I have for something that has no name.

In. Out.

The heat claws.

In. Out.

The pull screams.

In. Out.

My fingertips burn. I press them harder into the bark. The roughness of it, real, physical, present, is the only thing that feels like mine right now. Everything else is happening to me. The bark is something I'm choosing.

I choose it.

I keep choosing it.

I don't know how long it takes. Long enough that the heat drops from a roar to a hum. Long enough that my vision stops doing the thing it was doing, the sharpening, the wrongness of it. Long enough that my hands, when I finally look at them, are just hands. Short nails, scraped palms, shaking.

I get sick against the base of the tree, quietly, efficiently, the way I do everything.

Then I wipe my mouth and stand up straight and walk back out of the trees.

Someone must have said something. Klein, a runner, a look that lasted too long.

Catherine is standing at the edge of the field, like she came looking when I didn't come back. Not close enough to have followed me. I went off path, off track, into the trees at a speed and angle that no one could have matched. But she is here. Standing at the point where the grass meets the asphalt with her arms crossed loosely over her chest and her gold watch catching the morning light and her eyes on the tree line.

On me.

I don't stop walking. I don't change my pace or my face. I cover the distance between us the way I cover every hard thing, forward, neutral, already deciding what I'm going to say before I get there.

"Morning," I say.

Catherine looks at me for a long moment. Not at my scraped palms, not at the dirt on my shoes or the particular quality of my stillness or whatever it is my face is doing that I can't fully control right now. At me.

"Coach Klein said you left the track," she says. Carefully. Like she's choosing words the way you choose footing on uncertain ground.

"I needed a minute."

"Okay."

A beat.

"Has that ever happened to you before?"

The question lands differently than I expect, not accusatory, not suspicious, just open.

The way Catherine asks everything, like she is genuinely curious about the world and has never learned to be afraid of the answer.

I think about lying. I am good at lying. I have been lying since I was old enough to understand that the truth of my situation made adults uncomfortable, and uncomfortable adults made my situation worse.

But something about the way she is looking at me, steady, warm, already decided that she is on my side.

"No," I say.

The way I say it tells her everything about how frightened I actually am.

I watch her understand this. Watch her file it in whatever Catherine Montgomery files things, not away, not forgotten. Somewhere accessible, somewhere she'll return to.

"Okay," she says again.

Then: "Klein's going to want you back on the track."

"I know."

"I told him you had a side stitch."

I look at her.

She looks back. Unbothered. Like covering for a girl she met forty-eight hours ago is the most natural thing in the world. Like she made the decision before I came out of the trees and the only question was whether I'd be grateful or not.

I am grateful.

I don't know what to do with that either.

"Thank you," I say.

"Don't thank me." She falls into step beside me as I turn back toward the Field House. "Just tell me what a side stitch feels like so our stories match."

I almost laugh. I can't remember the last time someone almost made me laugh.

Coach Klein logs my split times without comment, the ones I produced before I left the track. He writes something on his clipboard and doesn't ask me directly what happened, just says we'll do the full assessment next week and hands me a schedule that has already been decided. I take it. I say thank you. I leave. The whole thing has the texture of a transaction I didn't agree to.

Catherine walks back to Blackwood Hall with me. She talks about the school, about Founders Weekend, about a junior named Priya who apparently runs a social hierarchy Klein doesn't know about and Evelyn absolutely does.

Catherine says Evelyn like the Headmistress doesn't need a title. Like whatever she is doesn't apply to her.

She doesn't mention the tree line. She doesn't ask any more questions. She is giving me the gift of being treated like nothing happened. I know it's a gift because I know exactly what it costs her not to ask.

In my room, door closed, Catherine gone to her first class, I sit on the edge of my bed and look at my hands.

Short nails. Scraped palms. The faded line of a watch I no longer own.

Ordinary hands.

I don't know what they almost did in those trees. I don't know what I almost became.

I think about my mother. Not with longing. Not anymore. With something sharper, a question that has been sitting in the back of my mind since I lay in the dark two nights ago and realized she had never once mentioned Bradford, Massachusetts.

Not once.

My fingers find the pendant at my throat. Cold metal, familiar shape.

My mother who numbed herself until she disappeared. My mother who I thought left because she couldn't cope, because she was weak, because I wasn't enough to make her stay.

What if she left because of something else entirely?

What if she knew something about what I am. What if she knew and said nothing because saying something was worse than saying nothing, and I have been walking around my entire life carrying something she understood and I didn't, and she chose to let me stay ignorant because ignorance was the only protection she could give me. Which is the kind of love that looks exactly like abandonment if you don't know what you're looking at.

I press my palms flat against my thighs. The bark roughness is gone. Just skin now. Just ordinary.

Outside, the forest breathes. I can hear it from here. I couldn't before. I can now.

Something has changed.

I don't know yet what it means.

But I know, with the same certainty that has kept me alive through seventeen beds and seventeen schools and seventeen versions of starting over, that I cannot let it happen again. Not here. Not where anyone can see.

CHAPTER 4
PUBLIC CONTROL

Lochan

The first day of classes always tightens the leash.

The scent is stronger this morning.

That's the first thing I know before I'm fully awake, before the ceiling resolves, before Barry's weight registers at the foot of the bed, before the compound sounds filter back in through the stone walls. The scent arrives first. It always does now. Sweet, warm, alive, belonging to no one in this building, no one in this world I can name, sitting in my chest like it has no intention of leaving.

I press my wrist to my nose.

It deepens.

Eight mornings. Eight mornings of this and I am no closer to an explanation and my wolf is no closer to indifference and the distance between those two facts is where I live now.

Barry is watching me from the foot of the bed.

He has been watching me since before I woke. I know this the way I know everything about Barry, not because I see it but because the tether between us carries information that doesn't need language. His weight. His attention. The particular quality of his stillness, different from sleep, different from contentment, the specific stillness of a familiar waiting for his wolf to catch up to something the familiar has already understood.

I don't look at him yet.

If I look at him, he will know that I know, and then the knowing will be something we share instead of something I can still pretend I'm managing.

I get up. I build myself into the uniform the way I build myself into it every morning. Black shirt. Dark slacks. Boots polished silent. The ritual of putting the human shape on deliberately, piece by piece, because a wolf who forgets that he chose the shape tends to find the choice unmade for him at the worst possible moment.

My father taught me that. My father teaches everything through demonstration.

In the window's reflection, my hair is parted until nothing wild remains. My eyes are still too bright. They're always too bright in the mornings, catching light wrong, the wolf too close to the surface before the day has built its walls back up. But the rest will pass. It always does. By the time I reach the corridor I will look like what I'm supposed to look like.

The heir. The Bradford line. Nineteen years of controlled, deliberate, exactly right.

Barry watches me do all of this without moving.

When I finally look at him he holds my gaze for exactly one second and then looks at the door.

He's ready before I am. He's always ready before I am.

The compound runs its morning the way it always runs its morning, guards rotating, corridors brisk with purpose, the specific efficiency of a household that has never once needed to be told what order looks like because order is the only thing it has ever been.

I move through it the way I always move through it, measured pace, neutral face. The corridor gives me space the way it always gives me space the way it always gives me space, not because anyone steps aside consciously, but because the compound's memory is longer than any individual wolf's manners. These walls have held Bradford heirs for two centuries. The stone knows the bloodline the way the forest does. By weight. By what it costs.

I nod to the men I pass. I receive what is given back. I do not stop.

Milo is at the kennel.

He has always been at the kennel in a way that stopped being explicable by job requirements years ago and has become something else.

A post. A watch. A man who has decided that being near the edge of the compound is where he needs to be and has never offered a reason and has never been asked for one.

He moves through his routine with the unhurried precision of someone for whom routine is a form of language. Latches. Bowls. Locks. Each motion exact.

He glances up when I pass.

Not at Barry. At me.

The question he doesn't ask sits in the space between us, visible as weather.

I give him a single nod. Respect and warning in equal measure.

He opens the gate a fraction wider.

Not warmth, not agreement. Access, because I outrank the rule, and Milo is precise about the difference.

Barry steps through without being told.

I follow.

The forest receives us the way it always receives us, without ceremony, without welcome, just the immediate adjustment of moving from one world into another. Compound sounds falling away. Forest sounds rising. The particular quality of air that has never been managed by human hands pressing in from all sides like a second skin.

I run.

There are three stages to every morning run.

First: the release. The compound peeling away with each stride, the human shape loosening its grip slightly, the wolf allowed to breathe without being asked to perform. Barry at my flank, the tether singing between us, the forest floor under my boots with the specific give of terrain that has known this bloodline longer than I have been alive.

Second: the reset. The body finding its rhythm. Breath and pace and the cold morning air doing what morning runs have always done, burning off what the night left behind, filing what needs filing, dropping what doesn't need to be carried into the day.

Third: the problem.

The problem arrives somewhere in the second mile, the way it has arrived every morning for eight days. Not as thought. As sensation. The scent rising through the compound smells, and the pine smells and the damp earth smells until it is the only thing in my nose, until my wolf lifts his head and points in a direction and my legs want to follow and I have to run the consequence chain instead.

If I follow: I find the source, or I don't. If I find the source and it is what my wolf believes it is, what the dream tells me it is, what eight mornings of an impossible scent tells me it is, then I have a different problem. A larger one. One with a name I am not ready to give it.

If I don't follow: I return to the compound with a wolf who is getting harder to manage every morning and no solution to the thing that is making him harder to manage.

I don't follow.

I return to the compound.

I have made this choice eight times.

It is getting more expensive every time I make it.

Barry stops running before I do.

He stops in the middle of the path, clean, absolute, all four feet planted, and he lifts his head and he reads the air with the particular attention that means he is not reading wind direction or prey or threat. He is reading something specific. Something that has arrived in the forest this morning that was not here yesterday.

I stop beside him.

Read the air myself.

The scent hits differently out here.

Not on my skin. Not the residue of eight dreams, eight mornings, the accumulated presence of something that has no business being in the compound. This is fresh. Present. Not memory and not a dream.

Real.

Recently real. As in within the last few hours. As in whatever carries this scent was in this forest this morning.

Close to the compound boundary. Close to the place where the path from the school grounds meets the tree line.

My wolf goes absolutely still. Not the managed stillness I practice in corridors and dining rooms and every human space that requires me to perform calm I don't feel. The real kind. The kind that comes before something significant. The kind the body does when it has stopped pretending and started paying attention with everything it has.

Barry looks at me.

I look at the direction the scent is coming from.

Neither of us moves.

The scent is already fading. She was here earlier. The trail is cooling. Whatever proximity produced this is no longer close enough to sustain it. In an hour it will be indistinguishable from the compound's baseline. In two hours it will be gone.

She was in the forest this morning.

Or close enough to it that the forest carries her.

I do not go in the direction the scent is coming from.

I stand in the middle of the path for thirty seconds with my wolf pointing at it like a compass needle that has found its north, and then I turn and I walk back to the compound because turning and walking back is the choice. It is always the choice. It is the only choice available to a wolf who understands what his world does with want it hasn't authorized.

Barry follows.

He doesn't lean into the scent trail.

He doesn't look back.

He is better at this than I am. He has been better at this than me since the first night.

The trees thin and the border appears, not naturally, but by design. A clipped hedgerow runs beside the path in an obedient line. Beyond it, trunks fall into neater spacing that doesn't belong to them. A boundary imposed by human hands. Nature doesn't grow like this unless someone makes it. I slow at the edge as the day's noise leaks in: laughter, voices, footsteps, life unfolding without awareness of what shares its borders. Duty first. Always. The moment I cross onto the grounds, the air changes. Not enough for anyone else to notice. Enough that my body does. The forest releases its hold without resistance. Stone and brick take over, clean lines, controlled distances, the sharp geometry of a place built to be watched. I straighten my posture without thinking. Lengthen my stride. Students move around me in loose clusters, voices bright and careless, bodies brushing past without hesitation. They smell like detergent and coffee and first day anticipation, metallic, restless, hungry for futures they think are theirs.

Human.

Human.

Human. The mantra holds my face in place as I move deeper into the quad. A boy bumps my shoulder without looking, momentum carrying him past before he realizes what he's done. "Sorry," he mutters, already gone. I nod once and keep walking. He doesn't notice the way my muscles lock for half a second. Doesn't feel the effort it takes to keep my hands relaxed at my sides instead of curling into fists. To keep my body from reacting the way it was trained to. That's the point.

I pass Blackwood Hall without looking up. The building sits too close to the trees, its stone darker, older, less forgiving than the others. It presses against my awareness even when I refuse to acknowledge it. I've learned that attention has weight. If I look, I risk noticing things I shouldn't. Then the pressure builds at the base of my skull, subtle, insistent. The next breath catches on the way in, as if the air has decided to hold me. I slow without meaning to. Noise dulls at the edges. Heat crawls up the back of my neck, fast and unforgiving.

And then, Magnolia. Not perfume. Not memory. Not anything sweet and harmless. This is green sap and bruised petals, rain and metal threaded beneath warmth, wrong seasoned and alive. It hits hard and undeniable, straight into the space under my ribs where instinct lives. It doesn't sharpen my senses. It doesn't demand pursuit. It recognizes. Sound fractures so cleanly it feels like impact. The quad dissolves into color and motion without meaning.

She comes down the steps of Blackwood Hall at an easy jog, one hand tugging her backpack higher, the other brushing hair away from her face. Casual. Human.

The effect is catastrophic.

My chest locks. Breath strangled mid-draw. Heat detonates beneath my skin and the shift surges forward, furious and unmoored. She slows at the bottom of the steps. Stops.

Looks up.

Our eyes meet.

Not spark. Not pull. Shock, clean and devastating, like touching exposed wire.

A laugh snaps somewhere to my left.

Someone curses. Footsteps shuffle. Life continues. My body doesn't. My hands curl into fists at my sides before I can stop them. I feel my nails threaten in my skin. My jaw locks until my teeth ache.

The tether snaps taut, Barry's alarm flooding my sternum like a physical shove. My throat tightens. My breath catches. The fist that was forming stalls mid-clench, forced still by the weight of him through my ribs. DOWN. I cannot afford this. Not here. Not now. If I fracture on campus, it becomes reportable. Reportable becomes council. Council becomes her. I force my shoulders to relax. I soften my stance. I fix my gaze past her and let neutrality settle onto my face like a mask I've worn so long it should be bone. Nothing has happened at all. She blinks. The moment fractures. Sound rushes back in, voices, laughter, the first bell chiming somewhere across the grounds. But the charge doesn't vanish. It hums between us, taut and electric, refusing to dissipate. Her gaze holds mine one heartbeat longer than it should. One.

That's all it takes to make restraint creak. I step back. Then another step, measured and controlled, even as every instinct screams in protest. I don't turn. I don't run. Running draws eyes. I retreat with the calm precision of someone who knows exactly what he's doing. Even when he doesn't. The trees rise to meet me at the edge of campus, their shadows swallowing stone and noise without question. The moment my boots hit dirt, the pressure shifts, easing just enough that I can breathe again. I don't stop until the forest has fully claimed me. Branches knit overhead. The canopy thickens. Light dulls into something manageable. Only then do I slow. Only then does my body remember how to breathe. I brace my hand against the nearest trunk, lungs dragging in air that tastes like soil and green and rain, and still, threaded beneath it, that wrong sweetness. Magnolia. It clings. Not fading. Not imagined. I wipe my mouth with the back of my hand like that will help. It doesn't. It's in me now.

CHAPTER 5

RECOGNITION

Winter

Heat crawls under my skin the moment I wake, wrong for September, wrong for morning, wrong for a room that still smells faintly of stone and old books. It sits along my spine and at the base of my skull as if my body has been left switched on overnight. I stare at the ceiling and breathe slowly until my heart stops trying to sprint. Which would be impressive cardio if it weren't also terrifying.

The dream won't let go.

It clings the way sweat does after a hard run, proof something happened even when the details refuse to line up. Motion. Pressure. A presence close enough that my body reacts before my mind can ask if it's allowed.

When I sit up, the smell hits hard.

Magnolia.

Not soap, not detergent, not perfume drifting under a door. This is presence, alive, green and warm, faintly sweet, like bloom under a sun that hasn't risen yet. It sits low in my lungs, impossible and undeniable, as if it followed me out of sleep and decided to stay.

My fingers go to my wrist without thinking. Then my collarbone. Then the edge of the sheet. Like I'm checking for a mark.

It's there too.

Everywhere.

I pull my hair over one shoulder and braid it without looking. The damp lengths snag halfway, knots hiding in the waves. I work them out with blunt patience, the way you do when panic won't help.

On the edge of the bed, I close my eyes and take three long breaths.

In. Out.

In. Out.

The heat isn't mood. It's a signal, my body's way of saying something is close.

The dream doesn't replay like a movie. It comes in fragments, each one too sharp to ignore.

A whisper at my ear, so close it feels like breath against skin.

Winter.

My pulse jumps. My muscles go tight. For one second I can smell wet earth and trees, like the room has been swapped out around me. Then memory slides in, slick and intimate, up the inside of my thigh.

Not a thought. A sensation. Certain. Familiar in the worst way, like a hand that already knows me.

My breath catches hard enough to hurt.

I jerk my eyes open.

Stone walls. Radiator hiss. Gray morning light.

Blackwood Hall, exactly as it is.

Catherine is asleep across the room, face turned toward the wall under her lavender silk mask, breathing slow and even. She looks untouched by the world, like she can sleep because she's never had to listen for footsteps in the hall that mean trouble.

I envy her so sharply it feels like a bruise.

The magnolia smell still lingers.

I swing my legs to the floor. My bare feet hit the wood and my skin prickles, as if the ground recognizes me from somewhere else. As if I've been here in a different way.

My body feels wrong, not sick, not hurt. Just restless, every nerve turned up one notch too high, like if I sit still the heat is going to find another way out.

So I dress like I'm managing a situation, not getting ready for the day. Leggings, a long-sleeve athletic top, sneakers. A jacket big enough to hide the lines of my body without swallowing me whole. Nothing that asks to be looked at. Everything chosen so I can move if I need to. The capsule wardrobe of someone who has always expected to leave.

In the mirror, I look the same, serious face, hair still a little wild, eyes too sharp for how early it is.

But there's tension under the surface that wasn't part of me yesterday.

I look… seen.

The thought lands fully formed, uninvited, like it's been dropped into my chest.

The clock says it's barely eight. Monday, first day. My body says it hasn't slept at all.

My phone lights with the message I already saw last night and didn't open again because it made my stomach clench.

WELCOME TO SAINT WILLIAM CROSS COUNTRY.

Under it: an attachment with my name already printed across the top of a medical release.

My throat tightens.

Baseline eval. Athletic Training. Eight-thirty.

The time sits in my head like a hook. Not because I'll miss it, because I won't. Missing it isn't a choice you get to make on scholarship.

I hate that my body understands that before my pride does.

Coach will want you at practice this week.

I don't reply about practice. I stare until my eyes blur, as if the world might remember it's supposed to ask first. It doesn't. Instead my stomach tightens, as if my life has started collecting appointments without my consent.

I lace my shoes quietly, grab my bag, and ease the door shut behind me before anxiety can climb all the way into my throat.

The hallway smells like lemon polish and coffee. Footsteps move in soft patterns, doors opening and closing, voices low like people don't want the building to hear them.

Blackwood Hall holds sound differently.

It doesn't echo. It absorbs.

Outside, campus is already awake. Students move in loose clusters, bright with first day energy. Laughter. Shoes scraping stone. Conversations about schedules and classes and futures that feel inevitable to them.

Fog sits low over the lawns, turning everything into a muted painting. The world feels quieter than it should, like someone turned the volume down just for me.

For a moment, I stand still and let the cold press into my lungs.

A bird lands on the railing beside me, close enough that I could touch it. It tilts its head, unafraid, studying me as if I'm worth the pause. "You're brave," I whisper. It doesn't fly away. Animals always did that. Strays used to follow me to bus stops and then sit as if they were guarding my feet, daring anyone to come close. My mom used to say it was because I smelled like trouble. Maybe she wasn't wrong. Or maybe she just knew what kind of trouble I was made of, and never figured out how to tell me.

The bird blinks slow, like it's deciding something.

I move away because staying put feels like inviting whatever I don't understand to finish walking up to me.

My body wants motion. It wants it so badly it aches.

So I run. Not far, not for time, just enough to bleed off the heat humming under my skin.

My sneakers whisper over stone as I cut down the Blackwood Hall steps, breath tight in my chest, fog beading on my lashes.

The sound of my feet should be the only thing I hear.

Halfway down, heat knifes up my spine, sharp and immediate, stealing my breath like a hand over my mouth.

Magnolia floods the air as if someone crushed blossoms between their hands.

My body stills.

Across the quad, a boy stands perfectly still, as if the whole campus has paused around him without anyone noticing. Dark clothes, hands in his pockets, posture too controlled to be casual.

His gaze is fixed. On me.

The space between us tightens, invisible and electric, as if the air has been pulled into wire.

My pulse stutters. The heat under my skin answers, signal flaring because whatever my body senses is suddenly right in front of me.

A girl at the bottom of the steps laughs and nudges her friend, then glances at me like I missed a cue.

I don't move.

His eyes flick, slightly, as if he's fighting the same thing.

Seen.

The word lands in my chest with the force of truth.

Not watched.

Not noticed.

Seen.

I blink once, hard, like I can reset the moment by force. Like I can make him just another person on campus.

He doesn't disappear.

The magnolia doesn't fade.

And when the noise of the world rushes back in, footsteps, voices, the ordinary chaos of a first day, something remains stretched tight between us, refusing to loosen.

I draw in a slow breath.

My fingers tighten on my bag strap until my knuckles ache.

I take one step forward.

So does he.

And the heat under my skin answers like it's been waiting.

Then he turns, breaking the moment cleanly, thread cut with a single motion.

Sound snaps back: laughter, shoes on stone, a bell chiming somewhere across the grounds.

My breath comes shallow. The air tastes different now. Magnolia after rain, bruised petals and metal, him, as if he left something behind in the space where he stood. My body insists on following him. My brain takes a vote and loses by a wide margin.

It takes everything, every ounce of willpower, not to sprint straight toward the treeline. I grip the strap until my knuckles ache, grounding myself in pain, in reality.

He's gone.

The spot where he stood is empty, but it hums, like the air remembers him.

I keep moving.

One step.

Then another.

I fall into the stream of students and let their noise cover me.

Somewhere behind me, wind combs through the trees.

And for half a second, it sounds like my name.

I cut toward the athletic buildings, slowing my pace until my breathing looks normal.

Walk. Breathe. Blend.

Athletic Training smells like disinfectant and rubber mats and order that doesn't ask permission. They measure everything, heart rate, lungs, joints, like my body is a form to be completed.

I sign where they point.

I do what they tell me.

I walk out with a timestamped clearance slip and the same heat under my skin as if none of it matters.

Baseline Evaluation complete, now off to class in the administrative building to see if I can keep up in that lane.

The first bell feels like a warning disguised as routine.

Doors swallow students in waves. Every hallway has its own current, and I have to learn how not to get pulled under.

At the edge of the quad, tucked near an archway of stone and ivy, there's a small security desk.

Or there should be.

The sign is there. The chair is there. A coffee cup sits abandoned like someone set it down mid-sip.

But no one is behind it.

People flow past like it makes sense.

My skin prickles.

In a place like this, absence is a choice.

I look away fast, because staring makes it real.

Environmental Systems 203 is in the east-wing building that smells like disinfectant and money. Everything is sharp, angles, light, voices bouncing off polished surfaces.

Inside, I slip into the classroom before anyone can really look at me.

The instructor's already there: tall, silver hair, posture that says he's seen a thousand first days and hasn't been impressed by any of them.

I head for the back row on instinct.

Back is where you can watch without being watched.

Everything here has been cold since the moment I arrived: the windows, the stair rails, even the air. So when I sit, I expect the seat to bite through my leggings.

It doesn't.

The seat is warm.

Not sun warm, not body-left-behind warm. Deep, steady, like heat rising from something alive.

My breath catches.

I shift, pressing my hand down slowly, half expecting it to fade once I notice it.

It doesn't.

The warmth spreads through the fabric, up my spine, settling low in my stomach. A quiet, insistent thrum, completely out of place in this chilled room.

A pressure blooms in my chest, recognition without memory.

The same signal that's been buzzing under my skin since yesterday.

I curl my fingers around the edge of the desk until the plastic digs into my fingertips.

Behind me, chairs scrape, soft and then softer. Not the normal chaos of students claiming seats, more deliberate.

Like people changing their minds.

I look over my shoulder.

A guy with a backpack half off his shoulder pauses in the aisle, eyes on me.

Not staring.

Clocking.

His mouth opens, then closes. His friend leans in, says something too low to catch.

And then, close enough for me to hear anyway, someone murmurs, "That's... odd."

The word lands and sticks. Odd. It isn't loud. It isn't mean. It's noted.

The guy shifts, then chooses a seat two rows forward. His friend follows. Two other students drift the same direction without looking at me, filling in around them like water finding the easiest path. Within seconds, there's an empty ring of space around my desk, not huge, not dramatic, just enough that I can breathe.

Relief, real relief, slides through me like warmth after cold. No one is close enough to touch me by accident. No one close enough to ask questions. No one leaning in, expecting something from my face.

It's quiet.

It's mine.

A memory flashes, sharp as a stitch in your side.

A bus stop, years ago. Cold metal bench. Exhaust in the air. Kids from school clustered at the far end, loud and bright. A stray dog wandering up and sitting at my feet as if it belonged there.

The kids noticed. Their voices dipped. "She's got that dog again," someone whispered, as if it wasn't an animal, as if it was a warning sign. They didn't come closer. I remember the way my body softened, the way I breathed easier with warmth pressed against my boots.

Not because I was lonely.

Because I was safe.

The memory fades as quickly as it comes.

The instructor clears his throat, and the class settles. His voice starts, steady, confident, but it reaches me through static.

Because the warmth isn't fading.

If anything, it's growing, as if my body is answering it. As if the signal under my skin has found something to sync with.

I swallow, throat tight.

I try to breathe like nothing is happening. Like I'm sitting in the back of a classroom like every other student.

But my skin is too aware. The air feels charged. The glass in the windows looks thinner than it should.

The instructor's gaze sweeps the room in a practiced arc.

When it reaches the back row, it pauses, not a stare, not accusation, just a beat too long. Like he sees the empty ring of chairs around me. Like he sees me.

Then he looks away and keeps talking.

My fingers dig into the desk edge until my nails ache.

The surrounding quiet should feel like comfort. It does. And that's the problem. Something is happening to me. I sit perfectly still, and inside, a part of me I've never met is waking up. I would very much like her to go back to sleep. I do not think she is going to.

CHAPTER 6

MAGNOLIA

Lochan

I do not run. Prey flees. Guilt runs.

I walk, measured, civilized, until the stone gives way to trees and my body stops arguing about turning back.

Behind me, Blackwood Hall recedes into morning traffic and bells and human laughter. Ahead, the forest closes ranks.

The moment the trunks begin to swallow the last of the academy's brightness, instinct tries to pivot me on my heel.

Turn back.

Go to her.

Claim, no.

Confirm.

The thought is poison. I cut it off before it forms.

Protocol: cover first, control second. Everything else can wait.

I push deeper into the woods, choosing ground that muffles steps and breaks sightlines from the perimeter cameras. What passes for a path isn't a path at all. It's memory, angles and gaps I've used a thousand times, the way a blade finds its sheath without looking.

My lungs burn; the heat turns metallic behind my teeth.

Magnolia follows. Not fading. Not thinning. Staying. A signature clinging to me where discipline should be.

I hate how my mind keeps reaching for her like a tongue to a broken tooth. I hate that even while I move away, I'm already mapping the campus around her: cover, exits, sightlines, the places she doesn't know to avoid.

She doesn't know what she stepped into.

The thought lands with a sharpness that isn't panic. Responsibility.

I slow, forcing my breathing into order, counting down, forcing my jaw to loosen, forcing my shoulders to drop, when the air shifts.

A pressure.

A change in the world's posture.

Barry.

He comes out of the trees without sound, not appearing so much as choosing to be visible: dark coat, massive shoulders. He crosses my path and stops so precisely it feels rehearsed. His stance widens, shoulder angled to cut me off like a gate.

I halt hard, boots biting wet earth.

For a split second the wolf surges, irritated, cornered, furious at obstruction. Then the tether hits.

Not words. Never words. A solid downward weight through my ribs. A command in pure sensation: Down.

My pulse stutters. My hands flex at my sides before I can stop them. Nails want to remember what they are.

Barry doesn't move. He just holds me there with the quiet force of his attention. He has done it before. He will do it again.

He is right. I am too close to the edge of myself, too bright, too loud, too scented.

The heat sits at the base of my skull, pressurized, waiting for the smallest crack in discipline.

I force my shoulders to drop. I force my jaw loose. I force the wolf back behind my teeth.

Barry steps closer and presses his shoulder into my thigh, anchoring contact, heavy enough to steady me, deliberate enough to insult me.

A familiar does not crowd his wolf unless his wolf is about to do something stupid.

I breathe through my nose, slow and controlled, counting each inhale like I'm counting my way back to myself.

In. Out.

In. Out.

The tether eases by degrees, not forgiving, allowing.

Good. Now move.

Barry turns his head to the northeast, and the forest answers with a chill that threads straight through my bones.

The perimeter.

Not the academy gate, not the iron mouth where buses stop and the world is told to walk the rest.

The real line.

Stone markers set deep in the woods, older than the school, carved with symbols humans never notice even when their hands brush them. A border that doesn't say keep out. It says behave.

We are too close. Barry's ears twitch.

His body goes still, not stalking, not hunting. Listening.

Patrol.

My blood runs colder.

If patrol tastes magnolia threaded through my breath, there will be questions. There will be reports. There will be eyes on me that don't blink and don't forget.

If they note it, they hunt the reason.

And if they hunt the reason, they find her.

Barry nudges me once, harder this time, a shove in my side that says: back. now.

I take one step away from the stones. Then another. Measured. Controlled. As if I'm simply finishing a run.

Barry stays close at my flank, a shadow that keeps my body honest.

The patrol never appears.

They don't have to.

Their presence is enough.

The forest tightens around the markers, and the rule asserts itself without anyone speaking it aloud.

A human on the wrong side of the markers turns into council business.

Magnolia rises again, sweet and alive, and my stomach turns with the violent urge to disobey.

Barry presses into my leg, steady as stone, and the tether floods me with one brutal truth:

If I go back, I will not be the only one who pays.

I turn away from the boundary.

I do not look toward the academy. I do not let myself imagine her at the bottom of the steps, heat under her skin answering mine like it was always meant to.

I keep moving. Back to the compound. Back to order. Back to consequences.

And all the while, the scent stays with me, soft as a bruise, impossible to scrub out.

Magnolia.

Today I'm meant to be seen, heir on stone, proof the pack is steady and the academy is safe. A calm face in public so no one thinks to look too closely for teeth.

But the heat is climbing, the wolf is too close to the surface. If I step back onto campus like this, I won't just fail my role. I'll break. And if the image cracks, they won't watch me. They'll watch what caused it. I won't let that attention land on her.

So I do the only thing allowed when ceremonial control breaks: I return to containment.

The compound walls rise out of the trees like a verdict. Stone. Iron. Old symbols carved into older arches.

Security that doesn't exist for protection so much as discipline.

The gate stands open, of course it does, because nothing here relies on locks the way humans do. It relies on obedience.

Two guards watch me pass. Neither stops me. Neither greets me. Their eyes flick once, quick and practiced, taking inventory: Face. Posture. Breath. Scent.

I keep mine buried.

In through my nose, slow enough to look human. Out through my mouth, silent enough not to sound like panting. Shoulders down. Hands loose. Mask rebuilt around heat like armor.

Barry stays close at my flank. Not a dog. Not a pet. A constant weight that keeps my body honest.

Inside, the air changes, cleaner, drier, disciplined. Footsteps in corridors. Voices clipped. Doors opening and closing with purpose. A place designed to make you remember what you are supposed to be.

Today it only reminds me what I'm failing to be.

Magnolia follows me through the gate anyway.

Not loud. Not obvious. Worse than that, subtle. Threaded in. A stain you can't see until you know exactly where to look.

I head for my quarters on instinct, already planning the routine: water too hot, clothes stripped to neutral, jaw set until my face forgets how to betray me. And then I see Milo.

He has been at the kennel since before I was born. He came up through the pack the way some men come up through families and others come up through wars, and no one has ever quite known how to introduce him in a sentence. Familiar. Liaison. Caretaker. The polite words the council uses do not name what he actually is: a man who has been here longer than the decisions he is asked to keep quiet about. He never married. He never moved into the compound proper. He lives in two rooms above the kennel and eats his meals alone, and the pack treats him the way you treat weather, with respect and without sentiment.

He's by the kennel, hands bare despite the cold, checking latches and bowls and locks in a rhythm so steady it feels like prayer. He glances up before I'm close enough for a human to smell anything.

Which tells me he can.

I stop at the edge of his space.

"Milo."

He doesn't look up from the latch. The routine is an excuse; the awareness is real.

"You're early," he says.

"I'm contained," I correct.

That gets his attention. His eyes flick to my face, one clean assessment, then to Barry at my flank.

Milo's mouth tightens by a fraction. Not judgment. Calculation.

"They'll have noted your absence," he says. Not a warning. A report. "Council's already assembled."

My blood does not cooperate.

"Where are the patrols posted?" I ask.

Milo's gaze slides past me toward the treeline, as if he can see the stones through walls.

"Standard perimeter," he says. "But they're watching harder."

Barry presses into my leg, steadying pressure. The tether tightens: down.

Milo sees it and says nothing. That's the closest thing to kindness he can afford.

"Wash," Milo says. "Breathe. Keep your head down."

He pauses, and the pause contains everything he doesn't say: don't give them a reason. don't give them proof. don't give them her.

My throat tightens around something like gratitude and something closer to rage.

"I can't," I say, softer than intended.

Milo's gaze sharpens a fraction.

"Can't what."

I look at the ground for half a second, not because I'm ashamed, but because if I look toward the academy my body will turn in that direction without my permission. Because even here, behind stone and iron, magnolia sits in the back of my throat like a dare.

"I can't pretend I didn't feel it," I admit.

Barry shifts at my side, heavy and anchoring, pressure through the tether like a hand on my sternum: down.

Milo doesn't flinch. He doesn't react the way a man should react to hearing something dangerous. He only exhales through his nose, slow and controlled, like he's seen storms start with smaller shifts than this.

"Then you're already compromised," he says quietly.

Procedure, not comfort. "So treat it like one."

He steps closer, long enough to lower his voice.

"Whatever you think it was, don't bring it into the room with you."

"I don't think," I cut in, too sharp. "I know."

Because my body already knows.

Because the recognition didn't ask permission from my mind.

Because it didn't feel like temptation.

It felt like an answer.

Milo studies my face for a long beat, then glances toward the corridor, toward council, consequence, the men who will smile and count every crack.

"Be careful," he says simply. "If you go near her again, do it like you mean to survive it."

Barry leans in at my side, heavy as stone, and the tether presses a warning through my ribs, slow, steady, hold your shape.

But inevitability has already taken root. I nod once, not promising anything, not confessing anything, only acknowledging the new geometry of my life.

"I have to know what she is," I say.

The words taste of treason.

They also taste like truth.

Upstairs, I strip my jacket off like it's evidence. I run water too hot and let it punish skin that won't cool. Soap, steam, control by ritual. I scrub until my knuckles go pink.

Magnolia doesn't leave. Not fully. It lingers faint and stubborn in the back of my throat, like the idea of her has already nested somewhere my discipline can't reach.

I dress again, tailored, precise, building the mask back onto my bones.

My reflection looks as it should: calm, composed, heir in black and iron.

Then Barry's weight presses against my leg and the tether tightens.

A reminder. Not of duty, but of danger. I open my door, and the corridor waits.

And I can still taste her, magnolia.

CHAPTER 7
BONFIRE

Something I've discovered about myself: I like playing music out loud.

Not in headphones. Not tucked under someone else's noise. Just open. Allowed to take up space.

Tonight it's soft pop drifting through my room while the last thin sheet of daylight slides behind the academy buildings. Blackwood sits tall and still, old stone holding the day's warmth, reluctant to let go. I perch on the windowsill and let myself breathe. Normal. Private. Mine, for now.

When it was just me and my mom, we shared a bed. Later, in foster houses, there were three bunk beds in rooms meant for one. Crying, footsteps, someone else's breathing in the dark. Nothing was mine.

Here, I have a door that locks. It still feels conditional, like the school could revoke the lock at any time and call it a policy update.

Cold New England air spills through the open window. It should make me shiver.

It doesn't.

There's warmth under my ribs, low and steady. It's been there since the first day, rising without warning, rising without explanation. I tell myself it's stress. New place. New rules.

It doesn't feel like stress. It feels like a thread tied just beneath my sternum.

My phone lights up.

SAINT WILLIAM ACADEMY BONFIRE: 8 PM
FIRST FRIDAY PARTY
OPEN TRAIL. WRISTBAND
CHECK IN. NO ID SCAN.

I stare at the words.

Bonfires are for girls who grew up belonging somewhere. Girls who don't treat freedom as a trick question. But I'm tired of hiding in rooms, treating them as the only safe shape I'm allowed. I want to see what happens if I step into the light and don't flinch.

Cross-country didn't ask politely. It arrived like paperwork already stamped.

Tuesday practice was exactly what Saint William makes everything: controlled. Times. Splits. Clipboards. A route I'm allowed to run and a route I'm not.

I showed up. Of course I showed up. Scholarship isn't optional.

But even doing everything right here feels like being cataloged.

My legs ache in that honest way miles leave behind. The kind that says you chose something.

And Wednesday they handed out uniforms as official Saint William identities. A maroon singlet with my name printed too cleanly, too permanent. The jersey wasn't heavy, but it felt like a tag. The kind of tag that doesn't come off without scissors and a story.

Tonight, apparently, I'm supposed to choose public.

I pull on boots. Grab my coat. My thermos.

Then I open the door.

The hallway is full in a way that makes my stomach tense. Doors slamming, laughter spilling down the stairwell, music turned too high. Friday energy I've only ever watched from the outside. I move with it.

Outside, the campus looks different at dusk. Buildings blur at the edges. Lawns stretch wider. Students drift toward the tree line, flashlights bobbing, someone dragging a speaker like it's a parade float.

I step off the last concrete slab and onto grass.

The closer I get to the trees, the tighter the thread pulls. Low warmth turning insistent, something in the dark tugging my sternum on a string.

Lanterns glow along the trail. It should look festive.

It looks like a threshold.

Right before the first lantern, there's a table.

Folding, half in shadow, with a single oil lantern burning steady. Clipboard, ribbons, stamp pad.

Two older students sit behind it. Not drinking. Not laughing. Working.

The sign reads:

BONFIRE ROUTE CHECK IN
CURFEW EXCEPTION WRISTBANDS

So much for no ID. Just a different kind of ID.

The girl behind the clipboard doesn't ask for names. She looks at faces.

"First year?" she asks lightly, pen already poised.

"Yeah."

"Dorm?"

"Blackwood."

She writes something that isn't Winter. Not my name. Some shorthand I don't get to read.

Then she reaches for my wrist and ties a pale ribbon there with quick efficiency. The knot cinches tight enough that I feel my pulse under it, edges soft but unyielding.

"Just so security doesn't stop you on the way back," she says. "They check wrists after curfew."

Behind her, a boy mid-laugh falls quiet when she glances up. He shifts aside without being told.

Students people move for.

I look down at the ribbon. Silver in lantern light. A soft cuff around my skin.

Counted. Cleared. Allowed.

It shouldn't bother me. It does.

Because it isn't decoration. It's proof I'm supposed to be here, and proof someone decided what "here" means.

I step past the table before pride can argue.

The trail narrows. The forest swallows campus light. Lantern glow. Crunching leaves. Cold air along my cheeks sharp enough to sting.

The thread tightens again as I near the trees, drawing me forward with quiet insistence.

Ahead, orange pulses between trunks.

The bonfire.

Smoke hits first. Then heat. Flames roar high enough to paint the lowest clouds gold. Students swarm around it in loose, messy circles. Music thunders through dirt and bone.

I hover at the edge.

And then the crowd shifts. Not a scene. Not silence. Just bodies making room without meaning to, the clearing already knowing where attention is supposed to go.

He appears on the far side of the fire.

Tall. Dark clothes. Shoulders held like he's containing something that refuses to stay contained.

He doesn't push through the crowd. It parts.

My breath falters.

Not because he's beautiful, though he is in a way that feels unfair.

Because something in me recognizes him.

He lifts his head.

Even through smoke and flame, I know he's looking at me.

The thread snaps taut. Warmth turning sharp, direction locking, a hook caught under my sternum.

Before my body can move, a voice cuts in beside me.

Low. Controlled.

"Don't."

I turn.

A girl stands there in a maroon blazer, academy crest catching firelight. Hair pulled back tight. Eyes steady.

Prefect.

"Not him," she says.

Her gaze flicks to my wrist. The silver ribbon.

"That band gets you the lit route," she adds. "There and back."

Her eyes shift past me toward him.

"It doesn't cover the tree line."

She doesn't sound cruel. She sounds certain, repeating a rule she's enforced before, more times than the rule deserves.

Across the fire, his gaze finds mine again.

It isn't long. It's enough.

My body tilts.

I step away from the flames.

The noise dulls behind me. Lantern light thins. The trees loom darker at the edge of the clearing.

There's a stone marker half buried at the tree line. Moss clinging to its edges. A symbol carved into its face.

The academy's permission ends at stone.

I could turn back.

Instead, I step past the marker.

Lantern glow drops away. The forest swallows sound, hungry. Leaves shift under my boots. Branches knit overhead. Cold air cuts sharper without firelight.

Something moves deeper in the dark.

Not wind.

A choice.

He steps into view.

Not fully. Not dramatically. Just enough for an outline. For breath. For presence.

Closer now, I see his wrist.

Not silver. A dark metal band catching moonlight, too deliberate to be jewelry. A clearance band.

My lungs forget the rhythm of breathing.

He doesn't move.

The stillness in him isn't calm.

It's restraint.

His eyes lock on mine, and the moment clicks into place like a door.

My mouth opens. No words come.

I never once considered what would happen if the dark answered.

He takes one step, not toward me, but into a slice of moonlight where the fire can't reach.

And my body follows.

One step.

Then another.

Three feet. Nothing and everything.

His gaze drops once to my wrist. The silver ribbon.

Something shifts in his expression. Recognition, sharp as a cut.

Then his eyes lift again.

"I shouldn't be here," I whisper.

His voice comes rough, quiet. "I know."

The words land heavy between us.

"Then why am I still standing here?"

He doesn't hesitate.

"Because I'm here."

The air tightens.

His phone vibrates. Once. Twice. Someone is counting him. His jaw flexes. His shoulders go rigid, the interruption landing as pain.

"I have to go," he says.

"Why?"

He looks at me, really looks, and whatever is in his eyes makes my stomach drop.

"Because if I stay," he says quietly, "I won't stop."

The warmth under my ribs surges so hard it almost knocks the air out of me.

He steps back. It costs him. You can see it in his shoulders, in the way his hands flex, remembering something sharper than fingers.

A shape shifts behind him in the dark, too big for the lie, intelligent eyes catching moonlight for half a second before it disappears again.

My pulse stutters.

He turns, fast and controlled, and the trees take him back without resistance.

And just like that, he's gone. The forest exhales. I stand in the space he left, breath fogging unevenly. The cold comes back first. Then the thread, tightening again, not pulling me forward now. Pulling back. Toward him. I turn toward the faint lantern glow and step back across the stone marker.

Lantern light touches my boots again. A beam of white light snaps across the path.

"Hey."

Not a drunk student. Security.

Jacket zipped to the throat. Walkie clipped to his chest.

His gaze goes straight to my wrist.

"Band."

I lift my arm.

He checks the knot. The color. The placement. Then he angles his flashlight past me, brief and sharp, to the stone marker behind my shoulder.

Then he looks at me.

"Stay on the lit route," he says. "You leave it again, I escort you back."

I swallow. "I didn't…"

He's already scanning the tree line, knowing what moves out there.

"Back to the fire," he says. "Now."

I walk. Music grows louder. Trees pretend they're just trees again, which is the most Saint William thing about them. But the ribbon burns against my pulse. Counted. Cleared. And somewhere beyond the lantern light, the thread pulls once more. Back.

CHAPTER 8
THRESHOLD

Lochan

I shouldn't have come to the bonfire. But choice never enters the equation. My wolf knew it before I did.

The shift starts long before the clearing opens, before the music builds courage into noise, before lanterns teach the forest to look harmless.

Bonfires are human ritual. Fire, bodies, heat mistaken for belonging. That's exactly why the academy approves them. Sanctioned chaos. A way to count who drifts, who drinks, who crosses lines and calls it freedom.

Tonight I'm meant to be visible: heir on display, calm face, proof the line holds.

So I arrive the way I've been trained to arrive everywhere: composed, deliberate, forgettable in the right way.

Lucky waits near the path, plastic cup in hand, laughing without drinking. His eyes find mine anyway, sharp and quick.

His look says: You disappeared earlier. You're here now. Don't do it again.

I nod once and move past him.

The crowd adjusts without noticing it has adjusted. Space opens. It always does.

The ribbon table sits at the mouth of the trail: same two older students, clipboard, lantern, stamp pad.

They look up together when I step into the light. Not surprised, not impressed. Alert.

The girl's pen hesitates. "Evening," she says.

I don't answer. I don't slow. I don't offer my wrist.

I already wear a clearance band, so dark it reads black in the firelight, not a curfew exception, not decorative, not optional.

The clipboard lowers.

The boy behind the stamp pad clicks the stamp once anyway, an empty, habitual motion, then makes a short mark on the list without looking up.

I'm already logged.

Out beyond the lantern spill, Barry stands where the light doesn't reach.

When the fire flares, his eyes catch for a second, then disappear back into the dark.

The clearing opens ahead. Smoke, alcohol, cologne, sweat. Human heat rolling thick and careless.

And beneath it, magnolia.

Not perfume. Not memory. Living bloom under cold air: wet green petals, sap sweet, rain metal underneath. It hits low and immediate. My ribs tighten. My wolf lifts its head.

Barry's tether presses through the bond, hard and simple.

Down.

Lucky calls my name once from the fire's edge. I hear it. I don't answer.

I stay long enough to be seen. Then I leave.

Not running. Walking. Measured. Away from flame and bodies and witnesses, far enough that if my hands flex wrong, no one will see it.

The noise dulls behind me. The forest sharpens.

Cold air. Pine resin. Damp soil. Leaves whisper over each other, conspiring around me.

My skin stays hot.

That's the first real problem. The heat doesn't belong to the fire. It doesn't fade when the fire does. It's mine.

And it's rising.

Barry's presence tightens in warning.

Hold.

"I am," I say under my breath.

The wolf isn't frantic. It's certain. That is worse.

The path narrows until lantern light disappears. The clearing becomes memory. The academy becomes something far away and irrelevant.

I stop where the trees break into a shallow pocket of moonlight. Not a clearing. Not social. Just a place that exists whether anyone stands in it or not.

Past the lantern line, there's no plausible reason to be here.

My phone vibrates in my pocket.

I don't check it.

Another vibration, then another, quickening.

Lucky again. A check-in turning into a command.

Return. Now.

Too late.

Magnolia drifts in on the wind. Soft. Close. My lungs lock.

The wolf does not snarl.

It reaches.

Here.

The wind shifts again.

And she steps into the break in the trees, silver ribbon catching moonlight, boots quiet on damp leaves, breath uneven in the cold.

For a split second, I understand why men burn kingdoms down.

Three feet. Nothing and everything.

She swallows. "I shouldn't be here."

My voice scrapes out of me. "I know."

The forest holds still, listening for what we'll do next.

She looks at the space between us, reading it as something physical. "Then why am I still standing here?"

Leaving would require tearing something out of my chest.

I give her the only truth I can afford.

"Because I'm here."

The words land and the discipline fractures. Barry's warning surges through the bond.

Hold.

She steps into the strip of moonlight and the warmth that rolls off her is not human. It isn't fire.

It's alive.

My hand digs into bark behind me hard enough to split skin. Pain sparks clean and grounding.

My phone vibrates again.

And again.

Lucky is no longer asking. He's signaling. I can feel the pattern behind it. The clock he keeps for me, the one that saves me.

Return. Now.

The wolf claws up my spine. I feel the shift try to take root in my jaw, my hands.

Her eyes stay on me.

Not afraid.

Not understanding.

That's the danger.

If she stays while I lose control, she becomes part of it. Not witness. Catalyst.

"I have to go," I say.

She doesn't argue. She's trying to memorize my face against the dark.

That nearly undoes me.

I step back. Every inch costs.

Barry's bulk slots into the space between us, silent, immovable. No growl, no threat. Just refusal made physical.

The trees close over me fast.

The second she disappears from sight, the craving hits. Not violence. Her.

It bends me forward. My hands shake. My vision goes razor clear. I force myself to keep walking, faster, because running would make my body choose teeth.

My phone vibrates again, then stops.

That's worse.

Silence means Lucky has turned his attention outward. It means he's gone to someone else.

Council is watching patterns tonight. First Friday. Optics. Presence.

Heir visible. Heir controlled.

If Lucky reports absence, it's recorded. If it's recorded, it's correlated. Time, location, who left the fire, who returned alone.

They won't accuse.

They'll observe.

Observation is worse.

Barry appears at my flank without a sound.

The tether presses hard.

Contain.

I drag air into my lungs and force it to behave. Shoulders down. Jaw loose. Hands open.

By the time the clearing's edge reappears through trees, my face is rebuilt.

Lucky spots me immediately. His posture shifts, barely, and he angles his body a half step closer, guiding me toward the center of the firelight without touching.

I step back into the heat and noise.

Laughter. Music. Smoke.

No one looks twice.

That's the point.

Lucky falls into step beside me, still casual on the surface. "You disappear again," he says lightly, "and I have to answer for it."

"Then don't," I reply.

His smile doesn't change. "That's not how this works."

No.

It isn't.

Across the clearing, I see the maroon blazer prefect near the trail entrance. Watching traffic. Watching wrists. Watching patterns.

Her gaze flicks to me.

Then past me.

Calculating.

The silver ribbon would have marked her. Open trail. Logged.

Security sweeps the outer path every twenty minutes. Wrist checks after curfew.

If she stepped past the stone marker, that becomes a problem.

My jaw tightens.

Legacy is permission. Her ribbon is a boundary. Two systems running parallel, not meant to intersect.

Lucky studies my face for half a second too long. "Everything good?" he asks.

"Yes."

Lie.

He doesn't press. He won't, here.

But he stays close, positioned between me and the dark edge of the clearing like a man who knows exactly where my body wants to go.

The council room will smell like smoke and discipline later. They'll talk about attendance. Donors. First impressions.

They won't say her name.

They don't know it.

Yet.

That is the only advantage I have.

I stay visible ten more minutes. Long enough.

Then I leave properly this time. Through the lit trail, past the ribbon table, under lantern light.

Counted.

Barry moves ahead into shadow.

The forest accepts me again without comment.

The pull under my sternum does not loosen.

It tightens.

This wasn't a coincidence.

It was alignment.

This was a threshold.

And I will cross it again.

CHAPTER 9

CHECKPOINT

Winter

The crowd closes around me the moment I step back into the firelight.

Heat. Smoke. Bass thudding through the dirt.

I'm standing on the outer ring, fire at my left shoulder, the lit trail and ribbon table somewhere behind the crowd near the trees. Close enough to feel watched. Far enough to pretend I'm just another body here.

I keep my wrist down.

Not because I'm ashamed of the ribbon. Because I hate what it means. How fast it turns me from student to subject. How quickly someone decides the safest version of me is the one that stays inside a marked route.

Catherine finds me with the precision of someone who has radar for isolation.

"There you are," she says, like I wandered off to flirt instead of getting stopped by security and pushed back into the light.

I open my mouth, but what comes out isn't the truth. It's the smaller thing that fits in public.

"I just needed air."

She laughs, easy. "Girl, the whole night is air."

Then the energy shifts

70

Not a hush. Not a scene. A recalibration you feel in your spine first, the crowd inhaling together and forgetting to exhale.

Conversations don't stop. They soften. Laughter drops half a note. Bodies adjust in ways that look casual if you've never had to read a room for survival.

I've always had to read a room.

Catherine's hand brushes my elbow, quick, almost careless, guiding me a half step into the shadow of a taller student, out of a clean line of sight from the trail entrance.

Her sleeve rides up.

Red ribbon. Not party red, not cute. Red people make room for.

Her smile stays on the fire, but her voice slips in beneath the music. "Don't make it obvious."

"Obvious how?" I keep my eyes forward.

"Wrist down," she murmurs. "Eyes off the red pocket. And don't drift toward the table."

My stomach tightens.

Near the trees, there's a pocket of people that doesn't move with the rest of the crowd. They aren't pressed together. They aren't shouting to be heard. They stand with space around them. Proximity is something they grant.

Red catches the light. Then another. Then another.

No one touches them. No one bumps them by accident. People curve around that pocket the way they curve around a wet paint sign.

Authority, my brain supplies, before I even know why. Not popular, not just rich. Something sanctioned.

My own ribbon sits pale against my skin. Silver. In the lantern glow it looks innocent, like a curfew band. But now it's the first thing I'm aware of, my wrist suddenly a passport and a warning at the same time.

I lift my thermos just to have something to do with my hands.

The music is loud enough to vibrate in my ribs and still I feel him before I see him. Presence at my shoulder, close enough to change the air.

His voice lands at my ear, low and amused, like he's allowed. "Keep your wrist down if you're going to stare."

My stomach drops, sharp and hot. The words find a bruise under my skin and press on it.

I don't turn right away. Rule one: don't show surprise. Don't hand anyone the satisfaction of knowing they got to you. Foster kid Olympics, gold medal event.

Beside me, Catherine's body stills.

Not fear.

Recognition.

When I finally look, he's already moving past, halfway gone like he never needed my reaction in the first place.

Light hair. Clean posture. Hands in his pockets like the world is something he's already bored with.

The fire snaps and throws sparks, and in that flare I catch his wrist.

Red. Not ribbon, not soft.

A band, glossy and official.

They yield.

He threads through and bodies shift automatically. Voices dipping, shoulders angling out of his path, the red cluster turning as one, ready to receive him.

A door opening without anyone touching the handle.

Catherine leans in, voice soft at my ear. "That's Jack Forrester."

"Who?" My mouth is dry.

She exhales slow. Careful. As if the name has weight she can't afford to toss around. "Student Body President."

"That was him talking to me?"

Catherine keeps her gaze on the fire, on the space he just passed through like heat through a room. "No," she says. "That was just Jack being Jack."

I wait, but she doesn't rush to sell me comfort.

After a beat, she adds, gentler, "It's complicated. You'll figure it out living with me."

My eyes drop without meaning to.

Silver.

I pull my sleeve down, fabric trying and failing to undo being noticed.

Catherine's attention snaps forward, sharp. "Okay," she says. "Now don't look."

Too late.

Because the conflict starts at the ribbon table.

Not inside the clearing, where the fire can pretend everything is play.

On the lit route, where the academy keeps its hands clean.

A guy barrels up the trail from the trees like he owns the dark. Big. Loud. Already flushed with entitlement. He tries to blow past the table without slowing, shoulder angled to clip the student posted there.

No ribbon visible. Or it's tucked, hidden. He thinks the system can't see what he won't show.

"Move," he snaps.

The student behind the clipboard doesn't flinch. Doesn't raise his voice.

"Wrist," he says, holding out his hand.

The guy laughs like it's a joke. "You serious?"

"Wrist."

Same calm. Same flat certainty.

The guy shoves him.

Not hard enough to knock him down.

Hard enough to make the moment real.

The student turns his head slightly, eyes tracking, and another older student steps in immediately. Bigger. Quieter. He doesn't hurry. He just shifts his stance, feet set like a hinge, and holds out his hand.

"Wrist."

The word doesn't sound like a request coming out of him.

The guy's smile goes mean. "Who the hell are you?"

The bigger student doesn't answer.

He just waits.

The guy swings.

Fast and stupid. All ego. An ugly arc toward someone who hasn't even lifted his shoulders.

His fist hits the bigger student's jaw with a crack that makes my stomach drop.

For one stunned beat, the trail holds its breath.

The bigger student turns his head back slowly, checking the world for alignment.

Then he hits him once.

Not a fight, a correction that is clean and devastating.

The guy drops like a switch got flipped. Knees first, then his body folding into the dirt. His mouth catches the ground and the sound is wrong, soft and final.

Blood flashes bright in the lantern light, one sudden bloom at his mouth that makes the scene look too real to be a party anymore.

People shout. Someone screams. Someone laughs too high, panicked.

And then security appears, too fast.

Three men step out from the trees like they were already placed there, jackets zipped to the throat, walkies clipped to their chests, flashlights cutting hard white lines through smoke and faces.

They don't ask what happened, they don't negotiate.

They separate bodies with practiced hands, hauling the bleeding guy up by his collar like he's not a person. A problem that needs removing.

A beam snaps down the line.

Wrists first. Faces second.

"Up," one of them barks.

Hands lift like a strange prayer.

I don't move fast enough.

Catherine's fingers close around my sleeve and guide my wrist up. Smooth, automatic. She's done it before. She knows what happens when you don't.

The flashlight hits my ribbon. Silver.

The security man's gaze slides off me immediately. The color answers everything he needs to know.

Relief doesn't feel like safety. It feels like being filed.

The beam moves on. Silver. Silver. Silver.

Then it catches red and his posture recalibrates, half a beat of deference he doesn't mean to show.

And the air shifts again.

Because Jack Forrester is standing just beyond the table. Close enough to be part of it, far enough to pretend he isn't. The checkpoint exists whether he's here or not, but tonight it's aligned around him.

He isn't helping.

He isn't reacting.

He's simply present, and that presence edits the room.

His gaze moves over the scene like inventory. Deciding what gets to stay and what gets removed.

Then he turns his head, slow, and his eyes land on me.

Not long, not dramatic. Precise.

The kind of attention that feels like a thumb pressed to a bruise.

My ribbon burns under my sleeve.

I only know I want to hide it, tear it off, keep it anyway, because as much as I hate it, it means I'm not lost in this system.

It means I'm recorded.

Jack's mouth curves, barely. Amused. Curious. Already deciding where I fit.

Catherine's voice tightens at my ear. "Winter. Don't."

I don't answer.

Because the bleeding guy jerks in security's grip and spits red onto the dirt.

The bonfire crackles.

The crowd surges back, hungry for the next thing.

And my body, traitor that it is, doesn't want to leave. It wants to understand what the ribbons mean. Why wrists matter more than names. Because the wrong color doesn't just get you noticed. It gets you corrected. And I have spent eighteen years learning the difference.

CHAPTER 10
CONTAINMENT

Lochan

I don't leave the bonfire. I escape it.

One second longer and I shift in front of her. Under firelight, under ribbons, under the eyes pretending they're here to drink instead of count. I feel the fracture the moment I step back from her. Pressure at the base of my spine. Jaw locking. Teeth aching, bone deciding what shape it prefers.

Barry is there instantly. Shoulder to my hip. Body a wall.

The tether hits.

Move.

I turn without looking back. If I look back, I go back.

The crowd stays loud behind me, but it reaches my ears wrong. Music turns into blunt impact. Laughter goes thin and distant, water over stone. I cut through the outer ring of students fast but not running.

Running is an admission.

I walk hard, head down, hands in my pockets so no one sees my nails darken at the edges.

A Bradford heir doesn't fracture in public.

The words are my father's. They sit in my marrow like law.

The trees take me in.

The moment the forest swallows the last spill of firelight, restraint breaks. The shift hits hard, no easing, no grace, instinct slamming into bone until it wins. Heat knifes through my forearms. Fabric tears at the seams as my hands split into paws mid-step. Breath rips out of a throat that can't decide its shape.

Shame burns hotter than the change.

I shouldn't have left her like that. Silver ribbon lifted under a flashlight, wrists up like a confession. One wrong step from being escorted and corrected in front of strangers.

I dig claws into the dirt until the earth gives.

The beast I've buried under discipline and lineage tears through every seam at once. Not for blood.

For her.

That's the sickness.

Barry appears without sound, a massive shape pacing my shoulder, shadow with weight. The tether holds. Downward pressure through my ribs, a command my body understands without translation.

Down. Hold.

I run.

Not to hunt. To burn the want out of my body before it burns through my skin.

Past the last lantern post, beyond the lit route, the forest turns older. Black trunks, knife-cold air, ground rising and dropping without warning. My body eats it because it was built for this, lungs tearing, heart slamming, muscles pulling tight and releasing in ruthless rhythm.

It should fix me. It doesn't.

Want keeps time with my stride, and her scent, sweet and sharp, wrong-seasoned and impossible, threads through my breath like I swallowed it on purpose.

I force my mind at anything else.

Duty. The compound. The crest stamped into every surface. My father's voice.

It slides off.

Because the only thing my body will hold is the moment she stepped into moonlight and stayed. Still choosing it.

A sound drags out of me. Rougher than a growl. Not threat. Refusal.

Barry shoulder checks me once, hard. Not affection. A warning with bones. The tether hits again.

Down.

I bare my teeth at nothing, then cut away. Deeper into the oldest part of the woods where the air tastes metallic and the trees grow too thick for witnesses.

I run until thought shreds into sensation.

Until panic thins.

Until the wolf's hunger stops feeling like it will crack my ribs open from the inside.

The shift recedes inch by inch. Slow, punishing, being dragged back into skin I never fully fit. Paws split back into hands. Spine stacks itself back in place with an ache that makes stars flicker at the edge of my vision.

I stumble into wet ground and drop to one knee, palms sinking into mud that smells like rot and salt. Human again. Barely.

My hair clings damp to my forehead. Copper coats my tongue. My hands shake once, just once, then I fist them until it stops.

It doesn't matter. I can still taste her.

Barry nudges my shoulder. Low. Steady. A question disguised as pressure.

Do we go back?

"No," I rasp. My voice sounds wrong out here. Too small for what I am in the dark.

"We're fine."

Barry doesn't move. He watches me with that fixed attention that feels like being held to account.

I swallow. "We're fine," I repeat, trying to make repetition become truth.

I stand, roll my shoulders, shake out my hands until the memory of claws feels like a lie.

The sky is thinning at the edges. Black bruising toward violet.

The hour that makes wolves honest.

I head toward the compound without thinking. Heel to toe. Weight even. Spine straight. Trained into legacy like a leash I never cut loose.

Barry falls in beside me.

We skirt campus. Always do. Not because students scare me.

Because the academy has eyes.

And eyes become stories.

And stories become leverage.

The compound lights glow through branches. Too controlled. Too exact. By the time violet bruises the sky into something like morning, I'm close enough to smell stone and iron beneath the trees.

I should feel relief seeing it. Instead, my stomach tightens. Because I can already feel him.

Power tightens the ground first. The subtle pull that makes the trees stand straighter, the air itself remembering who owns this stretch of land.

A guard at the terrace straightens. Radios hush mid-crackle, a dial turned down.

Barry goes rigid. Not fear. Respect, with a warning underneath.

Alpha Rowan Bradford steps onto the terrace, carved from stone. Coat immaculate. Posture clean. Eyes unreadable unless he wants them read.

He doesn't ask where I've been.

He looks at me like a flaw in glass. Not dramatic. Not angry. Just noted.

His gaze drops, briefly, to my hands. To the faint tremor I thought I buried.

Then back to my face.

"Inside," he says. Not a question. A command that settles into my marrow like gravity.

I follow.

Terrace stone is cold under my boots. The house looms. Clean lines, dark glass, old money pressed into architecture. The guards dip their heads as I pass. Not respect. Recognition.

Barry moves at my heel and no one calls him a dog because no one here is stupid enough to pretend.

Warmth hits my skin the moment I step inside. Not comfort. Kitchen heat already running.

The scent hits before I turn the corner. Marrow bones, rare steak, rendered fat, coffee black enough to be a threat.

It isn't hunger that twists me. It's instinct.

The wolf lifts its head again. Irritated by walls. Irritated by other wolves. Irritated by how close I am to scrutiny while still carrying evidence in my breath.

The house is awake in its usual way. Not speaking, awake. Working awake.

The dining room is long and old and too beautiful to relax in. Dark wood. Heavy chairs. Portraits that look like warnings.

Breakfast isn't a moment here. It's rotation.

Men drift in and out in layers. Those who train before sunrise, those who train after, those who don't train at all but still expect the world to move for them.

Conner won't appear at all. Sixteen and the youngest of us, the household has long since stopped pretending he keeps schedule. Nathaniel will collect him later. The chair he might have used is already passed over without comment.

Rowan is already seated.

Of course he is.

He eats like he leads. Unhurried. Exact. Steak carved into neat pieces, knife work so clean it feels like its own kind of violence.

Benjamin Knight stands at Rowan's right shoulder like a statue that breathes. Quiet, immovable. His attention tracks me once, then Barry, neutral as a camera.

Across the table, my uncle looks up over the rim of his coffee mug.

Nathaniel.

Sleeves rolled once. Hair slightly disobedient. Posture easy in the way only powerful men dare to be. He looks like a man who chose his life, not a man who inherited it.

He lifts the mug in greeting.

"Long night?" he asks, casual as weather.

His eyes are not casual. They flick once, fast, to Barry. Then back to me.

Rowan doesn't glance up.

"You're late," he says.

"I know."

A beat.

Then, without raising his voice: "Stay contained."

It lands like a hand at the back of my neck.

A warning that lands in my marrow. Not loud. Just law.

I sit without being told. The only defiance I can afford is making obedience look like a choice.

Barry settles at my heel, close enough that his warmth presses into my shin. Grounding. Tethering.

Rowan finally looks at me.

His gaze is weight. It presses against ribs and jaw and the thin line of control I've been holding all night with bloodless teeth. His eyes drop once to my throat, to my collar, checking for proof.

Then he looks away.

"A Bradford heir doesn't fracture. Ever."

My stomach knots.

"I didn't," I say.

Rowan's knife pauses mid-cut. He doesn't look up.

"You almost did."

I know what the solution looks like. I have always known. The compound has a name for want it cannot authorize. It calls that name Maris Harlan and considers the matter closed.

The correction is surgical.

Benjamin's attention tightens by a fraction.

Nathaniel's mouth curves. Not amused. Interested.

I keep my breathing even. Keep my face blank.

"I handled it," I say.

Rowan sets the knife down.

The sound is small.

The room stills anyway.

"Tell me why it happened," he says, finally looking at me, "without lying."

My tongue feels too big for my mouth.

Confess, and it becomes reportable.

Reportable becomes council.

Council becomes her.

So I say nothing.

Rowan reads the silence like he reads everything. His gaze sharpens. Still not angry.

Assessing.

"Whatever this is," he says quietly, "you will master it. Or it will master you."

Barry's head lifts slightly at my heel. Not a growl. A warning vibration only I can feel.

Nathaniel sets his mug down. Gentle punctuation.

"You were at the first bonfire," he says, like neutral conversation.

"I was."

"And you went alone."

Statement.

I don't answer.

Rowan pushes his plate away with measured finality.

"Eat," he says to me.

A reprieve wrapped in command.

I reach for the plate placed at my setting without anyone asking what I want, because wants have never mattered here.

My hands don't shake.

Not visibly.

Only Barry knows how hard I'm holding myself together.

I cut. Lift. Chew.

It tastes like iron and smoke and obligation.

Movement shifts at the doorway.

Lucky appears with the ease of someone who belongs everywhere without ever looking like he's trying. Hair damp from an early shower. Expression casual. His eyes go straight to mine.

You alive?

I give him nothing. I can't.

He steps in, greeting Rowan with a dip of his head that reads like respect and strategy in equal measure.

"Alpha."

Rowan acknowledges him with a glance that says: I see you. I remember you. Don't disappoint me.

Lucky takes a seat further down the table without being told.

Nathaniel's gaze flicks between us, quick and sharp. He sees alliances the way politicians see votes.

Rowan stands.

Benjamin moves with him.

The room rearranges itself around their motion without anyone thinking about it.

Before Rowan leaves, he leans slightly toward Nathaniel, voice low enough it shouldn't carry.

I still catch the edge.

"Keep your people out of the academy this week," Rowan says. Not a request.

Nathaniel's brows lift a fraction. "That's difficult."

Rowan's gaze goes colder. "Then make it easy."

Silence turns electric.

Nathaniel smiles faintly, agreeing to nothing and everything at once.

"Of course," he says.

Rowan looks at me once more.

Final assessment.

Then he walks out.

Benjamin follows.

The room exhales without realizing it.

Nathaniel lingers, eyes still on me, then speaks casual again like he didn't just get threatened over breakfast.

"You're going to class," he says.

"I am."

"And you're going to pretend you slept." Almost kind. Almost.

I don't answer. Pretending is what we do best.

Nathaniel pushes back and stands. As he passes behind my chair, he pauses just long enough to drop a sentence beside my ear.

Soft. Precise.

"You smell like you ran from something you didn't beat."

He already knows what Rowan will call the solution.

He's known it for years.

He just hasn't had to look at it directly until now.

My jaw tightens.

He doesn't wait for a response.

He continues on, leaving behind only expensive cologne and old politics.

Lucky watches him go.

Then Lucky looks at me again.

This time his voice is quieter.

"Where were you?" Not curiosity. Fear dressed as calm.

I keep chewing. Keep my face blank.

"I ran," I say.

Lucky's gaze drops, briefly, to Barry at my heel.

Barry doesn't move. Doesn't blink. Just watches.

Lucky's voice lowers further. "And?"

The wolf shifts restlessly against bone. Irritated by questions, irritated by proximity, irritated by how much of last night still clings to me.

"I stayed contained," I say.

Lucky's mouth tightens, wanting to believe it and unable to.

"Lochan…"

Hearing my name from him lands in my chest. Not comfort. Pressure. Responsibility.

I stand before he can say anything else.

Chair legs scrape.

Barry rises with me, seamless.

My plate is barely touched. It doesn't matter.

I look down at Lucky, just long enough to make the message clear.

Not here.

Not in this room.

Lucky holds my gaze.

Then nods once.

I leave the dining room.

The hallways are quiet but not empty. People move in patterns. The house runs on rules that never get spoken aloud.

I reach the back corridor where glass doors look out into the woods.

Dawn has thickened. The sky is bruised violet, trees black against it like ink.

I pause with my hand on the handle because for one split second my body leans the wrong way.

Not toward class.

Not toward duty.

Toward the forest.

Toward the place the night still lives in my blood like a trap.

Barry presses into my leg once. Firm.

A brace.

I exhale through my nose. Slow. Controlled.

I open the door.

Cold air bites my face.

And I understand, finally, why men like my father fear weakness more than enemies.

CHAPTER 11
GRAVITY

I'm on my feet before I know I've moved, my body already understanding that last night put me on a list.

The room is still dark, still soft, still pretending it can hold me. Catherine sleeps across the room under her lavender silk eye mask, breathing slow, the breath of someone who has never imagined the world might have teeth. I don't wake her. I don't even look at her twice.

Something in me won't let the room close.

My body is too awake, too alert, a live wire threaded under my skin while I wasn't looking, every nerve listening for a sound that hasn't happened yet.

Not the fire. Not the shouting. Not the blood.

Him.

The way he stepped out of the dark, the forest deciding to give itself a shape. The way the air sharpened when he looked at me, cleaner, colder, suddenly exact. The way he held himself with restraint chosen in both hands.

And the way I didn't look away.

I swallow hard. The memory doesn't budge.

It keeps surfacing in pieces. The cut of his jaw. The tension in his shoulders. The stillness in his eyes that wasn't calm so much as warning. A held thing. A dangerous thing. The kind of stillness that suggests if he ever let go, something else would step out.

There's a pull low in my ribs, quiet but relentless. Not pain, not hunger. A tug that keeps pointing outside, my body sick of waiting for my mind to catch up.

I try to sit.

I try to breathe.

Nothing works. My muscles are pacing even while I stand still.

So I leave.

Socks. Shoes. Hoodie. Hair up, ugly, fast, out of the way. I'm not building a version of myself today. I'm trying to survive one.

The hallway is empty. The academy is hushed in that post bonfire hour, after everyone spent the night pretending they're untouchable and now they're sleeping off the lie.

I make it three steps before the silence changes.

Thin. Almost nothing.

A whisper of static, clipped low, too close. Someone cleared their throat on the other end of a radio.

"…copy," a voice breathes.

Not a student prank, not dorm gossip. A patrol channel: professional, bored, not meant to be heard.

I don't react. I keep moving. I didn't hear it. I'm allowed to exist without being acknowledged.

Outside, dawn is barely a bruise on the horizon.

Cold air hits my face and I take it as punishment and relief at the same time. I head for the trail.

Coach handed out the route sheet at practice earlier in the week, treating it as normal. Cross-country, apparently, is just an extracurricular and not a system that stamped ATHLETE under my name without asking.

The entrance sits where campus stops pretending it's separate from the woods. Lantern posts. Rope lights. A sign that looks friendly until you read it long enough:

TRAINING ROUTE
STAY ON LIT PATH
WRISTBANDS REQUIRED AFTER DARK

It's daylight. The policy still has teeth.

At Friday's team meeting, it wasn't about running. It was about rules. Routes, curfews, injuries, reporting.

Coach didn't say "don't go past the rope light." He said it like everyone already knew. Stay on the lit path.

I start running.

At first it's just movement. Breath, rhythm, the clean math of one foot then the other. The honest ache in my calves. The way cold air scrubs my lungs.

This is what I know.

Running is the only place my body has ever felt like it belongs to me.

The trees close in fast. The academy falls behind. The trail turns to packed dirt and leaf rot and roots that try to trip you if you stop paying attention.

I don't stop paying attention.

The pull in my ribs doesn't fade. It moves into the rhythm like it's always been there, threading itself through my stride.

Then it tightens.

Not toward anything I can name. More toward being found.

The back of my neck heats, focused, exact. A fingertip pressing right between my shoulder blades.

I tell myself it's nothing.

No one is chasing me.

No one even knows I'm out here.

And still the air keeps feeling like it's taking attendance.

I hit the first bend where the lantern posts thin out.

That's where I see it.

A small black box mounted to a tree at shoulder height. Disguised as trail maintenance. Matte casing, tiny lens, pinprick light.

It shouldn't matter.

As I pass, it clicks, soft and precise. Not nature, not random.

A green light blinks once.

Then twice.

My stomach drops, quick and involuntary, my body recognizing a trap before my brain can name it. The pull in my ribs spikes sharp as a stitch.

I slow for half a beat, runner annoyed, survivor awake. My wrist tingles under my sleeve. The ribbon isn't there anymore, but the idea of it is.

I keep going, because stopping out here feels worse than being seen.

The trail dips and rises. Trees grow thicker, older. The air smells darker. Pine and damp earth and something clean underneath it, like cold stone.

The academy's training route starts to feel less like a suggestion and more like a leash they can tug from anywhere.

I push farther than the paper map wants me to.

The rope light ends ahead, clean line, clear boundary.

I see the rule.

And I break it anyway.

I take the cut where the rope stops, stepping off the approved path to test whether the woods will bite or the academy will.

The forest goes quieter immediately. Not peaceful. Watchful. Waiting to see if I'm stupid enough to walk into its mouth.

But the pull doesn't loosen.

It tightens.

A reel turning.

I slow to a jog. Breath fogs in front of my face. My skin goes cold. My ribs go hot.

And then I see him.

Not the boy.

Not the man.

The dog.

Except it's not a dog.

He's too big for that lie. Too silent. Too still. A dark shape half merged with shadow where the trail should not be safe and no one should be standing at dawn unless they belong there.

And his eyes, too intelligent, too human in the way they hold attention, make my scalp prickle with the certainty that I've been recognized.

His head is slightly lowered. Listening to something that isn't me.

Then his gaze shifts.

And lands on me.

The same impossible stillness I felt last night, only now it's in an animal's body. Not looking so much as measuring.

My whole body locks.

Recognition without reason.

He doesn't come closer.

He doesn't bare teeth.

He just watches, chest rising slow, counting my breaths.

My heart bangs hard against my ribs.

I don't move.

Because the truth arrives clean and cold.

If I run, I prove I'm prey.

If I stay, I prove I'm stupid.

The dog that isn't a dog shifts his weight once.

Just present.

A tether tightening.

And behind him, deeper than my eyes should be able to see, the woods look wrong.

Not wild.

Organized.

Paths back there that don't belong to hikers or students. The forest has doors.

My throat dries.

I back up one step. Then another. Slow, controlled.

I keep my eyes on him, because turning my back feels like signing something I can't read.

He doesn't follow.

He doesn't chase.

He only watches until the rope light comes back into view, until the lit route reappears like a line of safety the academy can claim.

The moment I cross back onto the approved path, the leash slackens, pressure easing at the back of my neck by half a degree. The route accepts me again.

I blink.

And he's gone.

Just not there. The woods erased him the second I stepped back into permission.

My lungs finally remember how to work.

I turn and run.

Hard.

Fast enough that the cold air burns.

Fast enough that my legs start to protest.

Fast enough that my body can pretend this is just training.

By the time I hit campus again, dawn has softened into pale morning. Sweat cools too quickly in the cold, making me shiver even as my pulse keeps stuttering. It never stopped being chased.

I don't go back to the room.

I go to the dining hall.

Because hunger is easier than whatever that was.

Inside, warmth hits first. The air smells like cinnamon rolls and smoked maple bacon.

Coffee. Butter. Money.

I hover at the doorway. My body expects someone to stop me, to ask what I'm doing here, to demand proof I belong.

No one does.

Which almost feels worse.

I move to the fruit bar on instinct. Abundance still feels like a trick. My hand is fast and practiced. Banana, two apples, slid into my bag with efficiency that isn't shame and isn't pride.

Just survival.

Then I force myself to do the normal thing too. Oatmeal. Spoon. A bowl that looks like breakfast instead of proof.

I find an empty spot at a long table and sit.

The room hums with quiet chatter. Silverware clinks. Chairs scrape. Someone laughs softly, even laughter mannered here.

I take my first bite.

And my body finally eases.

Not fully.

But enough.

Enough that my thoughts unclench. Enough that last night can slide into a box labeled bonfire instead of threshold.

I'm halfway through the bowl when someone sits beside me.

Not across.

Beside.

That's not how these tables work. People spread out. They keep a polite distance. They don't sit close unless they're claiming something.

I freeze with the spoon midair.

I don't look right away. I learned young. If someone wants your attention, don't hand it over for free.

He doesn't say hello. He doesn't ask if the seat is taken. He slides in with the confidence of someone space belongs to. Controlled. Clean. Certain.

Then, softly, making nothing of it, he speaks.

"You run like you're trying to disappear."

The words aren't cruel.

That's the problem.

They're accurate in a way that feels like being stripped.

I turn my head.

Jack Forrester.

Close enough that his shoulder nearly touches mine. Testing how much room I'll give him without fighting.

His wrist is half hidden under his sleeve, and after last night, after ribbons and routes and colors, I know that everyone who matters shows their color on purpose.

The fact that he doesn't makes my stomach tighten.

His gaze drops to my bag, the fruit tucked inside like contraband, and something like amusement flickers at the corner of his mouth. Then his eyes lift to my face.

Evaluating.

"Careful," Jack says, voice still low. "This place doesn't like when people try to outrun what's already decided."

My pulse starts again, sharp and quick, because my body recognizes danger faster than my mind does.

"Why are you sitting here?" I ask. "Are you following me?"

Jack's mouth barely moves, almost amused.

He tilts his head slightly, listening, not to me.

To something else.

Then he says, almost conversational.

"You were on the route at dawn."

It isn't a question.

Cold pours through me.

Because I didn't tell anyone. I don't even know anyone. And still he knows.

The spoon in my hand trembles once. I set it down carefully. Moving wrong would make the whole room notice.

Jack lets the silence stretch until it turns into a rope.

Then he stands. Smooth. Controlled. He never really sat down at all.

He disappears into the flow of breakfast.

I stay seated, oatmeal cooling in the bowl.

I didn't outrun anything.

I only proved I can be followed.

CHAPTER 12

SAY MY NAME

Lochan

Monday arrives the way Mondays do after weekends that cost something: too bright, too fast, already asking for things you haven't finished paying for.

I've been inside Evelyn Ashcroft-Forrester's office four times in two years. Each time the room has been exactly the same: books organized by subject rather than size, a window facing the east lawn instead of the main quad, a desk clear enough to suggest the real work happens somewhere else. She doesn't decorate with authority. She doesn't need to. The room already knows what it is.

She rises when I enter.

That's the thing about Evelyn. She always rises. Not deference. Acknowledgment. The distinction is precise, and she knows it.

"Lochan." Warm, unhurried, expectant without ever having summoned me.

"Headmistress."

She gestures toward the chair across from her desk. I don't take it. She doesn't press. She moves to the desk and turns the form toward me: endowment record, legacy continuation, my name already printed at the top in the font the school has used for thirty years.

"Formality," she says. "Your signature and you're done."

I cross to the desk. Pick up the pen.

The form is exactly what she said it is.

Which means this isn't about the form.

I sign where indicated. Set the pen down without rushing. Evelyn takes the form back and sets it aside with careful efficiency, already finished with it.

That's the other thing about Evelyn. She never looks away first. In two years I have not once made her flinch, drop her gaze, or unsettle the way people usually do when they understand what the heir represents.

I have never decided if that reassures me.

"How are you finding the new term?" she asks.

The question is warm. Textbook. The kind that comes with a smile already attached.

"Fine," I say.

"Good." She folds her hands on the desk, not clasped, just resting. "The start of term is always an adjustment. New students. New variables."

New variables.

The words land with a precision that isn't accidental.

I keep my face neutral. "Nothing I can't manage."

Her expression doesn't change. The warmth stays exactly where it was, practiced and genuine at once in the way that only comes from having done this for thirty years.

"No," she says. "I don't imagine it is."

A beat of silence. Not empty. The kind that has been placed there on purpose.

She doesn't say Jack's name. She doesn't say anything about the weekend or the crack that formed in me while the world kept moving around the shift.

She doesn't need to.

Whatever she was looking for when she put that form on her desk herself instead of sending it through channels, whatever she needed to see in my face before deciding, she has it now.

"That's all," she says. Still warm. Already moving on.

I cross to the door.

"Lochan."

I stop. Don't turn immediately. Give myself one beat to close everything down before I face her.

"Be seen smiling occasionally," she says. "Silence in someone your age reads as a secret."

I meet her eyes.

She looks back.

Neither of us says anything else.

I leave.

The door closes behind me with the particular quiet of a room that absorbed the conversation and kept it.

Outside, the corridor is exactly as I left it: ordinary, lit, the school going about its morning. I walk it the way I always walk it. Even pace. Neutral face. Both hands loose.

My jaw aches.

I hadn't realized how hard I'd been holding it.

The side door swings open into cooler air, courtyard noise, the scrape of a metal chair.

And I hear it.

Not her voice.

Not yet.

"Winter!"

The name cuts through everything.

My entire body locks.

I don't turn at first. I don't have to. My wolf is already moving toward the word, hooked through the ribs.

Winter.

It fits the second it lands in my head. Of course it does. Of course that's what she's called.

I turn.

She's smaller than memory made her. Not fragile, just contained, fine-boned in the way of someone who learned early not to take up more space than she was allowed.

Not prey.

Something you don't risk breaking.

Which is its own danger.

Beside her stands Catherine Montgomery.

I've seen her photo on briefing boards. Human liaison. Legacy blood with public power. The kind we track because pretending not to is how you get surprised.

Catherine's posture matches the file. Born knowing she belongs anywhere she stands.

Their conversation looks easy. Familiar.

My wolf bristles anyway.

Winter says something I can't hear. Catherine answers with a tilt of her head. Winter looks down at her hands, tight, nervous, and Catherine softens just enough for my wolf to notice.

A flicker moves through my chest.

Possessive.

Irrational.

Dangerous.

I step back into shadow, unseen.

I don't know why I'm standing here. I don't know why her scent still sits against my teeth, a memory I never earned.

I only know one thing.

Whatever happened in the woods didn't end there.

Pretending it did might be the first lie I've ever told myself.

Winter tucks a curl behind her ear and glances, quick, involuntary, toward the treeline.

She can feel something watching.

Catherine follows her gaze, says something too low to hear, dry and amused. Winter answers, but her shoulders stay tight.

The wind shifts.

Magnolia. Rain-metal. That living sweetness that doesn't belong in autumn.

My vision sharpens.

It would be so easy to step into the open. Close the distance. Let my body do what it keeps trying to do.

Benjamin's words drag through me, a hand on my throat.

Hold it together. At least until you get back.

If anyone saw me lose control here, if anyone watched the Alpha's son unravel over a human girl, they wouldn't just smell her on me.

They would find her.

And nothing would ever be the same.

The wind shifts again. The scent thins. The moment loosens, a held breath released.

I press my forehead to the brick, eyes shut tight.

In.

Out.

Again.

When I open my eyes, Winter and Catherine are walking away, deep in conversation. Winter doesn't look back.

It shouldn't matter.

It does.

I push off the wall and turn in the opposite direction. Away from the courtyard, away from the quad, away from the version of myself that still believes control is something you can hold forever.

Winter.

The word sits under my tongue, a secret.

I don't say it aloud.

But it's there now.

And it isn't leaving.

CHAPTER 13
OFF CAMPUS

Winter

I don't know when this will feel normal. Being expected.

In my old life, I could vanish and nothing would change. Here, absence gets noticed the way a missing badge gets noticed. Quietly, immediately, and with consequences. So I spend Monday moving. Focused, efficient, annoyingly early to all my classes.

Someone steps into my path in the library garden and I stop short, the moment breaking cleanly instead of shattering.

Catherine smiles, treating this as normal. People run into each other on purpose in Catherine's world.

"Hey," she says, already turning toward the library.

I hesitate, then follow.

Our steps line up easily. This was decided before I caught up to it. Catherine walks without ever worrying about being in the way. A student halfway through cutting across the path sees her, stalls mid-step, and slides around without looking annoyed. Her route has priority.

"There's a fundraiser tonight. The Bradford beginning-of-term donor event," she says, casual. "Off campus."

Off campus means gates, lists, wristbands that aren't for parties.

"Okay," I say, noncommittal.

"I have to go," she continues. "And you're coming with me."

I glance at her. She's smiling, but there's no teasing in it. Just certainty. She already mapped the evening out, and I'm a fixed point in it.

"We aren't allowed to leave campus," I say, because orientation made that sound like doctrine.

"I know," she says easily. "Rules are different when your dad is the Governor. It's hosted at the Mayor's house and my dad's in town for it. We'll make an appearance. Then we'll leave. Promise."

She says we without emphasis. It's the most natural word in the sentence to her.

"Seven," she adds. "I'll help you figure out what to wear."

I don't answer right away. She doesn't wait for one.

I keep walking, the rhythm returning, altered just enough that I can't ignore it.

Seven.

The day goes on without another distraction. I've gotten good at putting things away.

By the time I'm back in the room, Catherine is already dressed.

Music hums low from her phone. Clothes are spread across her bed, not messily, decided. She hands me a dress without looking. My opinion is a delay she's not scheduling.

We're out the door before I can renegotiate anything.

We don't walk out as students.

We walk out expected.

By dusk, the front steps are busy. Laughing girls, a couple of boys too loud, someone sprinting toward the quad with the panic of being late for their own life. But Catherine doesn't merge into it. She cuts through it. A prefect on the steps glances over, clocks her, and looks away on purpose.

There's a car idling at the curb. Not a rideshare. Not a student beater. Black paint that drinks the light. A driver in a dark coat with his hands folded, waiting for a signal.

Catherine doesn't hesitate.

I do.

The driver opens the rear door before we're even close. It's not courtesy. It's choreography.

"Evening, Miss Montgomery," he says. Soft. Certain. He's been saying it all week.

Catherine slides in with the ease of belonging in the back seat of other people's money.

Standing on the steps feels like standing in front of an audience, so I follow.

The door shuts, and the world muffles. The smell inside the car is clean leather and something faintly sweet I can't place.

Catherine checks her lip gloss in the dark window. To her, this is Monday.

My hands stay in my lap. My shoulders stay tense. I keep waiting for someone to stop us.

No one does.

Which feels worse.

The car doesn't take the main exit. It turns toward the side road, the one I've never walked because it isn't meant for feet.

The gate appears out of the trees. It's been there longer than the academy has been pretending to be modern. Iron bars, stone posts, a crest carved so shallow you only notice it if you're looking for things that want to be invisible.

A guard steps out of a small booth. He doesn't wave us through.

He looks in.

Not at Catherine.

At me.

His gaze catches the shape of my face and holds half a beat too long. Checking a reference. His fingers tap his earpiece once, a quiet confirmation, and the gate opens without a sound.

Catherine doesn't even look up. This part isn't real to her.

My stomach knots anyway.

No ID required, I think, then remember how ribbons work, how permissions hide inside polite systems. So much for no ID. Just a different kind.

The drive into town takes ten minutes, maybe fifteen.

The house, estate really, sits behind another gate. Less obvious. More expensive. A place that doesn't need height because it has history.

The driver pulls into a circular drive lined with gravel designed to announce you.

A valet is waiting.

Not a teenager, not weekend work. A man in a dark suit with a clipboard held against his chest, practically part of him.

Catherine steps out first.

"Evening, Miss Montgomery. The Mayor's expecting you," he says, already writing.

And then his eyes move to me.

Not curious. Not rude. Just categorizing.

"And your guest?" he asks, polite enough to be harmless.

Catherine doesn't say my name.

She says, "My roommate."

Not a name. An attachment.

The valet repeats it once under his breath as he writes. "Roommate."

He doesn't look up again.

Counted.

I register the house in pieces before I understand it as a whole. Stone at my eye line, a dark entryway, lights glowing behind tall windows. Greenery presses close to the walls, leaves brushing iron railings and window frames, allowed to grow only as far as beauty permits.

Inside, the sound changes immediately.

Not louder. Quieter. Music low enough that it feels intentional. Voices kept close, overlapping without rising. The space feels full without being crowded. Everyone is aware of how much noise they're allowed to make.

Catherine fits into it instantly.

Her hand finds the small of my back. Not comforting. Positioning. Turning me so I'm not in the open, not in anyone's clean line of sight.

A waiter passes and she takes a flute of champagne without breaking stride, fingers already comfortable around the stem. I hover just behind her shoulder, close enough to be included, far enough to disappear if needed.

The clothes Catherine picked feel unreal on my body. The fabric is soft, heavier than anything I own, the kind that doesn't wrinkle or cling or demand attention. It just exists. My hair is pulled up loosely, strands already slipping free.

I don't feel dressed up.

I feel intact.

People glance at us as we pass. Not openly. Just quick looks that linger a beat too long before smoothing over. Everyone here is white. Most of them are men. Older than us, for the most part. Comfortable in a way that has nothing to do with charm. They stand with their shoulders back, feet planted, voices low but unchallenged.

Silver hair catches the light across the room.

She isn't speaking. She doesn't need to be.

Her gaze finds mine anyway.

It holds a beat too long.

Then Headmistress Evelyn Ashcroft-Forrester looks away first.

It strikes me, watching her, that she's the only woman in the room standing alone. The other women cluster, lean toward each other, soften their laughter. The older men give her the same controlled space they give the red-band men at the bonfire. They don't approach her. They wait for her to approach them. Whatever permission moves through this room moves around her differently than it moves around anyone else here.

I file it without knowing what to file it as.

I'm not invisible.

But I don't factor.

Catherine stops beside a man with her eyes and her posture, cheerful on the surface, built underneath. He smiles with the certainty of a man who has never had to wonder if a room will hold him.

"Dad," Catherine says, already moving.

Governor Montgomery. I know it before the word finishes forming.

She turns back to me just long enough to make a casual introduction, touches my elbow, steering, not asking, and then:

"Remember that guy from the bonfire? Jack Forrester. Tall, blonde, aggressively good-looking?"

She rolls her eyes lightly. "He'll probably be here tonight."

A beat. "We have a situation I haven't briefed you on yet."

Her smile turns bright again. "So just act cool if he wanders over."

Her attention is already elsewhere, caught across the room.

I'm left standing where she abandoned me, hands empty, the hum of the room closing in slightly now that I'm no longer tethered to her momentum.

I shift closer to the wall, not because I'm hiding but because it gives me something solid at my back. From here, I can see the room without being pulled into it.

The men stand in loose clusters, bodies angled outward, conversations expanding instead of closing. They take up space without apology, hands relaxed, shoulders open. Their voices don't rise to compete. They don't have to. When they speak, others lean in.

The women move differently. Closer together, laughter contained, attention calibrated. No one interrupts without smoothing it over.

It's practiced.

A waiter passes again and this time I take a glass, mostly so my hands have something to do. The stem is cold against my fingers. I don't drink yet.

That's when I notice him.

Not because he's loud.

Because the room already knows where he is.

He isn't at the center of anything, but the clusters bend subtly in his direction. Conversations angling, bodies shifting without conscious intent. A man mid-sentence breaks off to greet him, quick and deferential. The greeting is mandatory.

Jack doesn't stop long enough to be held by it.

Dark jacket. Clean lines. Nothing flashy. Not flashy, just restraint that reads as confidence instead of caution.

He isn't scanning exits. He already knows who belongs here and who doesn't.

When his eyes meet mine, there's no delay. No surprise.

He holds the look openly, long enough that I understand this isn't a coincidence. He's aware of being seen and doesn't offer me a way out of it.

That must be Jack.

When he steps toward me, it's not abrupt. It's smooth, practiced, inevitable.

"Pretty cage," he says, glancing at the ivy. "Still a cage."

A couple of heads turn at the sound of his voice. Nothing dramatic. Just attention shifting, re-centering.

I follow his gaze without meaning to. From inside, the ivy looks ornamental. Controlled. Something designed to suggest wildness without ever risking it.

"I prefer the forest," he adds. "At least it doesn't pretend."

There's no flirtation in it. No testing. It lands as a position statement.

When I look back at him, he's already watching me fully. Not assessing whether I matter, but how.

"You're Catherine's roommate," he says. "Winter."

Hearing my name from him is jarring, not because of the familiarity but because he waited to use it.

"Yeah."

His expression shifts. Not surprise. Confirmation. A suspicion has just aligned.

"Hm," he says softly. "That makes sense."

It doesn't. I let him keep it.

He steps back first, already disengaging, attention sliding elsewhere with the same control he brought to me.

"Careful tonight," he says, almost absent. "This room notices more than it lets on."

Then he's gone.

The word shouldn't hit the way it does.

Careful.

It isn't the kind of warning that keeps you safe. It's the kind that puts you in your place.

I felt the same thing I felt at the trail table.

Filed.

I drift farther from the center of the room, toward a narrower stretch of wall where the crowd thins and the sound changes. The music feels more distant here, filtered through density I can't name. A window breaks up the stone, dark glass reflecting the room back at itself. I pause there, letting the cool of it seep through my sleeve.

People move around me without touching. Conversations slide past unfinished. Someone laughs, then reins it in. They've remembered where they are.

The house holds.

I take a breath. Then another. The tension Jack left behind loosens, drifting into something distant enough to manage. Familiar. I can do this. I can stand in a room and not matter.

I turn, meaning to keep moving.

The room shifts.

Not suddenly, not dramatically. Just enough that I feel it before I understand it.

Sound dulls. Space reorders. A pocket of stillness opens and closes somewhere behind me.

I stop.

It isn't the room.

It's him.

My body turns before I decide to.

Catherine appears at my side, seamless as ever. Her fingers close around my wrist, gentle and unthinking. Claiming.

It doesn't work.

The thread in my chest tightens, sharp enough that my breath catches. Not pulling me toward the forest, not asking me to move.

Just turning me.

Pointing me.

Across the room, Jack is speaking to someone else now. The sound of his voice doesn't register. The house doesn't register. Catherine's grip doesn't register.

Only the pressure does.

Rain. Pine. Faint sweetness.

Wrong indoors.

Right everywhere else.

I don't look for him.

I don't have to.

And somewhere in this house, I know, clean as a stamp, someone has already written me down.

CHAPTER 14
VETTING

I didn't go to class today because I couldn't trust my body to behave in a room with exits I wasn't allowed to take. Skipping didn't help. It only left more space for the same wrong rhythm to keep looping under my thoughts, insistent as a pulse I didn't own.

Tonight wasn't the time for fractures.

A new school year meant visibility. Standing where I was expected to stand, letting donors and wolves and humans all read the same story off my face. My father would handle the words. I would handle the rest.

Lucky is with me, stiff in a suit that fits him too well. To anyone who doesn't know better, he's a friend playing dress-up for a civic event. He belongs at my side, which is the only reason he's allowed.

The Mayor's house is louder than it looks. Low music, crystal laughter measured to the inch, bodies arranged in careful clusters, decorative and deliberate. The air feels handled. Pressed thin by too many people pretending it isn't.

The Mayor hosts it. Saint William owns it. The Governor attends.

My wolf goes quiet the moment we step inside. Not restless. Not bristling. Flattened.

I slow my breathing. Set my jaw. Let the mask lock into place without asking for it. I hate that my body remembers this so easily.

Lucky fidgets beside me. Tugging at his cuffs, his collar, then catches himself and stills, shoulders squaring a beat too late. I meet his eyes. A look we learned young. We'll survive this.

Lucky hates these rooms. Always has. He hated them when we were thirteen and our mother took him to his first one in a suit that didn't fit, and he hated them last spring when he stood at the back of a charity dinner pretending to be a server because it gave his hands something to do. He smiles his way through them because that is what the family requires of him, but I have watched him count exits since we were old enough to read the word, and I know that smile is something he is waiting to take off.

Tonight he is wearing it for me. He always wears it for me. One day I would like to know what Lucky chooses for himself, when no one is asking.

Something here is listening.

A server pauses mid-step as we pass, fingers lifting to her earpiece, receiving a cue. Above the doorway, a small black dome catches a sliver of chandelier light, camera, glass pretending to be decor. Nearby, a man at a side table glances down not at names, but at wrists, pen poised like he's counting categories.

The room adjusts around us without realizing why. Voices don't stop. They soften. Paths open in the crowded places. No one steps directly in front of me. It isn't respect. It's recognition without understanding.

Inherited gravity. The most exhausting kind.

Lucky clocks it too. Exits first, corners second, then the negative spaces where people aren't standing but could be. He isn't watching faces. He's watching flow.

I keep moving. That's part of the role. Smooth enough that no one feels challenged, threatened, or invited. Proof the line holds. Proof the wolves can be trusted to wear manners.

My father still isn't in the room. That should bother me more than it does.

"Feels off," Lucky murmurs, barely sound.

I don't answer. Naming it would give it weight.

The room feels expectant. Not tense. Waiting. It knows something is supposed to happen and is quietly checking the clock.

Then my wolf lifts his head.

Not rising. Orienting.

I breathe in without meaning to.

Rain.

Not the forest kind. Not soil and bark. Clean rain, just passed, just clung, like weather that touched skin and refused to leave.

And under it, that sweetness again, alive, wrong season, wrong room.

My irritation drops out from under me, sudden enough to leave a hollow.

That isn't possible.

I don't move. Don't turn. Around me, the party keeps performing, blissfully unaware that anything has changed. My body locks itself down anyway, because any sudden shift becomes a story.

The pull catches under my sternum. Not hunger. Not pursuit. Recognition with teeth.

Lucky shifts beside me. Not toward the room, toward me. His gaze flicks to my face and away. He doesn't want to look directly at the crack once he's seen it.

Anchor. Cover.

I let the room move until what I'm tracking enters my sightline on its own.

She does.

Winter stands near a stone column, half shadowed, a champagne glass held between drinking and occupation. She adjusts her grip on the stem, small, unconscious, and her gaze flicks once toward an exit that isn't meant for her. Then she stills again, contained in the way people get when they're trying not to take up space.

Exposed.

The scent sharpens the instant I see her. Rain again, that sweetness again, threaded into warmth and a quieter note underneath. The pull goes wire-tight. Exact.

My wolf surges forward not to challenge or claim, but to recognize.

I lock him down.

She has no idea.

Her face is open in a way it wouldn't be if she did. Eyes alert but unguarded, mouth relaxed, attention drifting without calculation. She expects the world to make sense if she watches it closely enough.

She lifts her gaze at the wrong moment.

Our eyes meet.

My jaw tightens once, an involuntary tell I hate, and the pull snaps so cleanly I feel it in my teeth. Her pupils flare, just slightly. A breath catches. I see the instant she tries to explain it to herself. Coincidence, curiosity, nerves. Human logic scrambling to keep its footing.

I break eye contact first.

If I don't, I will move.

I angle my body away, masking it as boredom, as disinterest, as exactly what they expect of me. Lucky shifts a half step closer, sleeves nearly brushing, a casual barrier to anyone watching.

The pull doesn't loosen. It tightens.

Winter shifts her weight, distracted, eyes following something across the room, and that's it. A half second where no one is watching closely enough.

I step forward.

Not fast. Not hesitant. Measured. Exactly where I'm meant to be.

She notices me three steps before I reach her. I see it happen, the flicker of awareness, the way her posture stills without stiffening. She turns fully, and the pull tightens again, sharp and clean.

Up close, it's unbearable. Rain. That sweetness. Warmth under cold. My wolf presses hard enough that my hands want to reach before my mind can refuse.

She doesn't step back.

That nearly undoes me.

"Hi," she says.

One word. Steady. No tremor. Curiosity, plus a feeling she hasn't learned to name.

"Hello," I answer, and the calm in my own voice feels like a lie I'm forcing into shape.

A beat. The room hums around us, oblivious. If anyone is watching, they see nothing but two people exchanging pleasantries.

"I'm Lochan," I say, because she needs something she can file. A name. A shape.

"Winter," she replies, immediate and unguarded, like her name belongs to her and always has.

It strikes clean through my chest.

"You should stay near the light," I say. Too direct to be polite, too controlled to be concern. "These rooms like to close around people they don't know."

Her brow tightens slightly. "Is that a warning?"

"It's information," I correct.

A flicker touches the corner of her mouth, almost a smile, gone before it can become one.

Behind me, I feel it. The shift in the air, attention snapping into focus.

I've stayed too long.

"It was," she starts.

I step back before she can finish. Before the pull becomes motion. Before the night breaks open.

And that's when it hits.

Not the pull.

Attention.

The kind that arrives sideways and sits too comfortably at my back.

"Bradford."

Jack doesn't raise his voice. He doesn't need to. My name lands between my shoulder blades, tested there by his voice.

I stop.

Turning too fast would confirm something. Turning too slow would look weak. I split the difference and face him with the same neutral ease I've worn all night.

He's inside the distance people keep for either deference or intimacy. He's dressed for anywhere that costs money. Relaxed posture. Clean lines. Nothing loud.

His eyes flick once, past me, toward Winter. A single check. Confirmation of a data point.

"You're early," he says, treating this as a conversation already underway. "I didn't think these things interested you."

"They don't," I reply. "They interest my father."

Jack's smile doesn't reach his eyes. "Right. Performance."

He lets the word hang there, then adds, mild as conversation and colder than it should be: "People notice patterns, Bradford. Especially when you cross a room, you never cross."

Before I can answer, Lucky steps in. Smooth, unhurried. He doesn't interrupt so much as reroute the air.

"Jack," Lucky says, tone easy, familiar enough to disarm without inviting. "Haven't seen you since the last council mixer."

Jack's attention shifts, recalibrates. He clocks Lucky properly this time. A fraction of surprise slips through before he masks it.

"Lucky," he replies. "Didn't realize you were back in town."

"Just passing through," Lucky says. A lie so clean it barely exists. "Thought I'd keep Lochan company."

Jack's smile thins. He eases back half a step, small, but real.

"Generous," he says. "He doesn't usually need supervision."

Lucky smiles. Real teeth. "No," he agrees. "But tonight feels like the kind of night you don't leave anyone alone."

The air tightens.

Jack studies him for one beat too long, then smooths himself back into ease. "Fair. I'll let you get back to your duties."

His gaze slides past me again, confirming once more, then he delivers it as a toast:

"Nice to meet the new blood."

He drifts away like he never stopped, already absorbed back into the room, already invisible again.

Lucky doesn't move until he's gone.

Then, quietly: "You good?"

I nod once.

Lie.

The performance resumes. The room continues. Music hums. Glass clinks. Laughter finds its footing.

But my wolf is up now. Fully aware.

And the worst part is how cleanly the hierarchy snaps into place when my father arrives, while that rain and sweetness remains, faint and unclaimed, a glitch the room can't correct.

Jack saw the breach. Lucky saw the crack. And Winter is standing in a room built to sort her, without knowing she's already been noticed.

CHAPTER 15

ADDICTIVE

Winter

The cold hits me all at once. Sharp enough to steal a breath and remind me where I am. Outside. Away. The door closes behind us with muted finality, the sound swallowed by ivy and stone, and suddenly the night is bigger than it was a second ago.

I draw my coat tighter, more reflex than need. My skin still feels warm, overstimulated, lagging behind the rest of me, part of me still inside.

The effort it takes not to turn around surprises me. He already stepped back. Already let the space open again. That was the point. Still, my body lingers in the shape it learned beside him. Calibrated to a height that made me tilt my head slightly, to a proximity that felt correct.

Too correct.

My shoulder aches with the absence of something that never touched it.

I keep walking.

Catherine is already halfway down the steps, heels clicking with purpose, coat swinging open, the night belonging to her. She's talking about a person from the room, some detail I should recognize, words sliding past without landing. My attention is busy with the quiet labor of forward motion.

One foot. Then the other. Don't stop.

Cold air fills my lungs again. Cleaner now, less perfumed, less charged. The pressure eases a fraction, redistributed instead of dismissed. Left pooled at the threshold behind us.

I tell myself it's normal. That rooms do that. That proximity can confuse the senses. That tall boys with calm voices and unreadable eyes are just people.

My body disagrees anyway.

It takes effort to move forward into the familiar work of not factoring. And I don't know yet why loss is the word my body reaches for.

The car smells like leather and fall air when we get inside. Catherine pulls away from the curb before I've finished settling, turns the heater up high, and doesn't put music on. The quiet stretches. My fingers curl into my sleeves, thawing slowly, sensation returning in uneven waves.

"So," she says, picking up a conversation we paused five minutes ago. "You met Jack."

I watch the house recede in the side mirror, lights shrinking back into decoration. Contained.

"I think so," I say.

Catherine hums. Confirmation, not surprise.

"He always clocks people early," she says. "Thinks it makes him interesting."

"Who is he?" I ask.

She smiles, quick and private. "Dangerous question."

I wait.

"Student Body President," she says. "Interned with my dad. Twice. He's already practicing for a future office."

"And you?" I ask.

Her grip tightens on the wheel for half a second, then loosens with practiced intention.

"I'm curious," she says lightly. "And he's easy on the eyes."

The streetlights pass in steady intervals, slicing the dark into manageable pieces.

"He said the house was curated," I say.

Catherine laughs under her breath. "Of course he did."

"He hates anything staged," she adds. "Claims he prefers the forest. Says it's more honest."

"And?"

She shrugs, eyes still on the road. "Jack is one of a kind."

I think of the way he looked at me. Not curious. Decided.

"He watches," Catherine continues. "Collects impressions. Files people away."

She glances at me then, quick, assessing. Then she hesitates. Just for a second. The kind of pause that means she's choosing between the careful version and the true one.

"Be careful around him, Winter. He's not the kind of dangerous people warn you about. He's the kind people learn about too late."

She turns her eyes back to the road, smile already smoothing the edges of what she just made true.

"He didn't make you uncomfortable, did he?"

It's careful, open, Catherine giving me room to answer honestly.

"No," I say. And it's mostly true. "Blunt."

Her mouth curves. "Yeah. That's Jack."

The car quiets again, engine humming steady beneath us. I let my head rest back against the seat, eyelids lowering for a second, the dark behind them still holding the room's shape. The height of him. The way my body noticed before my mind could.

"That crowd," Catherine says, softer now. "They're not as harmless as they pretend. But you handled it."

I open my eyes.

"I did?"

She nods. "You didn't flinch. Not even when the Bradford heir walked right over to you."

The compliment lands strangely. Not warm, not cold. Noted. She had been watching too.

We drive the rest of the way without filling the space. The night smooths itself back into manageability. The cold moves into my bones where it belongs.

Still, even as the car turns toward campus, part of me stays behind. My ribs tighten, the doorway still holding me by the chest.

The gates slide open and close behind us with the soft inevitability of routine. Saint William at night performs forgiveness. Lamps spaced evenly, buildings pressed into themselves, everything where it's supposed to be.

Catherine parks and lets the car idle. Heat hums.

"You okay?" she asks, still not looking at me.

The question lands softer than I expect.

"Yeah," I say. Automatic. Then, after a beat, "I think so."

She nods as if that answer makes sense. As if she's heard it before.

"First of many," she says lightly. "These things get easier."

I don't correct her.

We get out, the cold meeting us again, less shocking this time. Catherine locks the car and starts toward the dorm without hesitation, already back in her body, back in her world.

Inside, the building smells of cleaner and old heat. Someone laughs down the hall. A door shuts. Life continues at its usual volume.

In our room, Catherine kicks off her shoes and drops her clutch on the desk. She moves around me easily, humming now, energy unspent, and starts pulling pins from her hair.

I shrug out of my coat and sit on the edge of my bed.

The room feels smaller than it did this morning.

When the bathroom door closes, the quiet rushes in. Not silence. The absence of distraction. I lean forward, elbows on my knees, grounding myself in the familiar ache of muscle and bone.

My body is still holding on. Not excitement. Not fear.

Awareness.

I can still feel the shape of him beside me. The way the air adjusted. The way my breath caught without warning. It's faint now, dulled by distance and walls and reason, but it hasn't vanished.

Addictive. The pull.

The word startles me anyway. The fact that I came up with it startles me more.

I shake my head once, sharp, trying to knock it loose. New places do this, I tell myself. New people. New rooms. They make impressions. They linger longer than they should. Or so I have been informed by movies and people with normal childhoods.

Still, when I lie back and stare at the ceiling, my pulse refuses to slow completely. My senses stay tuned a degree too high, waiting for something that isn't coming. At least not tonight.

CHAPTER 16
BREACH

Lochan

My wolf wants to stay. Dragging him away takes more than it ever has.

I stood beside my father through the entire gathering at the Mayor's residence, under chandelier light and polite applause, my posture correct enough to pass for calm. He never looked at me directly, but that meant nothing. He cataloged without staring. The tension I couldn't smooth out. The hitch in my pulse when the room shifted. The way my attention kept slipping its leash.

Tonight mattered. Catherine Montgomery worked the donors with effortless precision, smile to smile, hand to hand, while her father held court. At the edges, pack elders lingered where human eyes slid past them, wolf and man blurred together in the same expensive air.

I nodded when required. Spoke when spoken to. Played my role.

All the while, my mind wasn't in the room.

Winter.

She wasn't near me, not close enough to touch, not even close enough to see clearly. And still I felt her as if we shared breath. When she moved somewhere across the residence, something inside me answered, immediate and disloyal.

Governor Montgomery spoke too long. My father listened with the patience of a man who understands silence carries more authority than interruption. My wolf pressed at the inside of my skin, irritated by noise, by confinement, by the lie of stillness.

When my father finally gave the cue, it was barely a shift of weight. The sentries appeared anyway, clean and practiced, and the flow of the room redirected around us as if it had been rehearsed.

As if nothing had changed.

The black Escalade waited at the curb. The rear door opened.

I didn't get in.

For half a second, the driver froze with his hand still on the door edge. Lucky's stride checked, just a hitch, then he covered it, too late for anyone watching closely to miss.

I turned away without a word and cut for the boundary on the south side of town, my pace sharp enough to flirt with a run. Lucky fell in behind me without hesitation, loyal enough not to ask where the night was taking us.

With every step toward the trees, my skin tightened, bones aching like they remembered another shape.

I knew Barry would be there.

So when he emerged from the dark at the boundary, massive and silent, it didn't surprise me.

What surprised me was how relieved my wolf felt to see him.

Barry didn't just come close. He placed himself with intention, between me and the road, his bulk slotting into the angle like protocol. Not comfort. Containment.

Lucky slowed when he reached us. Not fear. Recognition.

"Lochan," he said, quietly this time.

My name scraped. My wolf surged at the sound, impatient and sharp, claws dragging along the inside of my ribs. Barry mirrored it immediately, a low restless pace that matched the churn in my chest.

I tried to breathe.

Air went in. Caught. Refused to hold.

The pull toward the trees sharpened, no longer distant, no longer abstract. Directional. Insistent. Every step away from the residence felt like resistance now, like my body had spent the whole night fighting something inevitable.

Lucky's eyes tracked damage the way he always did. Throat, wrists, jaw. The places control breaks first.

"Your pulse isn't coming down," he said.

Heat rolled through me in waves, fast and disorienting. My vision narrowed at the edges, the night breaking into scent and sound and need. Barry pressed closer, shoulder brushing mine, anchoring and damning all at once. My skin felt too tight, like it was already splitting along invisible seams.

"This isn't adrenaline," Lucky said, flat and certain.

I shifted my weight, just enough to stay upright. Just enough to keep from giving in to the urge tearing through me to move, to run, to change.

Lucky swallowed once. "You didn't just lose control in there."

The pull tightened again, straight through my center. Barry bristled with it, muscles bunching, a physical echo of everything I was failing to contain.

Lucky exhaled slowly. "This is going to get back to Regan."

Regan. My father's Second.

"They'll accelerate the timeline. Maris Harlan back from missionary work," he said.

The words land the way verdicts land. Not loudly. Finally.

The name hit like a chain snapping tight.

My wolf recoiled, then lunged, fury ripping through me so fast it stole my breath. Barry growled low at my side, not a threat, not a warning. Just sound torn loose from the same pressure splitting me open.

I closed my eyes.

Whatever I'd broken tonight, it wasn't etiquette. It was something I wouldn't be able to put back the way it was.

Lucky didn't speak again right away, but I felt the calculation start in him anyway, the habit trained into us before we were old enough to call it choice. He looked past me toward the town lights still glowing behind the trees, toward doors that would open quietly once the right people started talking.

"This doesn't stay out here," he said finally.

I knew that already.

Nothing ever did.

Music still floated faintly from the residence, laughter riding under it, thin and unreal. Guests would be leaving now with the satisfied belief that they'd witnessed a successful evening, nothing more.

They were wrong.

Lucky shifted his stance, subtle and deliberate, already preparing for fallout. My father wouldn't ask questions tonight. He wouldn't send anyone after me. He'd let the information come to him the way it always did, filtered, precise, saved for rooms where decisions were made.

The pull hit again. Barry stayed too close, agitation bleeding straight into me, amplifying every instinct before I was ready.

Lucky's gaze flicked into the dark beyond the boundary.

"That introduction," he said carefully. "You didn't think anyone noticed?"

I didn't answer.

Because someone already had.

I felt it then, not the pull, not the forest.

Attention.

A presence with edges. Something that didn't belong to trees or night air. Someone lingering longer than necessary where the gravel met shadow.

A silhouette at the break in the path. A brief, dull ember of light, cigarette or phone screen, gone the moment I registered it.

Jack.

I didn't turn. I didn't need to. His interest had texture, sharp, probing, like a finger pressed against a bruise to see how deep it went. Jack wouldn't confront me yet. He'd watch the crack widen first, then decide where to apply pressure.

Lucky felt it too. His shoulders tightened.

"He's going to talk," Lucky said.

Jack always did.

And when he did, this wouldn't be about me losing control. It would be about optics. Promises. Who I'd embarrassed, and who I'd endangered.

The pull tightened again.

This time I tried to pull away from it.

I took two deliberate steps back toward the road, toward the town lights, toward anything that wasn't trees and dark and instinct.

My body refused.

Not a stumble. Not a misstep.

A yank, violent and humiliating, straight through my center. Vertigo punched up hard enough that my knees almost buckled. Left, toward campus, toward the Blackwood side of the woods, as if my bones had been threaded with a line and someone else had tightened their grip.

Barry reacted with me, shifting into my space, crowding the angle, blocking the road with his body like a living barricade.

I stopped.

Breathing hurt now. Every inhale scraped. Every exhale felt borrowed.

This wasn't panic. It wasn't hunger.

It was alignment.

The truth landed heavy and unmistakable. I could run all night and it wouldn't matter. I could put miles between myself and the Mayor's residence, between myself and my father, between myself and every promise I'd ever been raised to keep.

My body would still bring me back.

Not to the boundary stones.

To her.

Winter's presence pulled at me with the certainty of gravity, quiet and absolute. Not demanding. Not loud. Just there, shaping everything around it. I hadn't chosen it. I hadn't invited it.

But I'd answered it.

The memory landed sharp and unwelcome. The moment at the gathering, the way my voice hadn't shaken when I gave my name, even as everything inside me went still.

That hadn't been restraint.

It had been surrender.

I pressed my hand to my chest, feeling the violent rhythm there, the way my pulse refused to be reasoned with. Barry stayed close, a living echo of everything I was struggling to contain.

This was bigger than instinct, bigger than attraction.

Whatever promise I'd just broken wasn't one I'd made out loud.

And if my father learns what's pulling me, he'll decide what to do with her.

CHAPTER 17
CLAIM

Winter

My shoes are on and I am out the door before the campus fully wakes.

It doesn't feel like a decision so much as motion already in progress, like my body started moving and my mind is forced to chase it. I leave my phone on the charger, just in case Catherine tries to find me. She will. It's a new feeling, having someone care where I am. Not hovering, not possessive. Just caring. Present enough that I notice myself rehearsing explanations I might never need.

In the hallway, I pause once with my hand near the door. I know better than to go into dark places alone, especially when no one knows where I am. But knowing better has never actually stopped me, and that's probably something I should examine later. Right now I just go.

Outside, the cold is a full body interruption. My breath fogs as I walk, each step finding a rhythm that feels borrowed, not chosen. There's no spike of adrenaline. Just a steady pull, less like desire than orientation, like something inside me has already turned in a direction and refuses to turn back.

As if the air itself is leaning that way.

The ground gently insisting.

Light is just starting to filter through the branches when I cross into the forest.

Pale bands catch on frost and damp bark. The woods close around me almost immediately, the path narrowing, the world shedding its excess. My skin stays warm despite the bite in the air, warmth from movement and something deeper, slower, unrelated to exertion.

No voices, no questions, no edges to soften. It feels like what I imagine home feels like, which is its own warning.

The realization hits hard enough to stop me mid-step. I've never thought of myself as someone who belonged anywhere, not without effort, not without translation. Standing here with trees on all sides, I should feel exposed.

Instead, I settle.

I keep walking.

Time loosens its grip as the forest thickens. I stop counting steps, stop tracking the sun. The path curves and dips, familiar without ever having been memorized. My body moves on something steadier than intention, something that asks no permission and offers no explanation.

The rhythm is soothing until it isn't.

My pulse jumps, sharp and sudden, like it's responding to a signal I can't hear. Heat gathers low in my body, unfamiliar and unmistakable. My breath goes shallow. I'm overly sensitive to the atmosphere.

This is dangerous. I am not doing anything wrong. Both of those things can be true at the same time and I know it.

The words don't anchor. They skim and slide off. My legs start to wobble, not with weakness but with the strain of holding myself together too tightly.

I stop.

A wide tree stands just off the path, its trunk thick and scarred, roots lifting the surrounding ground like ribs. I lower myself against it, bark rough through my jacket, grounding in a way I didn't realize I needed. I tilt my head back and close my eyes, letting the forest breathe around me.

It isn't silent. It's layered. Wind through branches, the faint creak of wood, something small moving in the undergrowth and stopping again.

What am I doing?

Not mine. Someone else's panic, inside my skull.

Leaves whisper.

I open my eyes.

I see the dog first.

He's enormous, too big to be a dog if I'm being honest, and so silent I startle when he appears a few feet away, dark against the trees. His coat is thick. His stance is balanced and still, like he belongs exactly where he is. He isn't stalking. He isn't charging.

He's watching.

My heart jumps, then steadies. I wait for fear to follow.

It doesn't.

If anything, his presence feels deliberate, measured, as if he's on duty.

"Hey," I say quietly, unsure why I lower my voice. "You scared me."

He doesn't move. Just tilts his head, eyes intent and unsettlingly intelligent. My chest loosens a fraction, as if I've been guided here and he's confirming I made it.

Then I feel it.

Not sound. Not movement.

Attention.

It lands on me with the weight of a hand at my back, never touching, impossible to ignore. The air shifts. My breath catches.

He steps into view from my left, unhurried, like he's been here long enough to learn the shape of this place. Dark clothes. Jacket unzipped. Breath fogging faintly in the cold.

And the moment he arrives, the air changes. Rain threaded through the chill, and something faintly sweet beneath it.

Not perfume. Presence.

"Winter," he says.

My name settles differently in his mouth. Not tentative. Not curious.

Certain.

I push myself upright, suddenly aware of everything at once. The closeness of the trees. The absence of anyone else. The heat in my body that has nowhere to go.

"You followed me?"

"No." His gaze doesn't leave mine. "I came."

"Why?"

His lips curve. Not amused. Certain.

"You felt it."

The space between us tightens, charged with what neither of us names. He doesn't move closer.

That might be the worst part. My body leans forward anyway, a quiet betrayal I can't stop.

The dog shifts and sits at his side, solid and calm.

A name rises in my mouth, uninvited, almost familiar, then slips away before I can grab it, as if my body knows him and my brain refuses to cooperate. Great. Exactly what I needed today.

"I didn't plan this," I say, and hate how exposed it sounds.

"I know," he replies, immediately.

His gaze drops, briefly, to my throat, where my pulse jumps too visibly, and when it lifts again, something in his eyes tightens. Darkens.

"Winter," he says again, softer now. Careful. Like restraint is an active choice.

The word mine doesn't arrive as thought.

It arrives as sensation, low and undeniable, like a compass needle snapping into place. My breath stutters and then steadies, my body answering before I decide whether it should. Heat drops and holds, unmistakable in its calm.

Claimed.

Not seized.

Not taken.

Recognized.

I feel him register it, the infinitesimal shift in his focus, the way the air between us seems to lock into place like a mechanism engaging. Mutual. Immediate.

I don't flinch. I don't resist.

I let it land, this awareness of being held in someone else's attention, not loosely, not temporarily.

With intent.

His gaze doesn't waver. Neither does mine.

And in the stillness between us, hunger hums beneath certainty, quiet, insistent.

This isn't a moment.

It's a beginning.

CHAPTER 18

PULL

Lochan

I'm going through the morning motions when the urge hits, sudden, insistent, like surf breaking against rock.

I don't question it. I turn toward the forest and hold my wolf tight until the treeline closes behind me. Barry is beside me before I can register the decision.

The woods close in and my wolf surges. I stay human by sheer will, but I run, fast, reckless, branches snapping against my face, claws scraping inside my skin.

I know I'm being led.

The ground under my boots softens as the trees thicken. Pine needles give way to damp earth that holds an imprint if you stand too long. My breath fogs briefly, then disappears. Sweat cools along my spine; my jacket clings where branches have raked it. I shrug free of a snag without slowing, fingers numb enough that I barely feel the scrape.

My legs burn, but it's distant, secondary. The urge that yanked me from the house hasn't eased. It's only settled deeper, less frantic, more certain, as if time is no longer the threat.

Barry's shoulder brushes my calf as the path narrows, an anchor. Proof I'm not alone in this.

I keep running, because stopping still feels worse.

Then my pace shifts without me deciding it. The run lengthens instead of drives. Breath drops lower, steadier. The forest opens and closes in small ways my body anticipates before my mind catches up.

My wolf presses forward, but he isn't fighting me. The sharp, demanding pressure I'm used to is gone. What sits in my chest now is heavier, quiet, waiting.

Wanting sits low and unresolved.

I angle left without thinking, then right, duck beneath a branch like I've done it a hundred times. Roots split the ground and I clear them cleanly. My body knows where to place itself, and my wolf doesn't argue.

He settles, coiled, patient.

The pull tightens inward, narrowing the distance between where I am and what I'm moving toward. Barry stays aligned at my flank, not leading, not following, just exact.

I slow again, not because I choose to, but because running suddenly feels wrong.

The forest stills.

No birds. No insects. Just my breath and the soft press of Barry's weight beside me.

I stop.

The air changes, carrying warmth through the damp green. Sweet. Alive. Too close to be imagined. It catches at the back of my throat and my wolf lifts his head inside me, alert without tension.

Magnolia.

Winter is close.

Lower.

Closer.

I lock my knees and breathe through it, slow enough to look controlled. Barry doesn't look at me; his attention stays fixed ahead, unwavering.

I should wait. I should keep distance. I should do anything but close the gap.

I move anyway, quiet steps, careful weight, until I can see her.

She's sitting with her back against a tree, knees drawn in, hands loose where they fall. Nothing about her says alert. She looks comfortable, like the forest doesn't threaten her the way it threatens everyone else.

The urge to drop, crouch, kneel, anything but stand over her hits hard enough that my balance shifts. My throat tightens around it, intimate and humiliating.

Winter exhales. One shoulder rolls as she settles deeper against bark. Her fingers press into the dirt beside her, grounded, familiar with the earth.

She hasn't looked at me.

And still her body responds.

I let my boot scrape lightly against the ground.

Her fingers still. Her breath catches on the next inhale as if her lungs heard me before her mind did.

I hold the distance without measuring it. Far enough that I can still choose not to move. Close enough that every part of me knows how easily that choice could slip.

Winter's head lifts a fraction. Not startled, not searching, just orienting, as if she's adjusting to something she already feels.

Her gaze turns.

Our eyes meet.

No jolt. No flinch. Just quiet acknowledgement, her eyes level and unafraid in a way that makes standing upright feel suddenly like a mistake.

If I step closer, I don't step back.

CHAPTER 19
CONTACT

Winter

My pulse stutters as if it's misread the room. Just my luck. Heat climbs my throat anyway, fast, disloyal, and my feet go heavy, as if my body is bracing without asking permission. I pull in a breath that doesn't quite reach the bottom of my lungs.

When I look up, he's there.

Too close. Close enough that the air between us feels disturbed, claimed.

Something unsettled flickers across his face. Not anger, not arrogance. Confusion, threaded with the faintest edge of fear, and it throws me off in a way I don't understand. Like I've caught him at the exact moment he forgets the role he's meant to wear.

For a split second, it feels like I'm staring into something I shouldn't have access to.

No.

He can't be.

The eyes in front of me are honey, bright, flecked with gold, beautiful in a way that doesn't register as beauty so much as warning. Like light caught inside something that can burn.

My stomach drops, hard. Not butterflies, nothing sweet or fluttering. This is heavier, violent, as if my balance has been grabbed and shaken. The world tips; the edges of my vision blur as if I've stepped too quickly off solid ground.

For one breath, I think I might fall.

Then I don't.

My body corrects before panic can find me, weight shifting, knees locking, breath dragging itself lower as if I can force calm by sheer will. Everything inside me feels rearranged, but I'm not out of control. I know exactly where I am.

Heat moves low and fast, coiling through me with terrifying precision. My pulse becomes a sound in my ears, steady and relentless, a rhythm my body is determined to keep whether I want it to or not.

The big dog presses into my thigh.

Solid. Warm. Real.

The contact anchors me without ceremony. I register it distantly, an instinctive, absurd thought rising up and dissolving just as quickly: catching me, as if that's what he's here for. The weight of him is reassuring in a way that feels too easy, too familiar, like my body has already accepted something my mind hasn't.

I lift my eyes again.

And his are still on me.

There's a stillness to him that feels deliberate, practiced, like something wild taught itself how to wait.

It isn't emptiness. It isn't calm. It's restraint, held carefully, deliberately, as if he's learned exactly where to stop and what it costs him to stay there.

His beauty isn't loud. It doesn't reach for me. It sits there, quiet and unguarded, made stranger by the weight behind his eyes. There's sadness there, not sharp, not dramatic, but settled, as if it's been carried for a long time.

I don't mean to look lower.

My attention slips anyway, pulled by something that has nothing to do with curiosity and everything to do with gravity. I catch on the way his hands rest at his sides, loose by effort rather than indifference, the surrounding space charged with a kind of held back potential that makes my throat tighten.

This body could destroy things.

And he's choosing not to.

Something else intrudes.

Not a voice. Not sound. More like the sensation of words arriving fully formed, dropped into my mind without warning, intimate and wrong in the way overhearing always is.

What am I doing?

This can't be real.

She's not real.

The words aren't aimed at me, but they hit anyway, reverberating through my chest as if I've brushed against a live wire. They carry disbelief. Panic. The fraying edge of control stretched too thin.

And underneath it all, wanting, held so tight it almost hums.

I tilt my head, the movement instinctive, confusion threading through me as I take him in again. He's looking at me differently now, not startled, not alarmed, but with an intensity focused inward, as if he's trying to memorize something before it disappears.

Without deciding to, I lift my hand.

The motion feels inevitable the moment it begins. Simple. Overwhelming. My fingers rise slowly, cutting through the space between us, awareness sharpening with every inch they travel. I can feel the heat coming off his skin before I'm close enough to touch it.

To confirm he's solid.

To anchor myself to the thing that's knocked my world off its axis and somehow steadied it at the same time.

My hand falters.

Then:

Winter.

Winter.

Winter.

The name crashes into my thoughts, sharp and insistent, pressed there again and again, like knocking from inside my skull. It isn't a call.

Not his voice. His panic. Raw, unfiltered, barely held together.

I snatch my hand back as if I've been burned.

The sudden absence of movement between us feels louder than sound. My fingers curl against my palm, tingling, my breath catching too late to hide it. The wanting doesn't leave. It spikes, then tightens, coiling low and hot in my body, made more dangerous by the restraint wrapped around it.

His eyes widen, not in surprise, but in recognition.

Whatever just happened, he felt it too.

The dog shifts beside me, nails pressing into the dirt, a reminder of weight and warmth and earth. I ground myself through it, pressing my heel down, drawing a slow breath until my lungs stop shaking.

The forest remains still.

Unbothered. Unimpressed. As if whatever line we've just brushed against belongs to us alone.

I look at him again.

He hasn't moved. Not closer. Not away. His hands are still loose at his sides, but the tension in him is unmistakable now, control drawn tight enough that I can almost feel the strain of it from where I stand.

The name doesn't repeat.

The silence that follows is worse.

Because now I know.

Not what it means. Not what comes next. I reached for him, and he answered before he could stop it.

My pulse steadies. The nausea fades to a low, constant hum.

Wanting stays.

I lower my hand completely, letting it fall back to my side, fingers brushing my thigh where the dog still stands guard. I don't apologize. I don't explain. Whatever almost happened doesn't feel like a mistake.

It feels like a boundary we both see now.

And neither of us steps back.

CHAPTER 20

CLEARANCE

Lochan

I've forgotten everything I was born to know.

I barely remember my name.

I've never been looked at like this before.

Not like a crown.

Like a blade laid gently against my throat.

Her gaze is steady, unblinking.

My wolf lifts his head.

The air thickens the longer she keeps me there. Heat gathers low in my chest, slow, unmistakable.

I don't move. I don't blink. I let it happen.

As if I have a choice.

She should look away. Humans always do.

Winter doesn't.

Her attention doesn't sharpen or soften. It simply remains, unflinching, close.

As if she isn't bracing for anything, as if she doesn't feel the need to protect herself from me, or from whatever is waking under my skin.

That's when the wrongness clicks into place. Not fear. Not awe. Something too sure, too soft.

She should have moved. A human reaction would be distance.

138

I don't reach for her. I don't step closer. I don't dare to look away.

My breath stutters once. I smooth it down and pretend that means something.

Her attention stays on me like a weight, like a hand, like heat.

And the wolf in me recognizes that as familiar, which is impossible.

A chill runs through me.

In the next beat, Barry's ears shoot up.

The spell is broken. Barry doesn't give false alarms.

Then I hear it. Wood giving way where nothing should be moving.

Too heavy for deer.

Too careless for patrol.

My eyes release her. She doesn't feel ready to let me go.

I turn toward the sound, already moving, Barry angling ahead of me toward the path back to campus.

"I'll get you back," I say, voice low, rougher than it should be.

I start moving, then catch the hitch in her pace almost immediately. She tries to match me anyway, stubborn enough to make it quiet. Her breath shortens. Her steps begin to land a fraction late, boots scuffing where they used to strike clean.

I should slow.

I don't.

Distance is the only way I can keep my wolf from turning this into something else.

Distance lets me watch the path ahead. Shadows, movement, anything that doesn't belong.

I steer us toward the authorized route. Toward the place where humans mistake worn paths for safety.

Behind me, her breathing changes.

She doesn't complain. She doesn't ask to slow down. She just keeps up.

The sound of it, the effort she refuses to acknowledge, lodges under my ribs and stays there.

Then her step falters.

It's small. Almost nothing.

Her foot lands wrong.

I hear it before I see it.

The scrape. The shift in weight.

I turn too late.

She's already dropping, one knee catching the ground, then the other. No cry. No dramatics. Just controlled descent and a sharp breath she can't quite hide.

"It's nothing," she says.

It isn't.

I see it in the way she avoids putting weight on one side. The way her jaw tightens and her fingers dig into the dirt like she can negotiate with it.

I kneel.

Slowly.

Not because I hesitate.

Because I need to be steady.

I don't reach for her right away. I look at her first.

"Stay still," I say quietly.

Then I move.

One arm beneath her knees. The other at her back. Careful of the ankle she's protecting without realizing she is.

She inhales sharply, not pain, not fear.

Surprise. Then she's against me.

The weight of her lands like inevitability.

She fits.

Too easily.

Her warmth bleeds through my coat. Her hand closes in the fabric at my shoulder, not asking permission, not thinking about it.

I feel it everywhere.

My wolf does not fight me.

He goes still.

Not suppressed.

Not resisting.

Still.

This should feel like a mistake.

Instead it feels inevitable.

My grip adjusts once, secure, exact, and I rise without effort.

I do not look at her.

But the wolf exhales.

I have never carried anything that felt this dangerous to put down.

When I step out of the trees carrying her, the forest doesn't let me go easily.

The sky is no longer morning. Light has thinned to that late, cold gray blue, edges sharpening as day gives up. The air bites hard at the heat of her body pressed to mine, and the contrast makes my jaw lock.

Campus opens around us, too open. Too exposed.

A security light sweeps the lawn in a slow arc, indifferent as a lighthouse. It doesn't stop on us, but I feel the possibility of it like a hand at my throat.

The dorm windows glow with warm rectangles where students have already turned inward, tucked away from the cold. Behind me, the trees close rank, dark and watchful. Ahead: stone, rules, cameras.

And in my arms, proof.

"I can walk," she says, quiet but firm, as if saying it makes it true.

I glance down at her, at the way she's trying to sit straighter while her ankle stays tucked protectively toward her body. Her hair slides against my collarbone, long, wavy, slightly damp at the ends; it clings to my coat and chills where it touches my neck.

"I would love to," I say, meaning it. "But chivalry won't allow it."

A breath of a laugh slips out of her, not quite a chuckle, more like a soft release of tension, and my chest tightens at the sound.

I don't look at her again after that. If I do, I'll forget the lawn. The light. The cameras.

"Blackwood Hall," she says, breath thin. "Second floor."

I let her think she's giving me information I don't already have.

The dorm doors swing open and warmth hits us hard, too sudden, too artificial. Perfume. Detergent. Sugar burning in someone's diffuser. Voices ricochet down the hallway, laughter trapped between walls that feel too close.

I don't hesitate.

I move quickly because stillness is worse. Stillness invites questions. Stillness turns us into a scene.

I take the stairs two at a time, grip exact, her weight locked against me like my body is built for this and hates that it is. My pulse stays even. My mind doesn't.

Still in the trees.

Still counting consequences.

Still calculating how wrongly I've stepped.

By the time we reach her door, my breath hasn't quickened, but I've gone taut, stretched thin enough to feel brittle.

I lower her carefully, one hand steady at her back until both feet touch the floor. My palm spans the curve of her waist for half a second longer than necessary before I force it away.

She sways once, her balance fights to come back on instinct. Pride, maybe. Or survival. Either way, it makes me want to steady her again, too much, too close.

Carrying her should have been simple. She's light. Leaner than she looks. Muscle coiled tight along her thighs from running, from surviving. My arm still remembers the shape of her legs hooked over it. The way her hip fit against me as if it had been measured.

I didn't look down.

I didn't need to.

"Thank you," she says.

It's barely a whisper.

She looks up at me then, really looks, and waits. Not expectant. Just open. Like she knows there should be words here. A name. An explanation. A rule.

Words gather in my throat and die.

The space she leaves in my grip is immediate. My body keeps the outline of her anyway, as if it doesn't understand the contact ended.

So I do the only thing I can.

I step back.

I turn.

I leave.

The door closes behind me with a soft, final sound, and I'm halfway down the stairs before the weight of it hits, sharp and undeniable.

I ran.

After all of that, I ran like a scared pup, heart hammering not from exertion but from the certainty that if I'd stayed one second longer, I wouldn't have left at all.

CHAPTER 21

CARRIED AWAY

Lochan walks away as if leaving is an act of discipline.

Not the frantic kind. Not the guilty kind. The controlled kind. Measured steps, level shoulders, hands that don't shake, a face that doesn't betray what his body already admitted.

I watch his back until the hallway swallows him.

The door clicks shut behind me and the air changes.

I expect my body to remember it's alone. I expect to cool the second he's gone.

I don't.

I'm still warm where his hands were. At my waist, under my knees, along my ribs where my breath kept catching against his chest. Heat lingers like a handprint that refuses to fade.

And then the thought arrives, quiet and devastating. I don't remember anyone carrying me. Not once. Not as a kid, not when I was sick, not when I was too tired to stand. I learned early that if you couldn't walk, you got left. Which is a hell of a thing to remember at twenty past nine on a Sunday morning.

He carried me like it was normal. Like my body was worth holding.

Cradled, which is too gentle a word for me, as if I was something you don't set down carelessly.

144

My pulse stays too fast for a room this still.

I'm still there, in his arms, until my weight shifts.

My ankle flares, sharp and sickening. The world tilts.

Fine.

The ankle first.

I don't rip the boot off. I sit. I breathe once, slow and ugly, until my hands stop shaking. Then I unlace.

Each pull changes the pressure, and it's unbearable, as if the boot is holding the injury together out of spite.

I work it down in inches. Heel. Sock. Air.

The moment the boot clears, pain blooms outward, hot and immediate.

My ankle is wrecked. Swollen and glossy, skin stretched tight like it's trying to split. Bruising already bleeding up the side, angry and fast.

Cold. Wrap. Elevate.

The mini fridge hums when I open it, too loud in a room that suddenly feels like it's listening. I crack the ice tray with my palm. Plastic complains. Ice clinks into a bag, bright, wrong sound.

I press the ice to my ankle until the cold stings.

Punishment first. Then relief. Then something measurable.

Runner breath. Race breath. The kind that says: you can do hard things. You can finish.

I find a roll of wrap in the bottom drawer of my desk and I blink at it like it's a magic trick. Catherine stocks this room like she's prepping for disaster. I should be annoyed. I'm not.

I wrap my ankle tight enough to hold, not tight enough to numb my toes. Then I fold a sweatshirt and prop my heel on it until my leg is elevated as if it belongs to someone softer than me.

There.

Pain behaves when you give it rules.

My phone buzzes against the mattress. I forgot it was there.

Six messages from Catherine.

Where are you?

Winter.

Answer me.

Are you hurt?

I'm coming up.

Don't move.

My throat tightens. Care can feel like a corner when you're not used to it.

I type back with my thumb.

Ankle. Twisted. In my room.

Her reply lands immediately.

On my way.

I scroll past her name.

Further down is a number I never saved as Mom. Just digits, like naming her would make it easier to forgive the disappearing.

It's been almost six months. She's gone longer.

I hit call anyway.

One ring. Two. Three.

Ringing into a void that doesn't even bother pretending.

I end it before it can turn into hope and open a text instead.

You okay?

Delivered.

Nothing else.

The lock turns.

The door opens without hesitation, and Catherine is already inside, coat half off, eyes already on me like she's counting injuries.

"Winter."

Not a question.

Her gaze drops to my ankle. Her mouth tightens once. Then she's crossing the room and crouching in front of me, efficient enough to make panic feel embarrassing.

"Let me see."

"I already iced it," I say, because I can't stop myself from proving I'm fine.

"Mm hm." Catherine doesn't look up. She peels the edge of the wrap back and checks the swelling with two quick, careful presses, nothing dramatic, nothing gentle either. Competent. Certain.

"Okay," she decides. "You're done being brave."

She reaches into her bag and pulls out a small tube of anti-inflammatory gel like she carries it by default. Then a tighter wrap. Then a bottle of water.

Of course she does.

"Elevate," she says, and nudges my heel onto a folded sweatshirt without asking permission. She re-wraps my ankle with firm, even tension. Tight enough to hold, not tight enough to punish. When she's satisfied, she sits back on her heels and studies my face like she's checking for shock.

"You call Health Services in the morning," she says. "Not negotiable."

"I can walk…"

Catherine lifts one brow.

I stop.

"Good," she says, like my silence counts as consent. She stands, smooth, and tugs my blanket up over my shin with a quick, almost absent-minded motion that lands too intimate to be casual.

Then, softer, but still controlled: "You scared me."

The words hit wrong. Not anger. Not accusation. Just the simple fact that my absence mattered to someone.

I don't know what to do with that.

Catherine doesn't move from where she's sitting. She studies my face for one more beat, then she does something I don't expect. She reaches up, gently, and tucks a piece of hair behind my ear. The motion is unhurried, automatic, the kind of thing someone does for a person they've been doing it for their whole life.

"You're going to have to let me do this, you know," she says quietly.

"Do what."

"Worry about you." Her mouth lifts at one corner. "I'm an only child. You're the closest thing I'm ever going to get to a sister. So you don't get to keep disappearing on me and expect me to pretend that's normal."

She says it light. It doesn't land light.

Something in my chest does the thing where it tries to clench and fails. I have spent eighteen years being responsible for nobody and accountable to nobody and now this girl in a cashmere sweater is telling me I am owed to her. As if I am a person someone gets to miss.

I don't have an answer to that.

Catherine doesn't wait for one. She squeezes my hand once, brief, and stands.

Catherine checks her phone once, thumb moving. "I have to handle something early. I'll be out before you wake up."

"Fine," I say, too quickly, because I don't want this to become a thing.

Catherine points at the ice. "Twenty on, twenty off. Keep it wrapped. If it gets hotter, you go to Health Services."

I nod like I'm agreeing, not complying.

She pauses at the doorway, eyes flicking over me like she's filing the scene for later. Then she says, "Sleep," and leaves like she just closed a folder.

My phone buzzes once.

A blocked number. Official language.

I don't read it. I flip my phone over.

The nausea sulks back. The room steadies. And in the steadiness, the emptiness returns.

And in the emptiness, what happened won't let go.

My skin still remembers him, like my body keeps checking the same spot on a map. His arm under my knees. His hand at my waist. The steadiness of him, the quiet refusal to let me limp alone.

His chest under my cheek.

His breath.

The way my body softened without permission.

I tell myself it was adrenaline, the injury, the shock, the fact that someone carried me. A practical explanation my brain offers, unimpressed by romance and desperate for logic.

But my heart keeps sprinting, and sprinting isn't adrenaline anymore. Sprinting is pursuit.

And there's nothing to chase.

I dig Tylenol out of my bag like it's a surrender. Like I'm admitting something I hate to admit. Pain is not always something you can outwork. Sometimes your body demands care the way it demands oxygen.

Two pills. Water. Swallow. Simple, human, small.

I lie back carefully, ankle propped, ice balanced where it does the most good. I stare at the ceiling as if I'm waiting for instructions.

The room is too still. The air tastes like rain on stone, pressure dropping, weather coming.

My mother's rules arrive the way they always do at night. Not as thoughts. As reflex. Stay in town. Stay where there are streetlights. Don't talk to strangers. Don't go out at night. Don't mess around with animals. She didn't say them like normal warnings. She said them like survival, as if the world beyond sidewalks and crowds had teeth.

And tonight, my body has already disobeyed.

I close my eyes.

It's there immediately.

Not a face. Not a scene. A sensation: being held at the center of someone's attention so completely it changes the air.

My breath catches, sharp as a hiccup. My eyes snap open.

Nothing has changed. The ceiling is the same dark. The streetlight stripe is the same pale blade across the floor.

Except me.

Fine.

I try again. Slower. Like easing into cold water. Like I can trick my body into calm.

The second the dark covers my vision, it's there again, closer now. The warmth under my skin that doesn't belong to this room.

And then, beneath the jolt, the comfort comes.

Soft. Immediate. Wrong.

Like my body wants to rest under it.

Like my body wants to stay.

I open my eyes and suck in a breath like I've surfaced from underwater.

No.

I am not that girl. I don't melt.

But my body doesn't listen the way it used to. It keeps reaching for him like he's an answer to a question I haven't learned how to ask.

I press the heel of my hand to my sternum like I can force my heart back into obedience.

It doesn't work.

And the understanding lands so cleanly it makes me feel sick. This isn't going to fade by morning. This isn't a mood. This isn't a crush.

This is physical. Body level. A kind of knowing that doesn't ask permission.

I shift my ankle and hiss. Pain spikes, bright and honest, and for a second I'm grateful for it. Pain has a cause and a solution.

Ice. Wrap. Elevate. Wait.

The pull in my chest has no solution.

Only him.

The thought turns my stomach.

The building settles around me in small sounds. Pipes, distant water, a radiator ticking like it's thinking. Ordinary life insisting on itself. It should help. It should drag me back into my own skin.

Instead, the stillness gives my body room to replay him with cruel precision.

Sleep doesn't come like sleep. It comes like a slip.

One second I'm staring at the ceiling, counting my breaths, counting the throb in my ankle.

The next, the room is gone.

The woods are back, but not the way they were. Not leaves and branches and cold. The woods in a dream are sensation: damp air, dark earth, the pressure of something watching from everywhere.

I step forward and there's no pain.

My ankle obeys like nothing happened. The forest doesn't punish me for it.

I turn, and he's there.

Not approaching. Already there.

His presence fills the space the way weather fills a sky, quiet, certain. I don't see his face at first. I feel him the way I felt him against my cheek: heat at my waist, steadiness that makes my bones want to rearrange themselves around it.

My breath catches.

The dream doesn't ask permission. It moves me toward him without my consent, like gravity finally admitting what it is. Leaves shift under my feet without a sound. The air thickens, rain soaked and alive, and the forest leans closer as if it wants to listen.

His hand lifts, slow and inevitable, and I swear I feel it before it touches me, like my skin knows the shape of him from the inside.

Then the world narrows to one thing.

I look up.

His eyes fix on mine, shimmering green like deep water catching light.

Like something alive beneath the surface.

Comfort.

Want.

I jerk awake with my mouth dry and my heart sprinting, the room exactly as it was, my ankle throbbing like a metronome.

Outside, rain ticks faintly against the window, finally committing. The forest is out there beyond campus lights, existing the way it always has. Unbothered. Watching. Breathing.

My skin still remembers him.

As if the dream didn't invent anything.

As if it only showed me what my body already knows.

I stare into the dark until my eyes burn.

Then, because I need to know if it will be there every time, because some part of me is already learning how to reach instead of run:

I close my eyes.

Green eyes are already there.

CHAPTER 22
SUMMONS

Lochan

I leave her standing in the doorway because staying another second isn't an option.

I leave controlled. Every step measured, shoulders level, hands steady. My face betrays nothing my body already has.

The door clicks shut behind me.

The sound lands deeper than it should.

She is still on me. Her scent clings to my skin, threaded through my coat, caught in my breath like something I swallowed whole. Warm. Human. Sweet.

I swallow.

The forest waits ahead.

I don't look back at the building. At the lit windows. At the room still smelling like me.

If I look back, I won't stop.

And if I don't stop, I won't leave.

I cross the campus with my coat open, cold biting through the fabric. It doesn't clear her from me. My body is still mapped with the memory of carrying her, her weight, her breath, the quiet way she fit against my chest.

A few wolves clock me as I pass. Security posted where they always are, pretending to be bored, pretending to be students.

Their eyes follow.

I give them nothing.

I take the narrow path past the last row of lit buildings, into the fringe of trees where the air thickens, and the world stops pretending it's civilized.

There is no fence.

No sign.

Just a shift in the pressure of the air.

I cross without slowing.

The change takes me mid-breath. Bone reorders. Skin dissolves. The world snaps open, sound sharpening, scent widening.

Paws hit earth.

I run.

Not toward anything. Away.

From her door. From the heat of her body in my arms. From the part of me that didn't hesitate.

The trees swallow me whole.

I run until the campus fades to background noise. Until her scent stops chasing me and sinks into my blood. Until thought narrows to muscle and cold air and forward.

The wolf doesn't question.

He moves.

Dawn comes slow. The sky bleeds pale at the edges. The cold shifts texture. Birds start up.

Smoke and coffee ride the wind from the clearing.

That's when I hear him.

Lucky doesn't call my name. He stands just inside my line of sight, patient in the way only someone who knows me can afford to be.

"You have to come back," he says.

I shift because he asks. Because he's my brother. Because ritual doesn't wait for personal collapse.

Human skin feels wrong when it seals over me.

Lucky doesn't comment on how long it takes me to stand. Or the tremor I force still in my hands.

He turns. I fall into step beside him.

The compound lights cut through thinning trees. The air changes the second we cross back, less wild, more watched.

Barry holds position at the boundary. Silent. Immovable.

His gaze lands on me once.

Contain it.

Then he pivots and disappears into the dark.

Inside, the corridors are too bright. Every surface built to reflect control.

"You smell like the forest," Lucky says quietly.

Inventory. Not accusation.

"Shower," I answer.

"And then?"

I hesitate.

"Sunday brunch."

Saying it makes it sound like discipline.

The water is near scalding. I stand under it until my skin burns and her scent still doesn't leave. Until what's pulling in my chest stops feeling like anything I can outrun.

By the time I dress, the mask is back in place.

Not clean.

Contained.

Morning is bright when we step into the clearing.

Tables set. Cast iron steaming. Coffee thick in the air.

Ritual.

Heads lift when I enter.

Not polite.

Assessing.

Security wolves. Academic wolves. Wolves who pass as students. For half a second, several forget the mask.

They smell it.

Not her.

Me.

The night clings too close to the surface.

I take my seat without greeting anyone.

Lucky sits beside me. Barry settles at my feet.

Rowan remains standing at the head of the table, gaze moving across the gathering with unhurried precision.

When his eyes reach me, they stop.

"Did you sleep?"

"No."

"Where were you found this morning?"

"North woods."

"And who brought you back?"

"Lucky."

Lucky doesn't speak. He doesn't need to.

"You crossed the boundary last night," Rowan says.

"Yes."

"And returned with someone."

The air tightens.

"Yes."

I offer nothing more.

Rowan lets the silence stretch.

"Pack security reported from multiple posts," he says evenly.

Jack sits several seats down. Composed. Forward facing. Not looking at me.

The Forresters and the Ashcroft-Forresters branched generations ago over an inheritance dispute no one talks about anymore. The Ashcroft-Forresters kept the institutional power. Jack's side kept the appetite. Still, both lines find their way back to my father's table.

"This isn't an accusation," Rowan continues. "It's clarification."

"Understood."

"This won't be handled by assumption," Rowan says. "But understand this. What happens in the open belongs to the pack. Especially when it involves visibility."

I incline my head.

Rowan sits.

Conversation restarts in careful increments. Cutlery resumes. Cups lift.

No one looks at me directly.

Brunch dissolves quickly once permission is given. Clusters form. Wolves peel off toward posts and patrols and classes.

Lucky rises with me.

Barry rises too.

I don't look for Jack.

He finds me anyway.

He moves into my path with deliberate ease.

"Lochan."

Lucky's shoulder tightens. Barry stills.

Jack's gaze flicks briefly to Barry, then back to me.

"I didn't realize you'd be bringing proof of your temperament to brunch," he says lightly.

Silence holds.

"You don't look tired," he continues. "For someone who spent the night occupied."

Lucky exhales through his teeth.

"I saw you at the gathering," Jack says. "You looked at her as if you didn't need permission."

He leans closer.

"Careful. That kind of look invites interpretation."

I don't respond.

Jack studies me.

"Or did you forget," he murmurs, "what it looks like when an Alpha heir loses control in public."

I keep my face neutral. He's not finished.

Then, quieter, like he's decided something:

"She has no idea what she's walked into. That's useful."

Lucky steps closer. Not between us, but near enough.

"The Alpha wants you in his chambers," Lucky says quietly. "Immediately."

Procedure. Not emotion.

Jack's expression fractures for half a second.

Erased mid-move.

I turn without acknowledging him.

Lucky falls into step. Barry moves with us.

We leave the clearing. Move past the human-coded spaces into older stone and darker corridors where the estate feels less like campus and more like institution.

Evelyn will have heard about the brunch within the hour. She always does. Whether that helps me or hurts me depends on what she decides she saw when she looked at Winter at the donor party. I have not been able to read that decision yet, and Evelyn is not a woman who lets you read her before she is ready.

The Alpha's chambers sit at the edge of that shift.

Lucky stops at the threshold.

Protocol.

Barry presses briefly against my leg, then steps ahead.

The door opens before I touch it.

Rowan waits inside.

Benjamin Knight stands at his right. Still. Formal. A presence that makes rooms feel like proceedings.

No seat is offered.

Lucky remains outside.

The door closes.

Rowan's gaze holds mine. Not father to son.

Alpha to heir.

And for the first time since last night, I understand with brutal clarity.

Staying has a cost.

Leaving does too.

I know exactly what the approved version of my life looks like.

I just don't know how to want it.

Not now.

Not after I've smelled her.

CHAPTER 23

AFTERSHOCK

Winter

I wake with my heart already pounding.

The dream leaves no pictures behind, only sensation. Heat without touch. Closeness without form. The impression of him lingers the way a smell does after a door shuts, unmistakable and out of place.

For a second, I lie there, disoriented, trying to remember how I got here.

Then my ankle detonates.

Pain shoots up my leg, sudden and violent, stealing the air from my lungs. I curl instinctively, fists in the sheet as the ache deepens, hot and undeniable.

Whatever I was dreaming doesn't survive it.

My phone buzzes once, then again.

Catherine: You alive? Ice is in the freezer. Water on the desk. Don't you dare walk on it.

Before I can answer, another notification slides in, sterile and official.

SWA ATHLETICS / AT: Injury report received. Do not bear weight. Athletic Training will see you this morning. Reply with your location for escort/transport.

My stomach drops.

Not because of the ankle.

Because it's already a report.

Me: Blackwood. Room 214.

Light leaks around the curtains. Morning. Sunday. I stare at the ceiling while the room comes back in pieces. The faint crack above my desk, the shadow of the window frame.

And the small signs of Catherine's hands all over the night.

A water bottle sits on my desk where I didn't leave it. The wrap is out, not buried in the drawer. A fresh bag of ice sweats on a paper towel beside my pillow, ready as if someone reset it before it went warm. My boot is lined up under the chair, laces loosened. Tidy. Intentional.

Her bed is empty. Neatly made. Not gone, just not here right now.

I push myself upright, careful to keep my injured foot off the floor. The motion sends another flare through my ankle, bright enough that I have to pause with my palm braced to the mattress, waiting for it to dull.

The air smells like detergent and dust and something faintly floral from the soap Catherine uses.

Nothing else.

And the absence makes me want something I don't have the right to want.

I reach for the ice bag and press it to the swelling until the sting sharpens into something I can count.

My phone buzzes again.

SWA ATHLETICS / AT: Escort en route. Remain in room. Estimated arrival: 6 minutes.

Remain in room.

Like I'm a shipment.

Even on Sundays, Saint William doesn't let injuries linger. Not in scholarship athletes.

I set the phone down and look around, suddenly aware of how small this space is when you're told to stay inside it. I pull on a sweatshirt. I re-wrap the elastic bandage because it gives the pain boundaries. I keep my foot elevated as if Jordan is already watching.

A soft knock comes at the door, not casual, not hesitant. Precise. Two beats, a pause, two beats again.

I don't like how my body responds to measured sounds now.

"Miss Cates?" a man's voice calls, neutral and professional. "Athletics escort."

I open the door.

He's not a student, and not staff in the dorm sense either. Dark coat. An earpiece that's almost invisible. A small tablet held low as if it's an extension of his hand. The whole package screams "we don't say what we do for a living."

His eyes flick to my ankle, then my face, quick, contained.

"Good morning," he says. "I'm here to take you to Athletic Training."

Behind him, a compact wheelchair waits, sleek and clean, used often enough to stay ready but not often enough to look worn. He doesn't step into the room. He doesn't look past me. He keeps the threshold intact as if it matters.

"Do you need help to transfer?" he asks, as if it's routine.

I want to say no on principle.

My ankle throbs like a reminder that principle doesn't move you across campus.

"I can do it," I say.

He inclines his head, accepting the answer without commentary. He holds the chair steady while I shift my weight carefully, jaw clenched, breath controlled.

Once I'm seated, he drapes a light blanket over my knees with efficiency that suggests this is not his first injured scholarship athlete of the semester.

"Thank you," I manage.

"It's my job," he replies, and nothing in his tone invites further conversation.

We move through the dorm corridors faster than I should be able to move on an injury. Doors open and close. Voices drift. Someone laughs. Nobody looks too long. If they notice, they pretend they didn't.

Outside, the air is sharp and clean. Campus is in its Sunday hush, fewer bodies, slower steps, quiet that makes every movement feel more visible than it should. The escort guides me along paths that avoid the main traffic without looking like we're avoiding anything at all.

A cart waits at the curb, dark, quiet, branded with the school crest the way expensive things are: subtle, unavoidable. He lifts the chair's front wheels cleanly, folds it in one motion, and helps me into the passenger seat without touching more than necessary.

The cart pulls away.

The sensation is wrong, being moved without effort. Being handled by a system that already knows where I'm going.

We pass the corner of Blackwood Hall and I see him.

Jack Forrester. Standing on the steps with his coat unbuttoned and his hands in his pockets, watching the cart pass like he had nothing better to do this Sunday morning than be exactly there. He does not raise a hand. He does not nod. He does not pretend he hadn't been waiting for the cart to come through. He just watches, the way someone watches a horse going to a vet, calm as a person who has placed a bet on the outcome.

The cart turns onto the path before I can do anything with it.

We pass stone buildings and manicured lawns that make everything look harmless. Students cross in clusters, heads down, headphones in. The world continues.

The cart turns onto a side drive and stops at an old chapel.

Stone arches. Stained glass. The kind of quiet that used to be holy.

But the moment I'm inside, the illusion breaks. Flat screens, sealed cabinets, stainless carts, a wall of diagnostic equipment that looks like it belongs in a private hospital.

Saint William doesn't waste square footage on makeshift. It just likes its power dressed up as tradition.

My escort gives his name at the desk without being asked. The receptionist scans my wristband and gestures to an open bed as if she's been waiting for my arrival down to the minute.

The place feels half asleep and fully operational. Sunday hours, weekday standards.

I lower myself carefully onto the mattress, ankle elevated, and stare at the ceiling while my pulse tries to slow.

After a few minutes, footsteps approach.

Someone stops in front of the bed. I register shoes first, then a clipboard held low, then hands already reaching for the blood pressure cuff.

"Winter Cates?"

He doesn't wait for me to answer. Clipboard. Tablet. A quick scan of my wristband that chirps soft and satisfied.

"Jordan Williams," he says. "Athletic Training." His eyes flick to my ankle. "Let's see."

I glance down at the swelling, skin pulled shiny and thin. I hate how visible it is.

"I twisted it," I say. My voice sounds flatter than I expect.

Jordan's hands are warm and careful, testing in small increments instead of all at once.

"Tell me when," he says.

I do.

He stops immediately, easing off without apology or commentary. Just a recalibration, like my response was expected.

"That spot?" he asks.

"Yes."

He nods once and shifts his pressure slightly higher, lighter now. The pain dulls from sharp to insistent, still there, but no longer commanding everything.

"Good," he says. "Annoying, but good."

A breath slips out of me that might almost be a laugh.

He fits the brace with slow, practiced movements, smoothing it down so it sits right instead of just tight. He adjusts it once, then again, until the pressure feels even.

I notice how little he talks while he works. How he doesn't ask for a story. It makes it easier to stay where I am: focused on sensation instead of explanation.

When he straightens, he studies the joint for a moment longer.

"You've been walking on it," he says.

It isn't an accusation. Just an observation.

"Some," I admit.

He sets a pair of crutches within reach anyway, standard, prepared, then slides them back a few inches like he's deciding whether I'll actually need them today.

"Not for distance," he says, reading my face. "Just so you don't get brave."

He hands me a small packet of pills and gives dosage in clean, clinical sentences. I nod at the right moments, absorbing instruction the way I absorb pain: by turning it into steps.

"Any questions?" he asks.

A hundred.

None I can say out loud.

"No," I lie.

He accepts it like he expected it.

"Bed today," he says. "Elevate. Ice. No weight. If it gets worse, you come back."

Not call. Not schedule. Come back. As if the system has already cleared a space for me.

The escort is waiting by the desk when I'm finished, posture unchanged. He doesn't ask how it went. He doesn't ask if I'm okay. He guides me out the same way he brought me in, cleanly contained.

Back into the cart. Back across campus.

Blackwood Hall rises ahead, all stone and ivy and certainty.

He wheels me to my door, stops just short of the threshold, and sets the crutches within reach like punctuation.

"Do you require assistance transferring?" he asks.

"I've got it," I say.

He inclines his head again, accepting, contained.

"Rest, Miss Cates."

Then he turns and leaves without waiting for a reply.

I close the door and the click feels too loud.

The room is the same. The water bottle. The wrap. The damp bag of ice.

But I'm not.

I ease onto the bed, foot elevated, and reach for my phone long enough to cancel the rest of my day. My fingers hover over my mother's number out of habit, then stop.

I don't call.

I don't want to hear nothing again.

My phone buzzes.

Coach Klein: Jordan filled me in. We'll handle it. Stay off it today, no hero stuff. I'll check on you tomorrow.

I stare at the message longer than I should.

Then I turn the phone face down.

And let myself sleep.

CHAPTER 24
TERMS

Lochan

I don't expect anyone to be here when I return.

She is already in the sitting room.

Not waiting. Maris Harlan does not wait. She occupies space the way the compound occupies land, with the quiet certainty of something that has been here long enough to stop announcing itself.

She stands near the window, back to the door, hands loose at her sides. Dark hair pulled back. Academy posture that never fully left her even after graduation. Two years of missionary work in places with no mirrors, and she came back looking exactly like herself.

That is the most Maris thing I have ever known about her.

Barry stops at the threshold.

She turns before I speak.

"Lochan."

Her voice is even. It always has been. There is no performance in Maris Harlan, which is either her greatest quality or the thing that makes her impossible to reach, depending on the day.

"Maris." I keep my distance. Not rudeness. Protocol. We have never been careless with each other. "I didn't know you were back."

"Yesterday," she says. "Your father's people met me at the airport."

Of course they did.

She studies me the way she has always studied me, not with curiosity, not with wanting, but with assessment, as if she is checking the integrity of a structure she has been asked to inhabit.

"You look tired," she says.

"I'm fine."

Her mouth curves. Not a smile. The suggestion of one. "You always say that."

"It's always true."

She looks at me for a moment longer than is comfortable, then looks away. Her gaze finds the window, the dark tree line beyond the compound wall.

"They're going to move the timeline," she says. "I assume you know."

"I know."

"And?"

The word sits between us, small and patient. Maris has never needed more than one word to ask the hard question.

I look at her, really look at her, and think about what it would mean to want this. To find the arrangement easy. To let the future the compound designed fold around me like a coat that fits.

She is not cruel. She is not weak. She is exactly what this world asked for and she became it without complaint.

I think, briefly, of a summer afternoon when we were eight. Maris had collected a jar of beetles from the garden because she wanted to know if they preferred the dark side or the light side of a leaf. Her mother found the jar and made her tip them out, and Maris cried for the rest of the afternoon, not because she was being scolded but because the experiment had been ruined. She was a small girl who wanted to know how things worked. The compound has spent the years since teaching her not to ask. The fact that she still hosts her own quiet curiosity behind her eyes is the only proof I have that the girl is still in there.

That is not her fault.

"And nothing," I say. "I know."

Maris nods once. She doesn't push. She has never pushed. That, too, is either her greatest quality or the thing that makes this impossible.

She moves toward the door, stopping beside me with the careful distance we have always kept.

"I'm not your enemy, Lochan," she says quietly.

"I know that too," I say in a voice that is barely a whisper.

She is still for a moment. Long enough that I know she can smell it on me, the thing I haven't named, the thing the compound has already decided to name for me. She has always been perceptive in the way quiet people are.

She knows.

She leaves without looking back.

That restraint, I think, is the most honest thing she has ever shown me.

Barry watches the space she occupied.

I stay where I am and think about a girl who looks at something that should frighten her and is not frightened.

And the distance between those two women feels like the full length of my life.

The night doesn't end after she leaves.

I take the long walk through the sitting room, around the living area, down the stairs.

The doors close behind me with a sound that does not echo.

They're too thick for that. Iron-banded, set deep into stone that learned centuries ago how to swallow consequence without complaint. The chamber seals with practiced finality, as if it remembers what it was built for.

Inside, the air thins.

Not colder. Just stripped. Even sound behaves differently here, trained to travel only when permitted. My breathing feels too loud in a room that values restraint above all else.

The council chamber is arranged the way it has always been: dark wood polished to a muted sheen, iron worked into the walls like ribs, torchlight steady and disciplined. Light without warmth. Nothing invites comfort. Everything endures.

At the far end, elevated above the rest, stands the throne.

Rowan sits there now.

He doesn't rise when I enter. He doesn't need to. The room has already acknowledged him. The distance between us has already been measured, decided.

I walk forward until the stone beneath my boots darkens. Subtle, but unmistakable. The boundary between approach and address. I stop exactly where I'm meant to stop.

Never like this.

To Rowan's right stands his second. Upright, silent, watchful. Benjamin Knight. Not a participant. A function. His gaze flicks to me once, sharp and quick, then settles back into neutrality.

I wait.

Silence stretches, not because Rowan is deciding what to say, but because he's allowing the room to finish speaking first. This place has its own language: elevation and distance, the way it forces your body into awareness. It reminds you, with every breath, that your name means less than what you represent.

Finally, Rowan speaks.

"You understand why you're here."

It isn't a question.

"Yes."

The word lands cleanly. No elaboration. This is not a room that rewards explanation.

Rowan studies me the way he always has. Not searching for guilt. Measuring capacity.

"You let instinct move you where judgment should have intervened."

The words don't echo. They don't need to. They settle like ash, quiet and inescapable.

I don't answer immediately.

That, too, is training. Silence first. Stillness. Receive before you touch the blade.

Rowan's gaze doesn't leave my face, but something shifts anyway. Subtle, unmistakable. The Alpha remains, seated on the throne. The strategist speaks.

"That didn't happen in private," he continues. "It happened in open space. In front of witnesses."

Benjamin shifts behind him. Small, controlled. Not reaction. A recalibration.

"You crossed into public," Rowan says. "And you did it without hesitation."

I inhale slowly. Resin and iron. Old smoke embedded in stone. "Yes."

"That isn't like you."

I've heard that sentence before. With approval, with pride. Predictable restraint. Reliable containment.

"I know."

"Instinct doesn't bypass judgment in you," Rowan says. "Not without cause."

Cause.

The word hangs there. Heavy, unresolved. Systems can respond to named threats. They fracture under unknown ones.

Rowan leans forward slightly, elbows to the arms of the throne, narrowing the space between us.

"That's what concerns me," he says. "Not the act itself."

The stone beneath my feet feels harder, as if the room wants me to remember where I stand.

"You didn't stumble," Rowan continues. "You didn't correct yourself."

I see it again. The way my body moved before my mind finished objecting. The way the decision felt less like choice and more like alignment.

That is what unsettles me most. Not that I acted. That acting felt inevitable.

"You were carrying her," Rowan says.

He doesn't say her name. He doesn't need to.

"In daylight," he adds.

"Yes."

"In front of witnesses."

"Yes."

Benjamin exhales softly, barely there. Confirmation.

Rowan sits back. The throne creaks beneath him, old wood responding to familiar authority.

"You understand what that signals."

"I understand what it looks like."

"That isn't what I asked."

I lift my gaze fully. No challenge. No apology.

"It signals loss of containment," I say.

Rowan nods once, deliberate.

"And when containment fails," he says, "it invites interpretation."

Interpretation is where damage begins. Where narratives form without your consent and then become law.

"The council won't concern itself with why," Rowan continues. "They will concern themselves with what."

Yes.

"They'll ask whether this was an anomaly," he says, "or the beginning of a pattern."

Benjamin shifts again, closer. Not toward me. Toward Rowan. Alignment reinforcing itself.

"And you," Rowan says, "will be expected to answer that question. Not with words."

I swallow once. Even that feels too loud in here.

"I haven't lost control," I say.

Rowan considers it.

"No," he agrees. "You haven't."

The pause that follows is intentional.

"Which makes this more dangerous."

Instability in a reckless man is expected. Instability in a disciplined one is alarming.

"Instinct overriding judgment without explanation is not a failure," Rowan says. "It's a warning."

Torchlight flickers along iron brackets. For a moment, the shadows press closer, as if the room itself is listening.

"You were raised to anticipate pressure," Rowan continues. "To recognize it before it moves you."

Yes.

"And yet," he says, "it moved you."

Silence returns. Weighted.

In that silence, memory rises. Not invited. Triggered by the shape of the accusation and the implication beneath it:

You were selected because you were governed. If you are no longer governed, what does that make you?

Every wolf of age runs the trials. Not ceremony, not pride. The trials strip you down to truth: tired, hungry, cold, watched. Endurance, judgment, mercy. The things men claim until the world removes comfort and demands proof.

That year, terrain turned slick. Weather shifted. The group thinned as wolves fell back. Pressure tightened hierarchy the way it always does.

Grayson took command early. Not assigned. Assumed.

A younger wolf stumbled. Nothing dramatic, just the body failing before pride could admit it. Blood spotted the back of his boot where his heel had split. He tried to hide it.

Grayson saw anyway.

"Up," he ordered.

The boy straightened, shaking.

"If you can't keep pace," Grayson said, "you're dead weight."

Efficient and brutal. The kind of line men agree with because agreeing means you'll never be the one left behind.

The boy took two steps and buckled. Caught himself on a tree. Went pale.

"Move," Grayson snapped.

Something shifted in the group. Not rebellion. Just the collective knowledge that a call was about to be made that couldn't be unmade.

Grayson stepped closer, dominance rolling off him like heat. He wanted the moment. He wanted witnesses. He wanted the pack to see he could decide who lived and who didn't.

That was his flaw, stripped bare.

I didn't step forward to challenge him.

I stepped forward because if I didn't, a wolf would die so Grayson could prove he could make someone die.

"Enough," I said.

Not loud. Not dramatic. Calm. So calm it cut.

Grayson turned on me like the air itself had insulted him. "Don't."

A warning. A threat dressed as instruction.

I didn't name him cruel. I didn't force a war in the trees.

I made it practical.

"He'll slow us for an hour," I said. "He won't stop us."

Grayson's lip curled. "You want to carry him?"

"I'll take responsibility," I said.

Consequence. Cost. Ownership. The only currency that mattered.

Grayson didn't want responsibility. He wanted obedience.

"You don't get to rewrite my call," he said, stepping in close.

My hands stayed at my sides. My stomach stayed level. Everything built for control held.

"I'll answer for it."

That was when Grayson snapped. Not into claws. Not into blood. Into the thing before it.

He turned from me and pushed his dominance outward, calling for his wolf the way he always had. Certain it would rise because it always had.

And for the first time, it didn't.

Not resistance.

Refusal.

The woods went still in the wrong way. The way a room goes quiet after something unforgivable has been spoken. The way your body recognizes consequence before your mind catches up.

Grayson tried again.

Nothing.

His wolf didn't rise. Didn't flicker. Empty air.

Around us, the men froze. Not afraid of Grayson, but of what the world had just revealed: the eldest son reaching for authority and finding nothing to hold.

Rowan had been there, watching from the side the way he always does when watching matters more than intervening. His gaze measured Grayson first, then me.

Because I hadn't reached for my wolf.

I hadn't tried to prove anything.

I stayed governed.

That was the proof.

The exile came later. Quiet. Procedural. Removal dressed as necessity, because that's what it was. A wolf the land would not answer cannot remain at the center of a system built on the land's response.

They did not crown me because I wanted power.

They crowned me because I could carry strength and mercy in the same body, without needing witnesses.

The memory fades. The weight of it doesn't.

Rowan is still watching me like I'm a risk he can't name.

"There were expectations attached to your path," he says.

The tone shifts. Not strategist now. Alpha naming structure.

"They were not informal," he continues. "They were not symbolic."

No.

"They were built on the assumption that you would remain governed."

This is the part my father never warned me about. Not the rules, but the way they harden once spoken aloud.

"You haven't violated those expectations," Rowan says. "Not yet."

The pause that follows is deliberate.

"But you've exposed them."

Exposure. Not breach. The moment before both.

Rowan straightens. What comes next is not a threat. It is older than that.

"Maris Harlan has returned," he says. "The council considers the timing relevant."

He does not ask what I think of the timing.

He does not need to.

"You know what is expected of you," Rowan says. "You know what you are."

Yes.

He rises. Not ceremonially, just enough to end the room.

"You are free to go."
I turn.
"You are not free from what you are."

CHAPTER 25
STORM

Winter

Doctor's orders: bed for the next twenty-four to forty-eight hours. No weight on the ankle. No exceptions.

Jordan said it as if he was closing a file, not offering advice. As if stillness is a solution Saint William can enforce if it wants to.

So I'm stuck here.

Catherine being gone helps in the way empty rooms help. No questions, no bright voice, no eyes tracking how pathetic I look hobbling to the bathroom and back. But after an hour, helpful starts to feel like quiet.

Her side of the room is too neat. Blanket tucked with precision. Desk cleared except for a cup of pens lined up like they're standing at attention. It makes my mess look louder. Crutches against the wall. Brace on the floor where I kicked it off. The heat pack tucked under my pillow like contraband.

Her overnight bag is missing.

She warned me Friday, like it was casual. Like leaving for a few days was as ordinary as a meal plan. Reminded me again on Sunday, quick, brisk, already half elsewhere. A family appearance. Governor father. Photos, hands to shake, a version of Catherine polished and presentable.

Of course it's scheduled. Of course it's sanctioned. Catherine's life runs on calendars I don't get to see.

She left the room reset in her wake. Water where I'll see it. An extra wrap within reach. Fresh ice sweating through a paper towel in the mini-freezer. As if order can keep the world from touching me.

I shift, and my ankle throbs in response, offended I forgot it for half a second.

Outside, something taps the window. Not hard. Persistent. A branch testing glass like a hand on a locked door. The sky has been doing that low, heavy thing since yesterday. Pressure without release. New England weather doesn't arrive by accident. It circles. Considers. Decides.

I pull my laptop onto the bed, leg propped exactly the way Jordan showed me.

Emails first. Professors first. The normal thing.

To: Professor Whitaker
Subject: Absence

My fingers hover. I can already hear how I'm supposed to sound. Apologetic, grateful, careful not to inconvenience anyone. A student who makes herself small enough to be forgiven.

I type anyway.

Hi Professor Whitaker,

I sprained my ankle over the weekend and have been instructed to remain off it for the next 24–48 hours. I won't be able to attend class today. Could you please share any notes or materials I may need?

Thank you,
Winter

I send it before I can rewrite it into something that sounds like begging.

Then I do the same for my other classes. Copy, paste, adjust names. Building an alibi out of politeness.

My phone buzzes. I pick it up.

Catherine: I'm off campus most of the day. I left you fresh ice + water. Do NOT put weight on it. Text me if you need anything.

A beat later, another buzz. Different number, different weight.

Coach Klein: Jordan updated me. Stay off it today, no hero stuff. We'll reassess tomorrow. If you need transport or meds adjusted, reply.

My stomach drops.

Not because of the injury.

Because even when the care is real, the oversight is realer. Because updated means the file exists. It means last night didn't stay last night. It means my body belongs to a system the minute it becomes useful.

I don't reply. Not yet.

My thumb drifts, predictably, to the thread beneath Catherine's name. My last text from yesterday is still just delivered. Still nothing back. Six months is almost normal for her now, which is the ugliest part. How quickly absence becomes a schedule.

I lock my phone and toss it face down like I can put the void out of sight.

Outside, the wind picks up. The branch taps harder now, the glass answering with a faint tremor.

I tell myself it's just weather. Just pressure. Just Monday being Monday.

And then my body betrays me.

The flash isn't a picture. It isn't a memory. It is sensation with teeth.

Cold air in my mouth like I've bitten into snow. Sharp enough to make my eyes water. My breath catches; my hands clamp the blanket so hard my fingers cramp.

And under the cold, heat. Not on my skin. Under it. A low pressure in my abdomen that isn't pain and isn't hunger and isn't anything I have language for. As if I'm standing too close to something alive.

My heart stutters, then pounds.

For one fraction of a second, I know. Not think, not guess.

I am not alone in my own body.

Then it's gone.

Detergent. Dust. Catherine's faint soap.

My room again.

My mouth tastes metallic. My ankle throbs as if it's trying to prove I'm still mine.

"What was that?" I whisper, and the sound feels wrong in the stillness. Too loud, as if I've broken a rule.

Two knocks hit the door.

Crisp. Measured.

Two. Pause. Two again.

Like whoever is on the other side expects compliance the way the weather expects trees to bend.

I don't move.

"Winter Cates?" a man calls through the door.

Neutral. Professional. A voice that belongs to a badge.

How does he know my name?

"I'm here," I manage.

"I have a delivery for you."

Delivery.

My brain tries to drag it back to normal. Mailroom, package, something Catherine ordered. But my body doesn't believe in normal right now.

"I'm instructed to hand it to you directly," he adds, polite as a formality. "Authorized given your injury. I need to confirm receipt."

Confirm.

Receipt.

I reach for the crutches. The brace holds, but pain licks up my leg when I shift wrong. The hallway feels suddenly too close, like the building is listening.

At the door, my hand hesitates on the knob.

"I can leave it at the desk," he offers, voice still even. "But I was instructed to place it with you."

Place it with you.

Not for you.

With you.

I open the door a fraction.

A man stands there in a dark jacket with a crest stitched low on the chest. Subtle, the way expensive things are. Not campus security. Not maintenance. Something between.

His expression is calm, courteous, bored in the way people get when they're executing a task that doesn't require emotion.

He holds a small black box and an envelope with my name printed cleanly across the front.

He doesn't step forward.

Doesn't glance past me into the room.

Keeps his eyes on my face like that's the rule.

"May I?" he asks.

The chain latch feels thin. Like theater.

I unhook it and open the door fully.

He hands me the box and the envelope without crossing the threshold. His fingers don't brush mine. Even contact has boundaries.

"Thank you," I say, because my body knows how to follow scripts even when my mind is screaming.

"Of course." His gaze flicks to my crutches, then returns to my face. "We hope your recovery is swift."

Too smooth. Too practiced.

He turns and walks away without waiting for anything else.

The hallway swallows him like he was never there.

I lock the door. The click is loud.

My hands shake.

The box is light.

Inside: a folded blanket in expensive dark fabric, a jar labeled Herbal Recovery Balm, and a packet of tea.

A get-well kit. Neat, thoughtful, curated.

The envelope is heavier than it should be.

No return address.

Just: MISS CATES in the same clean print.

I sit on the edge of the bed and open it.

Cream stationery. Thick. Old-world on purpose. Paper that wants you to feel the money before you read the words.

Miss Cates,

We were sorry to learn of your injury and hope your recovery is swift and uncomplicated.

Please consider the enclosed a small gesture of goodwill during your convalescence.

You will be contacted in due course regarding a formal introduction.

Until then, we trust rest will serve you well.

No signature.

No organization.

Just politeness arranged like a lock.

Sorry to learn. Not heard. Not told.

Learn implies attention. Process. Decision.

In due course. Not if. Not should you wish. The sentence has no space for refusal.

A file has been opened.

I am being notified.

And somewhere underneath the dread, I am thinking of Headmistress Ashcroft-Forrester. The way she looked at me at the assembly. The way she looked at me at the donor party. Both times like a woman taking inventory. I have no proof this letter is from her. I also have no other suspect.

My phone buzzes again.

I snatch it up too fast.

Catherine: Storm's rolling in. Emergency kit is in the bottom of my closet if you need a flashlight. Use whatever.

The casualness hits like a slap. Like she's texting about weather and batteries while my room is being visited and my name is being printed onto paper like a decision.

I type: Someone came to the door.

Delete.

I type: Did you send this?

Delete.

I type the safest thing.

Me: OK.

Then I flip the phone face down again.

Outside, the first real rain hits the window. Not a sprinkle. A flat slap. Wind-driven and sharp. The sound changes instantly from threat to presence.

The branch scrapes the glass.

The building hums with it, a low vibration in the walls. Somewhere down the hall, a door slams. Someone laughs too loud, like they're trying to outrun the weather with noise.

I look at the envelope. The blanket. The balm.

Not gifts.

A marker.

A reminder that I've been noticed.

And then my mind lines it up. Clean, ugly pattern recognition.

Flash.

Delivery.

Storm.

I open a new tab on my laptop and hover over the search bar.

My fingers pause above the keys.

Because if I type the wrong thing, it becomes real. A story with a shape. Something I can't pretend I don't know.

Rain hammers the glass again. The sky goes darker than midday has any right to be.

The note sits on my bed like an instruction I never agreed to.

My ankle throbs. The pressure behind my eyes builds.

And the question arrives fully formed, sharp and unavoidable:

Who is watching me?

CHAPTER 26

EXILE

Lochan

Lucky and Barry are waiting outside the chamber door.

I walk down the corridor without looking at anyone. Shoulders square. Hands steady. My wolf is not. He keeps saying one word, low and constant: run.

Lucky stays two steps behind me. Silent. Barry brushes my calf once, reminding me I still have a body in this place.

The walls feel closer than they did an hour ago. Nothing on the compound is safe for how I feel, not anywhere familiar.

I don't look at the guards. I don't look at the doors. I don't give anything the chance to look back.

At the end of the corridor, where stone gives way to wood, I say one word.

"Cabin."

Lucky nods.

That's it. We don't debate it. We don't pretend there are other options.

Outside, the wind has teeth.

It moves through the compound like it owns it, lifting grit and leaves and the feeling of warning. The clouds hang low and bruised. The storm isn't here yet.

But it has decided.

We cut toward the tree line without speaking. The second the trees close around us, my wolf surges.

Lucky glances back once.

I nod.

Skin gives way. The shift is a function, not a spectacle. Bone pulls, breath sharpens, the world opens.

Wet earth. Pine resin. Iron in the distance. The sky pressing down.

Relief hits first, then urgency.

We run.

The compound falls behind in fast rhythm. Branches whip past. Ground drops and rises beneath us. The forest thickens, then thins, then swallows everything man-made.

Still, I don't feel free. Freedom implies nothing is following you, and something always is.

The storm keeps pace. Rain scent building in the air. Pressure increasing.

I refuse to think of her. The refusal doesn't hold.

Winter.

Not her face, not her voice. Just pressure, the way lightning lives in your teeth before it strikes.

My wolf huffs, unsettled.

Run to her.

Run away.

He doesn't know the difference.

Neither, apparently, do I.

We cross a shallow stream, climb higher, push deeper. The treehouse doesn't appear until you're almost beneath it.

That was intentional. We built it to stay disappeared. Two boys with a stolen hammer and more stubbornness than sense. Four summers later, it became something that hid itself.

We call it the cabin.

It's a grown man's treehouse lashed into old trunks, rough boards cut by hand, beams hauled in sweating silence. It looks like it grew there.

Lucky shifts first at the base and takes the ladder. I follow. Barry circles once below, checking the air, then climbs after us.

Inside smells like sap, smoke, old rain.

Like boyhood.

Lucky lights the lantern without asking. Golden light fills the rough walls.

Supplies sit where they should. Grain sealed tight. Dried meat. Water. Blankets. Stove ready.

We never planned to run.

We planned for reality.

Lucky bolts the door.

Barry settles near the opening, angled toward both door and window.

I take the far wall.

My wolf won't quiet.

Lucky waits until the silence finishes working through me.

"They called you," he says.

"Yes."

"The council." Not a question. I don't correct him.

"They summoned," I say.

Lucky's jaw tightens.

"What did Rowan say?"

"He didn't need to say much."

Lucky nods.

It's started.

"Yes."

He exhales slowly. "They'll want stability."

"They always do."

Lucky doesn't look away. "A betrothal."

"And when it gets back," he continues, "they'll call in the approved answer."

I say nothing.

His eyes flick once toward the compound.

"Maris Harlan," I say.

Lucky nods. Not sorry. Just certain. "Founders Weekend. They'll want it visible."

The future my father chose for me before I knew I could want something else has finally arrived with a name and a date.

My wolf reacts before I do. Heat under skin. A swallowed snarl.

Lucky notices. "How soon?"

"They'll move quickly."

"They'll frame it as honor," I say quietly, rage tightening every word.

"And Jack, he was close enough to see everything," Lucky says.

Of course he was. Jack never misses a shift in air.

"What does he want?" Lucky asks.

"Leverage."

Lucky nods once. That's enough.

Silence returns.

Then, "And her," Lucky says quietly.

Not a name. A center.

"She doesn't belong in this."

"That's not how it works."

Thunder rolls closer. I feel it before I hear it.

Not the storm. Her.

Pressure, as if someone is pressing their palm against the opposite side of a door and holding it there.

My wolf stills.

"What is it?" Lucky asks.

I hesitate.

Then: "I feel her."

"Now?"

I nod.

It isn't direction or distance. It's awareness.

"If you contact her," Lucky says carefully, "they'll know."

"I think they already do."

That's the coldest part.

Silence isn't neutral anymore. Silence is a message.

My wolf presses forward, restless. Not frantic. Certain.

"What do you need?" Lucky asks. Not instruction. Choice.

I look at my phone on the table.

It feels heavier than it should.

"I have to text her."

Lucky nods.

Permission. Witness. Warning.

I pick up the phone. I don't write what I want. I don't write tenderness. I write something that can survive being read by someone else.

I type:

I hope your ankle is healing.

Take care during your recovery.

I read it twice.

There's nothing in it. That's the point.

Send.

The message disappears.

Lucky doesn't ask what I wrote.

"We'll stay," he says. Not suggestion. Decision.

The storm hits hard then, rain slamming against the roof, wind shaking the trees. The treehouse sways. Not unsafe, just alive.

Lucky lights the stove. Warmth pushes back against the cold.

Barry keeps watch.

I sit on the cot.

My wolf finally stops pacing. Not because he's calm. Because he's listening.

My phone stays silent. That should feel like relief. It doesn't.

Sleep takes me without permission. Not rest. Not peace. A drop into something deeper.

Then magnolia. Not blooming, not arriving. Just there.

She stands too close for space to exist between us.

My breath brushes her neck. She stills.

My hands rise without asking. Not invitation. Acceptance.

One at the curve of her neck. One at her shoulder.

Heat hits hard enough to blur thought.

My wolf goes quiet. Not calm. Aware.

I don't move.

That is the point.

Her pulse answers mine. Steady. Present.

The air holds.

My forehead hovers near her temple. Close enough to feel warmth. Not close enough to touch.

Nothing escalates.

Nothing gives way.

The moment remains exactly where it is.

And that restraint is what makes it dangerous.

I wake without jolting.

Magnolia lingers in my lungs.

The storm roars outside.

My phone sits where I left it.

Silent.

My wolf is not pacing.

He feels like something that has recognized its place.

I stare at the dark and understand something I didn't want to understand yet.

This isn't building. It's built.

And whatever they summoned today, the council didn't slow it down. They made it real.

CHAPTER 27

PATTERNS

Winter

By Tuesday morning, the storm has stopped pretending.

It presses itself against the building with intent, a sustained force that doesn't come in bursts but in layers. Wind drives snow sideways across the window until the glass looks sandblasted, opaque, erased. The world beyond it has been stripped down to motion and white noise. Trees bend under the weight of ice, branches cracking with a sound that lands in my chest even through brick and insulation. Somewhere along the quad, metal strikes stone again and again in a dull, uneven rhythm, as if the campus has developed a pulse and it is a bad one.

The dorm groans in places I didn't know it could groan. Pipes knock. The radiator hisses too loudly, nervous. The building feels alive in a way that suggests stress rather than safety.

My room is warm. Too warm.

The heat sits heavy and unmoving, stale against my skin. The contrast between inside and out makes me restless, like my body knows it's been sealed in while the world moves without it.

My ankle throbs beneath the blanket, a deep, steady ache that refuses to fade. It's no longer sharp. It's worse than that.

It's persistent.

A reminder.

188

You didn't imagine last night. You're still carrying it.

My phone vibrates on the desk.

Then again.

Then again.

I don't reach for it immediately. I already know what it will say.

SAINT WILLIAM ACADEMY ALERT
TUESDAY CLASSES CANCELLED
SEVERE WEATHER CONDITIONS
TRAVEL NOT ADVISED

The notifications stack until the screen dims. I roll onto my side and stare at the wall instead, at the faint hairline crack running from the corner toward the light fixture. I've memorized it over the last several hours. I could trace it blind.

I haven't slept.

Every time I close my eyes, the same image surfaces, uninvited and unsoftened.

Green eyes seeing right through me to the deepest parts I haven't discovered yet, making me feel warm and safe. The way my body reacts before my mind has a chance to intervene, heat and tension coiling through me like instinct waking up.

I squeeze my eyes shut harder, as if pressure might erase it.

I sit up carefully, my ankle flaring as I shift. The pain grounds me, sharp enough to cut through the loop in my head.

The message is exactly where it has been all night. No follow-up. No elaboration.

I hope your ankle is healing.

Take care during your recovery.

That's all.

No question mark. No invitation. No warmth that would make interpretation easy. Just courtesy. Clean, distant, unassailable.

I read it again anyway.

The words don't change, but the space around them does. The absence feels louder in daylight. Not colder. More deliberate.

My gaze drifts to the desk.

The package sits where I left it, small and neat and unassuming. My name printed cleanly on the label. No return address. No sender. It arrived yesterday, after the storm had already started to gather itself. The knock at my door had been polite, professional. A campus worker in a waterproof jacket, face damp from snow, holding it out like this was routine.

"Delivery," he'd said, eyes flicking briefly to my ankle before he corrected himself.

Inside were things chosen with care and knowledge. A new ice pack, still sealed. Athletic wrap. Pain reliever. A single sachet of tea, the kind meant for throats tightened by cold and sleeplessness.

Not a gift.

Provision.

The part that won't let me rest isn't the items themselves. It's the certainty behind them. Someone knew I was hurt. Someone knew what would help. Someone knew where to send it. Someone made sure it arrived even as the campus shut itself down.

My room feels smaller now, as if the walls have been leaning in while I wasn't paying attention.

I swing my legs over the side of the bed and sit there for a moment, breathing through the ache in my ankle. Outside, the wind surges again, rattling the glass like it's testing for weakness.

Staying here would be easy.

The storm has already provided justification. Classes cancelled. Travel discouraged. Everyone instructed to remain inside if possible. This is a day where staying in bed looks responsible instead of avoidant.

But the longer I stay still, the worse it feels.

Not fear. Pressure. As if remaining here is a choice someone else has already made for me.

I've never been good at that.

My mother raised me to be capable in ways that don't look impressive until required. You don't wait, she used to say. You figure it out. You move. You don't count on the world being gentle.

I stand carefully. Pain flares, bright and sharp, then dulls into something manageable. I wrap my ankle with practiced hands, adjusting the tension until the ache becomes background noise. Then I dress quickly. Layers without ceremony. Thermal leggings. Jeans. Thick socks. Sweater. Coat. Hat. Gloves. Scarf wrapped tight.

I tuck the ice pack and wrap into my bag, not because I need them right now, but because leaving them behind feels like leaving a piece of myself in someone else's care.

The dorm hallway is empty. Heat hums through vents. Lights buzz. No footsteps, no doors, no laughter. The building feels like a place people are hiding in on purpose, as if the storm has turned everyone into secrets.

I move down the stairs with one hand on the railing, ankle complaining at each descent. At the front entrance, I push the door open and the cold hits me with a physical shove.

Wind steals my breath. Snow needles my cheeks. The air tastes like metal and ice. My scarf jerks sideways, and I clamp a gloved hand over it, holding it in place.

Campus is half empty. Advisories everywhere. Not posted signs, but emptiness that warns you. No students cutting across the quad. No figures moving between buildings. Just the weather and the dark outlines of things being softened, erased, swallowed.

The library sits across campus. On a normal day, it's nothing. Ten minutes. A walk I don't think about.

Today it feels like a dare.

I step out anyway.

Snow is deeper than it looks, hiding ice beneath it. Each step is a calculation. My ankle flares when I land wrong, sending bright pain up my leg. I grit my teeth and keep moving. The wind pushes at my shoulders so hard I have to lean into it like I'm wading through water.

For a moment, I think of all the times I've done things alone because there was no alternative. Moving apartments. Fixing things that broke. Walking home in weather people called dangerous because being late had consequences. There is a specific kind of competence you build when you can't count on someone else. You don't negotiate with conditions. You adapt.

I am used to doing whatever it takes on my own.

A gust hits hard enough to tilt me. I stumble, ankle screaming, and grab a lamppost. My lungs burn. Snow collects on my lashes. The world is white motion, soundless except for wind.

Then it eases, just enough.

I push forward again, head down, eyes fixed on the library's dark stone shape cutting through the storm.

When I finally reach the doors and pull them open, warmth wraps around me like a different climate. The sudden stillness makes my ears ring. Snow melts off my coat in slow drips, loud in the quiet.

The library is empty.

Not just quiet. Empty. Reading lamps glow over unoccupied tables. Chairs sit pushed in with unnatural neatness. No backpacks. No laptops. No bodies.

A single librarian sits at the main desk, posture composed, hands folded near a keyboard. She looks up as I approach, gaze steady. Her eyes flick to my ankle, then return to my face with practiced neutrality.

"Archives," I say, voice rough.

She doesn't ask why. She doesn't tell me to go home. She slides a clipboard toward me.

"Second floor. Room C. Sign in."

The page is almost blank. My name will be the first entry today, which should feel ordinary. Instead it feels like a record being created.

Upstairs, the stacks form narrow corridors of paper and shadow. The air smells like dust and glue and old pages. My footsteps echo faintly, then get swallowed by the carpet. The emptiness makes the building feel bigger and more controlled at the same time, like it is holding its breath.

Room C is at the end of a short hallway. A small plaque reads SPECIAL COLLECTIONS: ARCHIVAL ACCESS.

The door is unlocked.

Inside, the archive room is closet-sized. Four walls. No windows. A table bolted to the floor. A rolling chair. A desk lamp casting warm light in a tight circle. Shelves lined with boxes and binders, labeled in careful handwriting.

The door clicks shut behind me.

I expect my chest to tighten. I expect panic.

Instead, I relax.

It is strange, how safe a sealed room can feel when the world outside is loud and exposed. The storm can't reach me here. No one can see in unless they choose to. The air is still. The light is warm. The space is finite, containable.

The comfort is sad in a way I don't have time to name.

I hang my coat on the chair and sit. My ankle throbs under the table. I switch on the lamp, and the circle of light tightens the world into something manageable.

Then I start.

At first, the research is clumsy. I don't have a clean question. I have pressure, a sense of being watched, and a need for context.

I pull the nearest box: CAMPUS FOUNDING RECORDS.

Minutes from early board meetings. Donor lists. Names that look like they belong on buildings. The handwriting is elegant, old, script that implies confidence. The same surnames appear again and again, threaded through decades like an unbroken cord.

Bradford.

Montgomery.

Forrester.

Harlan.

Not always the same first names. Sometimes sons, sometimes brothers, sometimes marriages that tie lines together. But the families repeat the way weather repeats: predictable, seasonal, unavoidable.

I flip to land deeds and maps.

The earliest map shows the academy as a small cluster of buildings pressed against dense forest inked in heavy strokes. A boundary line is drawn with obsessive care between campus and woods, and the notes in the margins call it conservation, protected land, ecological preservation.

But the line isn't drawn like a suggestion.

It is drawn like a warning.

Later maps update the language. The line remains. The campus expands, but the forest line stays firm, as if the land itself refuses certain changes. Some margins mention "old boundaries" and "historic demarcation." Words that sound academic. Words that cover something older.

I open a thin binder labeled REGIONAL FOLKLORE.

The paper inside is brittle. The stories are not sensational. They are practical, almost plain.

Warnings about not crossing the tree line after dusk.

Accounts of travelers being "returned" to roads they swear they never found.

A recurring phrase about "the old order" that keeps the land balanced when humans get greedy.

Wolves appear, but not as monsters. Not as fairy tales. As structure.

I flip to another page and the handwriting changes. Faded. Different ink. A margin note someone added decades after the original entry.

Once, the line was held by women, the note reads. Then it wasn't.

That's all. No context. No explanation. No record of what changed or who decided. Just an aside in a margin, the kind of detail an archivist couldn't quite bring themselves to leave out and couldn't quite bring themselves to feature.

I read it three times.

The phrasing snags me in a way I can't immediately name. Once it was. Then it wasn't. Like a fact stripped of cause. Like the most important sentence in the entire archive has been written as if to be overlooked.

The language is careful. Reverent. It treats wolves like weather and law: a force that exists whether you believe in it or not.

Hierarchy emerges through repetition and omission. Certain roles are referenced as if they are understood.

First sons.

Stewards.

Heirs.

Not kings, not presidents. Heirs. The word is old enough to taste like iron.

One page mentions "the line of the woods" and the "holder" who keeps it. Another mentions that the forest answers only to those who can hold restraint and strength together. The phrasing is too specific to be a poetic accident.

I stop and stare at the line until my eyes blur.

Restraint and strength.

Lochan's stillness flashes through my mind, uninvited. The way he held himself as if moving too quickly would cost him. The way he looked at me like he was deciding whether to speak at all.

My stomach tightens.

I'm not thinking wolf. I'm not ready to name anything.

But I'm starting to see shape.

Years where photographs skip certain events.

Articles that reference "private ceremonies" with no details.

A repeated avoidance of the forest, spoken of only as land, never as presence.

It isn't the information that chills me.

It's the omission. The way the archive seems curated to allow a certain kind of knowledge and deny the rest.

I reach for a box labeled ACCESSION: RESTRICTED MATERIALS and lift the lid.

Inside is a thin folder with a red stamp: CONSULTATION REQUIRED.

My fingers hover over it.

I open the door and step into the hallway.

The library is still empty. The silence has teeth now. I walk back to the desk, each step too loud.

"I have a folder marked consultation required," I say.

The librarian doesn't look surprised. She doesn't ask what it is. She simply lifts her gaze, calm and measuring.

"That material isn't for general access," she says.

"I'm doing research."

"For what course?"

"I'm not," I admit, and the honesty tastes like risk.

Her eyes flick to my ankle again, subtle but unmistakable, as if my body has become a form of identification. Then she smiles, thin and professional.

"You can request it," she says. "We'll see."

We'll see.

Not no. Not yes. A polite delay shaped like control.

I nod and walk back upstairs, back into Room C, back into my small, windowless comfort. The moment the door clicks shut behind me, I breathe easier, which is its own kind of indictment.

Back in the chair, I return to what I can access.

Local histories. Campus founders. Family trees embedded in alumni notes. Old property records. It becomes a web: land and blood and institutional power braided together so tightly you can't tell where one ends and the other begins.

The wolves aren't presented as mythology.

They're presented as a social order that the human world learned to coexist with, then learned to hide behind polite language.

Preservation.

Stewardship.

Ecology.

Tradition.

Words that let you say everything without saying the real thing.

And Lochan, in that web, stops feeling like an anomaly.

He becomes legible as a figure the system recognizes. Someone people move around instinctively. Someone whose restraint is not a personality quirk but a requirement.

A role that has existed before.

I don't have answers. Not the kind that would let me stand up and say I know what he is.

But I have orientation.

Which is worse, in some ways, because orientation means I can no longer pretend I'm just confused.

I reach for a thin box labeled PHOTOGRAPHS and slide it closer.

Loose prints, edges curled, some mounted on stiff card stock. Faces posed. Buildings half built. Snowy steps and black coats and formal gatherings with rigid smiles.

Then my fingers stop.

A photograph near the bottom pulls at me like gravity.

I lift it carefully.

A woman stands near the center of the frame. Young. Composed. Her face is wrong in a way that makes my breath hitch. Not because it's unfamiliar.

Because it isn't.

Cheekbones. Mouth. The set of her gaze. The shape that my mother carried, and that I carry in different ways, like inheritance written in bone.

She looks like my mother.

Not identical. The hair is styled in a way that dates the image, the clothing old, but the resemblance is threaded through it so unmistakably my hands tremble.

Beside her stands a man positioned slightly forward, the composition subtly arranged around him. Not by accident.

He isn't smiling. His posture is straight, controlled, unyielding. Not tense. Not defensive.

Commanding.

The resemblance to Lochan isn't in a single feature I could list. It's in presence. In the way the photo seems organized around him. In the quiet authority that makes everyone else look like they're waiting for his approval even in a still image.

There is no label. No name. No date.

Just the photograph.

I set the photograph down and flip to the consultation log at the front of the box.

Most entries are faculty names. Dates going back decades. Careful handwriting in careful ink.

Near the bottom, one line different from the rest. Not a faculty name. Not a researcher.

Ashcroft, E. - Personal research. Materials returned intact.

No date. No department. No explanation for why a headmistress was reading founding records in a restricted archive.

No explanation for why the entry sits directly above a folder marked CONSULTATION REQUIRED.

My pulse pounds in my ears. My ankle throbs. The room feels smaller, not because the walls moved but because the world beyond them suddenly gained depth and teeth.

This isn't about him, my mind says, clear and flat.

It's about me.

I didn't come here to find myself. I came here because I couldn't stay in my room replaying his eyes and a polite message and a practical gift that proved I was visible to someone I hadn't met.

But the photograph doesn't offer me Lochan's secret.

It offers me my own.

I sit there, holding the print, elbows on the table, the desk lamp making the image glow like it wants to be remembered. The storm continues its assault on campus, muffled by walls, distant now but still present in the vibration of the building.

In this closet-sized room with no windows, I stay still.

And I realize I didn't stumble into something hidden. I stepped into something that already knew me.

<h1 style="text-align:center">CHAPTER 28</h1>

ADJUSTMENTS

Lochan

Sleep comes in scraps between watches.

I jolt awake flushed, heat in my face that doesn't belong in this cold. Lucky doesn't stir. First light clears the trees, thin, sharp, and my body answers it before my mind catches up.

We move.

The shift takes me mid-breath. Bone sliding clean. Skin pulling tight. The world snapping into sharper pieces. Cold air cuts across my tongue. The storm hasn't finished leaving; rain still shakes loose from branches, wind snapping through the canopy in short, angry bursts.

I run.

The ground is slick but known. Roots remember me. Mud gives under my weight and holds. I place my paws where the land expects them, where it will yield instead of betray. My lungs fill fast, clean and burning, every breath a negotiation between speed and silence.

Barry tracks me without needing sight. Close enough to register. Far enough not to crowd. I feel him when I cut left, when I lengthen my stride, when I shorten it again.

We don't brush. We don't speak. We don't need to.

The forest bends around us. Wet leaves slap my flanks and slide off. Scent layers thick and overlapping: storm-water, bark split open by wind, wet stone, then the faint iron note of something older, settled. That note sharpens as I near it, not louder, just clearer.

The boundary arrives before it can be seen. Not a line. Pressure.

My pace eases without decision. Spine lowering. The ground firming beneath me, less forgiving, more deliberate. Paths worn in the way the forest never is. Trimmed back where sightlines serve a purpose. Left wild where they don't.

Barry veers off toward the kennels before the house comes fully into view. No pause. No question. He angles away cleanly, already shifting his weight for the last stretch.

I let him go.

I keep on alone.

The house rises out of the dark like it always does. Stone heavy with rain, one solid shape set into the slope, unmoved by weather or time. The storm breaks around it instead of against it. A few windows burn with light.

Not welcoming. Working.

I shift back before the steps.

The motion is practiced enough to hurt and not matter. Heat drains. Cold rushes in. Skin too sensitive. Nerves loud. My breath stutters once, then evens when I force it to.

I stand long enough for balance to hold, rain sliding down my spine.

Then I take the steps.

Inside, the air changes immediately. Dry. Controlled.

The house swallows sound the moment my feet hit the stone. Water drips from my hair, my sleeves, darkening the floor beneath me.

I don't shake it off.

Voices carry faintly from somewhere deeper inside. Measured, not private enough to be accidental. I catch cadence, not words.

That's enough.

I move past the entry without looking.

The common room is occupied. Wolves scattered through the space, none of them relaxed. Someone sits too straight on the edge of a chair. Someone else stands with weight shifted like they might leave if given the excuse.

Heads lift as I pass.

No one speaks.

No one asks where I've been, why I'm soaked through.

That silence presses closer than questions ever have. It doesn't follow. It stays where it is and lets me walk through it.

I take the stairs out of habit, the first two steps too fast.

I catch myself before the third.

One. One. One.

The correction sends a twitch through my thigh. I let it burn itself out without reacting.

Halfway up, I feel it. Attention without a source. Not new.

Just nearer than it should be.

I don't search for it. Searching would make it visible. I keep my eyes forward and my pace even.

At the landing, I peel my wet shirt away from my back. Fabric clings and resists. Water runs in a thin line onto the floor. I fold the shirt inward and carry it instead of leaving it behind.

At my door, I stop.

Not because I need to.

Because my body does it before my mind can argue. My palm presses against the wood, pressure firm enough to quiet the tremor in my arm before it can travel.

The door is cool beneath my hand. Solid. Familiar.

The house waits.

Nothing follows. No summons. No interruption. No voice saying my name as if it belongs to them.

I go inside anyway.

The room is unchanged. Spare. Quiet. Exactly as I left it.

I close the door and stand there longer than necessary, listening to the absence of sound, the way the quiet holds instead of loosens.

Permission. Not relief.

I strip off wet clothes slowly, deliberately, like time belongs to me. I don't rush. I don't hesitate. I move like there's nowhere else I'm expected to be.

There is. I act as if there might not be.

After I change, I take the corridor that usually cuts clean through the center of the floor.

Halfway down, two wolves step out of a side room and stop short when they see me, like they misjudged the timing. One says my name, then doesn't finish whatever he meant to add. They move aside without meeting my eyes.

"Morning," one of them says, late.

I nod and keep going. Their footsteps don't follow.

The training doors are shut. Not barred. Not locked. Just closed, with a handwritten notice taped at eye level.

Inspection this morning.

No signature. No timeframe. Fresh paper. Old tape.

I read it once and step away.

The house drains time in small, unaccountable increments. One minute here, five there. Enough to matter. Not enough to challenge.

Conversations thin when I pass. Then resume a beat later with the same words, repeated like nothing interrupted them. Someone shifts to block a side exit without appearing to. Someone else redirects a small group toward the opposite stairs.

I pass Jack near the stairwell.

He's still talking. Still smiling. Still not looking at me. The man beside him laughs quieter this time, like he's been given something useful.

I don't stop. I don't acknowledge him. I don't give him the satisfaction of adjustment.

Instead, I choose a route that keeps me visible without putting me anywhere that counts. It costs me ground. It costs me time. The calculation sits heavy in my chest. Familiar and exact.

This isn't confrontation. It's demonstration.

The summons doesn't arrive the way it has in the past. No knock. No runner.

A note waits where I'm meant to see it, slipped beneath the edge of my door without disturbing the frame.

Cream paper. Heavy stock. No seal. No flourish. My name written in a hand I don't recognize, precise enough to be impersonal.

Council session extended. Attendance required. No time. No room. Just required.

I read it once and leave it where it is.

Downstairs, the house has shifted again. Not dramatically. Deliberately.

Chairs in the common room moved closer together. Tables cleared that usually aren't. The long windows facing the drive are uncovered, letting light fall where it normally doesn't. Wolves sit where they've been placed instead of where they prefer.

I take a seat at the edge of the room and wait.

No one tells me to move. No one needs to. Space around me feels measured and approved. A junior passes with coffee on a tray, sets a cup within reach without meeting my eyes, moves on.

I don't drink it.

Time stretches. Not idle. Managed.

Footsteps come from the upper corridor. Slower than usual, heavier. The kind that doesn't hurry because there's no reason to.

The council filters in without ceremony, taking their places like they've never done anything else. No one looks at me directly. No one avoids me either.

That balance is deliberate.

This isn't the chamber my father used before. This space is for reports and updates. For orderly language. Not for serving sentences.

Rowan enters last.

He doesn't nod. Doesn't acknowledge me. He takes his seat at the head of the table and opens a folder that wasn't there a moment ago.

"We'll begin," he says.

No one objects.

The agenda unfolds without naming me.

That's the point.

Territory reports. Resource allocation. Patrol routes, lingering too long on areas I usually oversee. Neutral words in calm tones, cumulative in effect.

I listen.

Someone mentions a delivery in passing. Not to me. Near enough. Polite. Institutional. Already completed.

When someone references the storm, it isn't about damage.

It's about timing.

About strain on infrastructure. About how quickly conditions shift. About the importance of having oversight in place before they do.

A councilor clears his throat and mentions "temporary adjustments" to movement within the grounds.

Not closures.

Adjustments.

Another adds that the measures are precautionary, given recent developments. He doesn't say what developments.

No one asks him to clarify.

My name doesn't come up. Instead, my routines do.

Efficiency. Redundancy. Ensuring no single point of failure carries too much weight. Overlapping responsibilities "for the next few days." "Only prudent."

Rowan listens. Says nothing.

When the meeting breaks for a short recess, no one stands. They stay where they are, murmuring in low voices that don't carry. A few eyes glance my way and then look past me, like checking a mark on a page.

I rise anyway. The room quiets just enough to notice.

I cross to the window and stand where light hits my shoulders. Not challenge. Position.

Outside, the grounds look unchanged. Same paths. Same trees. Same sky clearing in patches where the storm has passed. The illusion of normalcy is almost impressive.

Behind me, someone says my name.

I turn.

A councilor, young enough to still choose his words carefully.

"We'll need you to adjust your schedule," he says. "For now."

The hours I usually disappear from have been accounted for.

"For how long?" I ask.

A beat too long.

"Until further notice."

Rowan's gaze lifts then. Not to meet mine. To rest somewhere near my shoulder. Close enough to count.

I nod once. "Understood."

That's all they need.

The recess ends. Chairs shift. Papers move. The meeting resumes without me being invited back to the table. Not dismissed. Accounted for.

I remain standing where I am, visible and quiet, a variable held at the edge of the equation.

They finish with logistics. Dates. Reminders about unity and discretion. The importance of avoiding unnecessary displays of force.

Rowan closes the folder.

"That will be all."

The council disperses like the meeting never mattered. Chairs scrape. Papers slide into folders. Voices soften into small talk that doesn't include anything real. They step around me with practiced neutrality.

Rowan is last.

He stands, and the room follows the motion without meaning to. He doesn't look at me until the others are gone.

"They're closer," he says.

"I noticed."

His eyes hold on me a beat too long. Not accusation. Not warning. Inventory.

Then, quieter, as if the walls are part of the council too: "Be careful."

I don't ask what he means. He doesn't offer.

When he leaves, the room feels too large. Too many exits. Too much space.

I stay where I am, breathing slow until my body stops searching for the next instruction.

Only then do I move.

I don't go upstairs. I don't go toward the grounds.

I return to the window and look out at the drive, at the wet trees beyond it, at the land pretending it hasn't been measured. The storm has gone. The air is clear.

Everything looks permitted.

Inside my chest, the pressure doesn't lift.

The thought lands. Quiet, heavy, unavoidable.

Someone has already reached her. Not a guess. A recognition. Polite. Institutional. Already done.

Evelyn moves first. She always has. By the time the council voices a concern, Evelyn has already drafted the response, signed the paperwork, and quietly arranged for the outcome she wanted. If Winter is being approached, it is not by accident, and it is not by Jack, and it is not by my father. It is by the woman who has been deciding what this academy does with girls like Winter since before I was born.

My hand curls into a fist without permission. Tendons stand out along my forearm.

I force the fingers open again, slow.

Don't give them anything visible.

I step back from the window. The room's air tastes too dry. Too controlled. I roll my shoulders once, small enough to look casual, and feel how tight my muscles have been holding without my consent.

I leave the room the same way I entered it.

Even pace. Neutral face. No shortcuts. No sudden turns.

I take the corridor that keeps me in sight, pass wolves who pretend not to watch, and let the house swallow the sound of my steps.

By the time I reach the stairs, my jaw aches from how hard I've kept it set.

I don't go toward anything useful.

I go where I'm expected to be.

CHAPTER 29

CONFIRMATION

Winter

I steal the photo.

I check out a book I don't want and slide the print between its pages, careful with the corner as if it matters. My ankle throbs at the desk, swelling tight, skin stretched. My body refusing to let me disappear into my head. The librarian stamps the due date without looking up. I don't register the title when I leave.

The walk back across campus is slow. Not because the storm has softened to mist, but because my ankle keeps dragging me back into my body, each step a bright reminder that I'm still here, still intact, still expected to be normal.

In my room, shock sits like a held weight. Heavy. Quiet. It doesn't ask questions.

I sit on the edge of my bed and open the book.

The photo looks different outside the library. Sharper. Less forgiving. The woman's face doesn't soften into maybe. It stays exact.

My mother didn't leave me anything like this. No pictures in drawers. No letters in boxes. She was raised without a family herself, and then she raised me like that, too: with nothing you could open, nothing you could hold, nothing that proved we belonged to anyone but ourselves.

And when she disappeared, when her absence became routine instead of temporary, the lack didn't resolve. It kept widening.

I've never even seen a baby photo of me. Not once.

So this. This face that carries mine, carries hers. Lands wrong.

Not familiar.

Matched.

Resemblance you don't debate because your body recognizes it before your mind can object.

I've already accepted impossible things. I don't always know how. I notice when certainty arrives without permission.

Lochan flashes through my head anyway, uninvited. The way he rewrote possible around him without trying. How I accepted the wrongness of him because my body insisted it was real.

And Bradford, one sentence in an old Saint William history volume, buried in the founding chapter. A line I couldn't forget because it didn't belong with the rest:

More wolves than people were residents when the town was founded.

I didn't believe it. I didn't know what else to do with it.

I slide the photo back into the book like putting it away will make it less true.

It doesn't.

The book sits on my bed, innocent the way objects are when they don't have to answer for what they carry. I look anywhere else: my desk, my lamp, the damp sweater slumped over the chair, the window where the last of the storm hangs in the air like breath.

My ankle throbs again, and for a second I'm grateful for pain because it's simple. Honest. It doesn't change shape.

I tell myself I should eat. I tell myself I should text Catherine, ask if she's coming back tonight, ask something normal. My phone is face down on the nightstand. I leave it there. Normal feels like a language I can't reach.

I open the book again.

Not carefully. Not like I'm studying. Like my hands have their own curiosity.

The photo is warm from being near me, or maybe that's my mind trying to make this domestic. Manageable. I slide it out and lay it on the page. My fingers hover over the woman's face without touching.

Completely normal thing to do with a stolen archive photo, obviously.

I look for an explanation the way you look for one when you don't want to believe your eyes.

Not magic. Not a mystery.

Coincidence. A trick of resemblance. A family of faces that repeats across decades because faces do that.

My gaze drops to the text around the place I found it. Dry. Institutional. Dates stacked like they're harmless. Names inserted like they're just information. Footnotes. Sources. Cross-references.

It's worse than rumor.

It's written like fact.

My ankle flares as I shift. Heat shoots up my calf sharp enough to steal breath. I brace my palm on the mattress and wait until the pain dulls into a steadier ache.

When it does, my eyes go back to the page.

A line is underlined in pencil. Not mine. The pressure is light, almost polite. In the margin: a small symbol. Asterisk, star, something that isn't printed.

My throat tightens.

I flip forward.

The same symbol appears again.

And again.

Not everywhere. Enough to be deliberate. Like someone tracked a thread through the text.

I turn pages slower now, hunting for the places neutrality slips. The moments the writing fails to stay academic.

And it does.

A sentence uses pack where it should say group. Predation framed like economics. Livestock losses presented as a pattern, not an incident. A pause in cadence like whoever wrote this tried to smooth a sharp thing into an acceptable one.

Outside my door, someone laughs in the hallway. A normal sound. A human sound.

It makes my skin prickle.

I turn a page and find Bradford again, expanded this time. Census counts. Notes about "discrepancies between recorded residents and observed population." A sentence trying to make strangeness sound like weather.

Wolves were noted in greater number than expected for the region, often outnumbering the town's human inhabitants during its earliest recorded winters.

It reads like someone explaining snowfall.

I read it twice because the words refuse to resolve into meaning. A third time because my brain insists there has to be another interpretation.

Lochan rises again, not as a distraction but as gravity: his face half lit, the way he looked at me like he was trying not to, the way the air changed around him. Nothing romantic about it. Altered. Like distance and sound didn't obey the same rules around him.

I don't say wolf out loud.

I don't even think it cleanly.

My mind circles the edges the way you approach something dangerous in the dark. This. Him. Bradford. The photo.

It isn't a conclusion.

It's alignment.

I close the book halfway, photo inside, and press my palm down on the cover like containment is a choice.

My heartbeat is steady, which makes everything worse. I want panic. I want an obvious reaction, something that would justify stopping.

Instead, I feel quiet.

Focused.

Like a part of me has decided this is a problem that needs solving.

The thought that rises isn't dramatic. It's procedural.

If this is in a book that I can check out with a student ID, then it isn't hidden.

It's managed.

And if it's managed, someone decided what I would and wouldn't be allowed to know.

I open the book again.

Not because I want to.

Because I can't stop.

I turn another page, and before my eyes can adjust to the text, I know something that isn't written there.

The realization lands whole. Finished. Not a thought I follow. Not a conclusion I reach. Just present, fully formed, as if I walked into the middle of a sentence already being spoken.

I freeze with the page half lifted.

This isn't my thought.

It doesn't arrive like thinking.

It arrives like entry.

I know there's a truth in this book I'm not meant to find.

My thoughts hesitate. They argue. They backtrack.

This doesn't.

It arrives complete.

My pulse kicks hard. My ankle flares at the same time, pain spiking up my leg as if my body is trying to interrupt whatever just happened. I press my foot into the mattress and grip the book, grounding myself in paper and weight and texture.

I scan the paragraph again, hunting for the sentence that explains what I know now.

It isn't there.

The text hasn't changed. The words sit exactly where they were. Neutral. Academic. Unaware.

But the knowledge remains.

Not words.

Direction.

The sense of a truth withheld on purpose.

My mouth goes dry.

I flip back a page. Forward again. Faster, trying to catch the mechanism that slipped past me. My ankle protests. I barely register it.

This isn't research anymore.

This is access.

I don't hear voices. I don't see anything new. No cinematic flood of information.

Only the unmistakable awareness that something crossed into me without asking.

Someone is thinking about this.

Not abstractly.

Actively.

I sit back against the headboard, breath shallow, book open in my lap. My heart is racing now, fast and insistent, but beneath it there's a steadiness that scares me more.

Whatever this is, it isn't stumbling.

It knows where it's going.

I close the book slowly, deliberately, like the motion might matter.

The pressure doesn't vanish. It doesn't intensify.

It waits.

A line drawn behind my eyes.

Then it happens.

Pressure cinches at the base of my skull, sharp and immediate, as if my head has narrowed.

It's not memory.

It's borrowed sensation.

Not darkness.

Motion.

Wet ground rushing beneath something built to take it. Breath low in a chest that isn't mine. Muscles working in a rhythm I don't recognize but somehow understand.

No fear.

No hesitation.

Only forward. Only now.

My stomach lurches.

I gasp and the image fractures, tearing apart mid-stride. I clutch the bedspread, fingers digging in hard enough to hurt, and force my eyes open.

My room snaps back into place. Too bright. Too still.

My ankle screams as I twist, pain blooming white-hot up my leg. A sound rips out of me before I can stop it. Raw, unguarded.

I fold forward, breath coming too fast, and wait for pain to drag me all the way back into my body.

It doesn't fully work.

Something lingers.

Not the image.

The after of it. The certainty of movement, the certainty of direction, the knowledge of where something is headed without knowing how I know.

My hands shake. Not panic.

Adrenaline without a target.

"That wasn't," I start, then stop.

Vision is wrong. Memory is wrong. Dream is worse. Those belong to me.

This didn't.

I sit there with my spine pressed to the headboard, the closed book in my lap like a held breath. My heart pounds, but underneath it is that same cold steadiness.

Whatever reached into me didn't take anything.

It checked something.

Outside my door, laughter again. Normal enough to feel cruel.

I stay very still and let the truth land, because pretending it didn't happen will only make it happen again.

This isn't imagination under stress.

This is access without permission.

I barely make it to the bathroom before I vomit.

It's violent and sudden. My body rejecting a presence it can't name. I grip the sink edge as it happens, knuckles white, ankle flaring as I brace. My throat burns. My eyes water.

Nothing about it is graceful. My body is saying no.

When it's over, I stay bent over the sink, breathing hard, staring at my reflection like I don't fully trust it yet.

My face looks pale.

Ordinary.

Human.

But the wrongness doesn't lift.

And somewhere beyond the walls of this room, I know, cold and certain. A presence already knew I felt it.

CHAPTER 30
REMEMBER

Lochan

I can't stop replaying the words said in passing.

The delivery has been successful.

They didn't look at me when they said it. That was the tell: the way truth moves when it thinks it has already won. I kept my expression neutral. Still. Receptive in the way I was trained to be.

Barry pads at my side, close enough that his shoulder brushes my leg. He hasn't left me since the meeting ended. Not when I paused. Not when others passed. Not when eyes followed me longer than politeness allowed.

Once, they would have objected. Now they pretend it's normal.

That's how I know the room has shifted.

I keep walking. Don't slow. The path away from the chambers slopes toward the outer grounds, gravel crunching under my boots. Hands loose. Measured. Anyone watching sees exactly what they expect to see.

The heir apparent. Composed. Contained.

Inside, restraint is working overtime.

Winter.

They don't know what she is. Not yet. They don't need to. Proximity has always been enough for them: nearness mistaken

215

for access, curiosity dressed up as oversight, assessment framed as responsibility.

It's never the accusation that gets you. It's the reach.

Something hot and dangerous flashes through me and I clamp down hard before it can find my face. This is how mistakes are made. This is how blood gets spilled in the name of order.

Barry shifts half a step closer. Warning or anchor. With him, it's always both.

I breathe through my nose. Count my steps. Let open sky dilute what the chamber tried to do to me. Stone, glass, authority, pretending it doesn't need teeth.

They reached toward her.

That's the truth beneath everything else. Not formally. Not openly. But intention has weight, and I felt it when I stood to leave. A collective lean. A recalibration. The subtle shift that says: we will be involved now.

Involved becomes assessed. Assessed becomes contained.

I won't give them that.

Not confusion.

Not reaction.

Certainly not her.

Barry's presence has already unsettled them. A watcher they didn't authorize and can't dismiss. The argument about whether a "dog" belonged near council chambers died quietly.

He proved himself the way the forest always does. By being right.

Lucky would have broken something already. That's the difference. Lucky burns. Barry holds. And right now, holding is the only reason the room didn't feel the full weight of what crossed my mind when Winter's name passed their mouths.

I adjust course just enough to look incidental.

Supplies for Barry. That's the excuse. No one questions caretaking. No one questions dogs.

The kennel sits far enough from the main buildings to feel like an afterthought, and close enough to be indispensable.

The irony isn't lost on me. I was the heir before Barry arrived. I became dangerous after.

The kennel isn't what it used to be.

Most wolves don't bother with it now. Too domestic. Too small. A relic from when containment still pretended to be care.

But there are reasons I come here that have nothing to do with cages.

Milo will already know.

He always does.

The kennel is still where it's always been.

That doesn't mean it's still seen.

It sits at the edge of the lower grounds, half shadowed by trees that were never cleared because no one could agree who should give the order. It hasn't been rebuilt. It hasn't been improved. Time didn't preserve it. Time abandoned it.

Once, this place mattered practically, not ceremonially. Dogs were kept close then. Not as pets. As partners. Warnings. A bridge between forest and people that didn't pretend it belonged cleanly to either.

That kind of usefulness doesn't survive once power decides it prefers silence.

Hierarchy replaced cooperation. Protocol replaced instinct. Dogs became inefficient, too loyal to a bond instead of a system. You couldn't order them to forget who they answered to.

So they were phased out.

Quietly. Politely. With language like modernization and streamlining.

The kennel became formality. A few guards. A few aging animals. Enough to claim the practice hadn't been abandoned.

Enough to lie.

Barry walks beside me, too large to be mistaken for anything this place was designed to hold. His presence shifts the air like weather pressure before a storm. Heads turn as we pass, never long enough to challenge.

No one asks why he's here.

They stopped asking questions about this place years ago.

I slow as we approach the fence, letting my stride soften into something habitual. Feed is stacked near the entrance. Liniment. Old blankets folded too neatly to be used.

Caretaking reads as harmless. Dogs read as harmless.

Barry stops when I do, not because I tell him to. Because he understands pauses the way some men understand commands. He lifts his head once, scenting the air, then lowers it again.

He isn't guarding me. He's choosing to remain. That difference matters.

Inside, sounds are muted. Low barks. A shuffle of paws. Straw and disinfectant layered over something older that never quite leaves.

Time lingers here differently. Not preserved. Left alone.

We pass older runs, doors bolted, wood weathered silver. A hand painted sign hangs crooked on one post, letters faded past legibility. No one has bothered to take it down.

Neglect is its own form of containment.

Barry pauses again. Ears angle forward. Not alert. Assessing.

I follow his attention and see a figure moving at the far end of the building, slow and familiar.

Good. This place still keeps its ghosts.

I angle toward the supply shed, deliberate in my movements, reaching for a sack I don't need. My hands know the motions. Untie. Lift. Set aside. It gives anyone watching a narrative to hold.

Heir collects supplies for his oversized animal.

Nothing to see.

Barry settles beside the door, patient in a way that isn't trained. He doesn't watch me. He watches the building and the spaces between sounds. The pauses where things decide whether to happen.

He has never been leashed.

If I violate whatever principle he answers to, he could leave.

That knowledge has weight.

I shoulder the sack and turn, letting my gaze lift casually, just enough to catch the older man's eye as he approaches.

No signal. No acknowledgment yet.

Just recognition moving through a face that learned long ago not to show too much.

This is where dogs were once chosen.

This is where answers used to come from.

And this is where the wolves stopped listening.

Milo is already there.

He always is.

He doesn't turn when he hears us. Doesn't tense. Doesn't reach for anything. He keeps sorting feed like time moves differently for him.

"Still growing," he says, nodding once at Barry. Not a question.

Barry dips his head just enough to acknowledge him. Not deference. Recognition.

I crouch to check Barry's leg, fingers brushing fur thick as winter. There's no injury. I knew that already. Ritual more than inspection. A reason to be here that doesn't require explanation.

Milo waits.

He's good at that.

"I need salt blocks," I say. "And oil."

"For the coat?" he asks.

"For the joints."

Milo hums. Sets a crate aside. "He won't stay long," he says, like an observation. Not like advice.

Barry flicks an ear.

First warning.

I straighten slowly. "He stays as long as he chooses."

Milo finally looks at me then. Not startled. Not impressed. Just measuring.

"That's what I said," he replies.

We stand in the kind of quiet that presses instead of empties.

Milo sets the crate down carefully, like sound might matter.

"Every man who believed himself different," he says, not looking at me, "began that way."

Barry shifts behind me. Not closer. Not farther.

I don't answer.

I don't start with Winter.

So I start with the council.

"I want to understand something," I say.

Milo doesn't stop what he's doing. That tells me I haven't crossed a line yet.

"How much interest does the council usually take," I continue, "in… personal matters."

He lets out a breath that might be a laugh if it weren't so humorless.

"That depends," he says. "On whether it stays personal."

I nod once. Fair.

"And if it doesn't?" I ask. "If it's inconvenient. Unplanned."

Milo looks at me.

"Wolves?" he asks.

I hesitate, long enough to be honest.

"Or humans."

Recognition moves through him. Not shock. Not outrage.

History.

"There's always been a gray area," he says slowly. "Or people liked to pretend there was."

Barry shifts. I feel it through the floorboards.

"And who decides when it stops being gray?" I ask.

Milo sets the crate down. Careful. Final.

"The council," he says. "Unless Rowan decides first."

That lands harder than anything else.

"And if those two disagree?"

Milo studies me, not with sympathy, with precedent.

"Then pack comes before son," he says. "That's the rule everyone pretends they won't need."

Silence.

I don't argue. I don't react.

I ask the last question. The one I came here for without admitting it.

"How long," I say, "do they usually wait before deciding it's their business?"

Milo's answer is immediate.

"They don't," he says. "They notice. They discuss. They prepare."

He meets my eyes.

"And by the time they speak, they believe they're late."

I don't tell him about the thoughts. Not directly.

I tell him enough by standing here.

He studies my face for a moment.

"Your mother sounded like that," he says.

I still.

For half a second, I am eleven years old again, watching her leave the council chamber with her back too straight and her hands too steady, and I understand a thing I have been refusing to understand for years.

No one talks about my mother anymore.

I don't give him anything.

Milo doesn't ask for it.

"She never explained it," he adds, quiet. "But I watched what it did to the room around her."

He wipes his hands on his trousers.

"Whatever you're circling," he says, "it cost her."

His eyes lift, and the next words are almost gentle, almost.

"So be honest with yourself, Lochan. Are you asking about council interference,"

He pauses.

"Or council erasure."

Milo reaches for another crate. Lifts it. Sets it down. Slow, buying time he already knows he doesn't have.

"You're asking the wrong question," he says finally.

I don't move.

"The council doesn't interfere in romances," he continues. "They interfere in outcomes."

That lands.

Milo looks past me, not at me.

"There was a time," he says, "when certain female wolves were different."

Not rare.

Not powerful.

Different.

"They could shift like the rest of us," he goes on. "But they didn't stop there."

My spine tightens.

"They heard more. Felt more. The bond didn't sit between them and their mates."

A pause.

"It ran through them."

Barry's weight shifts. Slow. Heavy.

"The forest answered those women," Milo says. "And the men bonded to them stopped answering anyone else."

I keep my voice even. "So they were killed."

Milo finally looks at me.

"No," he says. "Not at first."

Worse.

"They tried to manage it. Isolate it. Dull it. Separate the women from the forest. From each other. From the men who would have torn the pack apart to keep them safe."

My jaw tightens.

"And when that failed?"

Milo exhales.

"Then they taught everyone to forget."

The silence that follows isn't empty.

It's braced.

"They don't call it a genocide," he says. "They call it a correction."

Something in my chest tightens sharp and sudden, like my body has recognized a shape it was warned about but never shown.

"And the men?" I ask.

Milo's mouth thins.

"They either broke," he says, "or they were removed."

Barry goes still beside me.

This time, I do too.

CHAPTER 31
TELL ME EVERYTHING

Winter

Two weeks after the storm, I stop moving the way I used to.

Not carefully. Not deliberately.

Just forward.

I find myself halfway across campus before I realize I've left my room. Standing in places I don't remember choosing. Pausing where I've paused before, like my body has memorized something my mind refuses to name.

This is new.

Growing up, acting before thinking wasn't romantic. It was how you missed exits. How you trusted the wrong people. How you didn't make it back.

Now it happens anyway.

The sensations arrive without warning. Not thoughts. Pressure. A tightening behind my ribs. A sudden awareness of my pulse, my breath, the space I take up in the world. Sometimes it hits in the middle of nothing. Sometimes mid-conversation, mid-sentence, like something brushed past me just out of sight.

I keep waiting for it to resolve into something recognizable.

Fear. Attraction. Illness.

It doesn't.

It just is.

I slow near the edge of the quad without knowing why. My feet stop where they've stopped before. I tell myself it's habit. Muscle memory. The mind is good at inventing reasons after.

But the truth is quieter.

I'm waiting.

For what, I don't know.

If I said any of this out loud, they'd smile first, reassuring, careful, and then they'd start writing things down.

So I don't say it.

I keep moving.

I keep pretending it's temporary.

But I have shifted, and I can feel it in the way my steps keep betraying me, carrying me back to the same paths, the same sightlines, the same empty spaces where absence feels charged instead of empty.

A full day of appointments should help. Structure feels like a lifeline lately. Something to move through without asking myself why I'm moving at all.

First stop: medical.

The infirmary smells like disinfectant and citrus, clean enough to feel performative. Like they want you to register care the second you walk in.

Jordan is already at the desk. Not lounging. Not waiting. Working. Tablet angled toward him, stylus in hand, eyes flicking up the moment the door opens like he's been tracking my timestamp without needing to.

"You're early," he says.

"I couldn't sleep," I answer, then immediately regret offering that much.

Jordan's expression doesn't change. Not warm. Not cold. Logged.

"Sit," he says.

The exam room hasn't changed, paper crinkling under my weight, the window looking out onto a campus that has already moved on. Students cross the quad below, bundled against the cold, laughing too loudly for a weekday.

Jordan doesn't ask how I am.

He asks for data.

"Pain," he says, eyes on the screen. "One to ten."

"Four."

"At rest?"

"Two."

"Weight bearing?"

"Five. Sometimes six."

He nods once like I've confirmed what he expected. His hands move to my ankle, warm, precise. He presses along the joint in small increments, not testing for drama but for thresholds. He watches my mouth more than my foot.

"Tell me when," he says.

"I am."

He adjusts without comment. Tries again from a different angle. Efficiency dressed as gentleness.

He measures swelling, checks range of motion, taps notes into his tablet between each step.

"How many times have you removed the brace?" he asks.

"Only to shower."

"Crutches?"

"When I have to."

"That's not an answer."

I swallow. "Most of the time."

"Good."

He rolls an ultrasound machine closer.

My stomach drops. "What's that for?"

"Baseline," he says, already applying gel. "Comparative imaging."

Of course.

Saint William doesn't do probably. It does evidence.

He glides the wand along the tendon, eyes on the monitor, face unreadable.

"It's not torn," he says finally. "No rupture. No fracture indicators."

Relief hits hard enough to make me dizzy.

He wipes the gel away, checks my pulse with two fingers like I'm equipment he knows well.

"Dizziness?" he asks.

"Sometimes."

"Nausea?"

"No."

"Headaches?"

"I don't think so."

"You don't think so?"

"I don't know anymore."

He studies me. Assessment, not comfort.

"Any episodes of loss of time?" he asks.

"What?"

"Missing minutes. Gaps. Blanks."

My heart kicks hard. "No."

Too fast.

He doesn't comment.

"Storm aftermath can disrupt the nervous system," he says. "Sleep disturbance. Elevated cortisol. Hypervigilance."

"And the other things?" I ask before I can stop myself.

His stylus stills.

"What other things."

It's not curiosity. It's procedure.

My mouth goes dry. "Nothing. Sometimes it feels like I know what's coming before it happens."

"Predictive stress response," he says smoothly. "Your body anticipating threat."

He says threat carefully.

"And if it's not that?"

He closes my file with a soft snap.

"Then you come back," he says. "You don't self-diagnose. You report changes. Understood?"

Report.

"Understood."

"Physically, you're cleared. Full activity as tolerated. One week structured rehab. I'll schedule check-ins."

Assigning. Not suggesting.

"And if anything worsens, blackouts, disorientation, you come back immediately."

Not call.

Come back.

I slide off the table. The floor feels solid under my feet. Predictable. I hate how relieved that makes me.

Jordan watches the way I stand, the way I distribute weight.

"And you'll remain available today," he adds casually.

"For what?"

"Follow-up," he says.

I nod and leave.

In the glass cabinet by the door, my reflection looks normal. No visible cracks.

Which means whatever this is hasn't reached the surface yet.

And that somehow feels worse.

The rest of the day is meetings, forms, a study block I scheduled weeks ago and never canceled. I let structure carry me.

By late afternoon I'm in the library, surrounded by quiet that feels too deliberate to be comforting. I tell myself I'm here to work, but my laptop stays closed. Instead I pull archives, old yearbooks, scanned event programs.

Faces in stiff rows. Faculty portraits repeating the same careful expressions decade after decade.

It catches me off guard, how often Catherine's surname appears.

Montgomery.

Not highlighted. Just threaded through everything. Donor plaques. Committee lists. Dedication pages.

Her family ties go way back.

I keep thinking I'll recognize something when I see it. A pattern. A resemblance. Some visual proof that explains why my body keeps pulling me into the same places.

Nothing does.

Whatever I'm looking for isn't here.

Or it is, and I don't know how to see it yet.

By the time I leave, the quad lights are on. The cold has sharpened. I walk straight back this time.

Our room smells faintly different when I open the door.

Citrus and something floral.

Catherine.

She's sitting cross-legged on her bed, laptop open, hair damp like she showered recently. She looks up.

"There you are," she says.

"Hey."

"You okay? I mean, obviously you're walking, so that's a win."

"Infirmary cleared me."

"Great. Love that for you."

A beat.

She tilts her head.

"Now tell me everything."

A thought passes through me, sudden and disarming.

This is what having a sister might feel like.

"I went for a hike," I say. "I fell. Lochan helped me back to campus. Crutches. Storm. The end."

"That's not everything," she says lightly.

"It's the order it happened in."

"That's not what I asked."

Silence stretches.

"He stayed," I say finally. "Longer than he needed to."

"Stayed how?"

"Walked me to my room. Waited while I found ice. Made sure I could move."

"That sounds decent."

"It didn't feel casual."

Her expression shifts.

"Lochan Bradford," she says.

My stomach tightens.

"You should know that little rescue moment put about a hundred eyes on you."

I blink.

"Not just because he's unnervingly hot," she adds. "Or because he's richer than God. But because he doesn't do that. Ever."

She gestures vaguely.

"He doesn't speak to anyone outside his circle. He's private. Aggressively so."

She pauses.

"I've met him a few times. Family events. He shook my hand. Said, It's nice to meet you. Next time, It's nice to see you again."

She shrugs.

"That's the full Lochan Saint William Academy experience."

Even hearing his name does something to me. Not romantic. Alert.

"This isn't the first time Lochan and I have shared a moment," I say.

She stills.

"Define moment."

"We've crossed paths. Before the storm."

"Did he say anything?"

I shake my head.

"People will make their own assumptions," she says. "What do you want them to assume?"

"It felt like I already knew him," I say.

She nods once.

"Okay. That settles it."

"What settles it?"

"We are absolutely not sitting here psychoanalyzing this sober."

"There's no alcohol on campus."

"I know."

"And town is a two-hour walk."

"Good thing we're not walking."

I sit up. "We're not?"

"Jack says there's a thing off the border. Nothing fancy. Drinks. Bad music. Probably regret."

That gets my attention.

Catherine sets her brush down on the dresser, then doesn't pick anything up to replace it. Her hands rest there empty. She glances at me in the mirror, and for a second her face is doing something I don't have a name for.

"Winter, I..."

She stops. Whatever she sees in my reflection makes her change her mind.

"Never mind. It's nothing."

She picks the brush back up. The moment goes.

"You've been cooped up," she says. "You're cleared. You're spiraling. I'm restless. This is preventative care."

I open my mouth to argue.

Nothing comes.

She waits.

Something in my chest loosens.

I reach for my coat.

I don't let myself think about where we're going.

Only that staying feels worse.

I follow her out anyway.

CHAPTER 32

LEASHED

Lochan

The shack sits where rules go to pretend they're freedom.

Not on campus. Not quite the town. Not quite the forest. Close enough to everything to be convenient, far enough to deny responsibility if something goes wrong. Which is exactly why it exists.

Lucky calls it an unwinding. To me, it's optics.

A place for the pack to see me being normal, beer in hand, shoulders loose, laughter at the right moments, so they can file it away as evidence that nothing has changed.

It has been days since the council chamber, and already the air feels altered. As if someone moved a chair in a room and expected no one to notice. As if the pack has begun speaking around what they refuse to name.

I don't drink.

Lucky does enough for both of us, not to get sloppy, but to get loud. To get loose. To make the night feel salvageable, as if normal is something you can summon with bad music and cheap liquor.

Conner, my youngest brother, is here. Sixteen, shoulders too broad for how young his face still is. Eyes tracking exits like he's trying to copy me without understanding why. Two of Rowan's younger loyalists hover close, boys who don't ask questions because they don't want answers.

231

Blood stays close right now. That's the rule no one has said aloud, but everyone is obeying.

Barry doesn't come inside.

He waits beyond the shack's back edge where the dark thickens and the tree line starts to take ownership of the ground. I feel him there anyway, the same way I feel weather before it breaks.

Lucky bumps my shoulder hard enough to test whether I'm real.

"You're doing that thing," he says, too amused for what he's actually asking.

"What thing."

"Standing here," he says, sweeping his cup in a lazy arc, "like you're not in the room."

"I'm in the room."

Lucky smiles like he knows better. "That's not what I mean."

If I answer, I'll confirm what he's already decided. That the council is tightening. That Rowan is quieter than usual. That I can still hear a sentence I wasn't meant to hear:

The delivery has been successful.

I shift my weight, eyes on nothing, mind on one thing.

Not the shack. Not Lucky. Not the watching wolves pretending to be relaxed.

Her.

I don't know why my body won't let her go. Only that instinct has never respected anyone's timeline, not the council's, not mine.

Then the door opens.

Cold rushes in, sharp and clean, carrying a scent that doesn't belong here. Not smoke. Not liquor. Not sweat.

Human. Bright. Wrong.

My spine locks.

The room keeps moving, music thumping, laughter cracking, boots scraping. But I go utterly still.

Winter steps inside.

And for a single beat, before anyone's eyes can land on her long enough to make meaning out of it, I understand something with a clarity that feels like violence:

There is no version of this where she stays unseen.

My chest tightens. Not panic. Calculation.

Every choice from here forward will be read as confirmation. Every distance as refusal. Every step toward her as escalation.

I don't look at Lucky. I don't look at Conner. I look at her. And I don't move.

That's the mistake.

The room is already tilting. I feel it in the way attention shifts, the way bodies adjust without admitting why. Curiosity first. Then recognition. Then the story.

Lucky clocks her immediately. His jaw tightens. Weight shifting, ready for instruction that doesn't come.

Conner freezes.

He's young enough not to know what he's seeing, only that it matters. His eyes flick to me, searching for permission. For rules.

I give him nothing.

And that's when Jack sees it.

He leans back against the bar, casual, deliberate, the picture of ease. He doesn't look at her at first. He looks at me, measuring the space I haven't crossed.

Then he turns.

His gaze lands on her like a question he already thinks he knows the answer to. Too long. Too open. The kind of look men use when they believe the rules are flexible and the heir is choosing not to enforce them.

I feel the ripple.

A few heads turn. A laugh breaks at the wrong time. Someone nudges someone else. Meaning starts assembling itself without permission.

Jack lifts his glass slightly. Not a toast. A signal.

Interesting, it says.

That is the cost of waiting. Not for me. For her.

Conner doesn't throw his glass. He doesn't shout. He doesn't even look angry.

He sets it down too hard. The sound cuts through the room sharper than a yell. Not loud. Final.

Conversations stutter. A chair scrapes. Someone says Conner's name under their breath, warning or plea, I can't tell.

Conner is already on his feet. He doesn't look at me. That's how I know this isn't permission. It's instinct outrunning restraint for the first time.

He steps once. Then again. Not toward her. Toward Jack. Too direct. Too honest. No social padding.

Jack's smile falters. Not fear. Not yet. Calculation. He hadn't accounted for this variable. He'd assumed the younger brother would stay seated. Stay small.

"Easy," Jack says lightly, palms lifting just enough to look reasonable. "I was just saying hello."

Conner stops a few feet away. Close enough that everyone can feel it now.

"You were staring," Conner says. No accusation. No threat. Statement of fact.

The room goes very still.

Jack chuckles, glancing around like he expects backup. "Relax. I didn't realize we were enforcing eye contact rules tonight."

Conner's jaw tightens.

"You don't stare at things you aren't prepared to answer for."

A few people shift back. Someone mutters again, sharper this time.

This is the moment I should move. I don't, because if I move now, it becomes dominance. Public. Undeniable.

And Conner needs to learn what that costs.

Jack takes a step closer.

Wrong choice.

Conner's hands curl at his sides, not fists, not yet, but the air around him tightens. The scent hits a second later, sharp and untrained.

Fear.

Not Jack's.

Conner's.

He doesn't know how close he is to crossing that invisible line.

Lucky swears under his breath. I move. Quiet. Controlled. Enough.

I'm there before Conner realizes he's been flanked, my hand closing around his wrist, not hard, but absolute.

The contact grounds him immediately. Too immediately.

He sucks in a breath like he's been underwater.

"Enough," I say. Quiet. No room for argument.

Conner nods once.

He steps back.

The room exhales like it's been holding its breath for permission.

Jack raises his glass again, smile thinner now. "Didn't mean to cause trouble."

I look at him for the first time.

Really look.

"You didn't," I say.

And let the silence finish the sentence for me.

Conner retreats another step. The moment folds back into itself like it was always meant to. Noise resumes in careful increments, laughter returning too bright, music suddenly too present.

Lucky claps his hands once, sharp and loud enough to cut through the fragile quiet.

"Alright," he says, already smiling, already moving. "That was exciting for half a second. Now someone put money on the jukebox or I'm picking the next song and you'll all deserve it."

Relief answers him.

The room follows.

It always has.

But my attention isn't on any of that.

It's on the distance Conner crossed without measuring. The way he moved before thinking to ask himself why.

That wasn't loyalty. It wasn't bravado. It wasn't even anger.

It was a response.

I feel it in my chest first, a tightness I didn't authorize. Like a muscle flexing without instruction. Like a reflex answering before I've finished forming the question.

I turn my head.

Slow. Deliberate.

Winter stands near the edge of the room, jacket still on, hands tucked into her sleeves like she's trying to take up less space. She hasn't spoken. She hasn't moved.

But she's aware.

Not fear. Not curiosity.

Orientation.

She looks up. Not at Conner. At me.

And recognition passes between us that doesn't belong to sight or sound.

Recognition: clean and brutal.

That was for me.

The thought isn't hers. It isn't mine. It arrives finished, the way truth does when it's done waiting.

Conner didn't know what he was responding to. That's the worst part. He didn't feel threatened. He didn't feel challenged.

He felt pulled.

I glance at Lucky. He's reading the room now, tracking angles, tracking exits. He hasn't looked at her once.

Which tells me everything.

This isn't a coincidence.

It's alignment.

And it's already costing us more than anyone here understands.

I step back into place beside Conner, close enough for him to feel me without being touched.

He steadies.

The change is immediate. His shoulders drop. His weight settles like something that had been braced finally found somewhere to lean.

That shouldn't happen.

He didn't act because he wanted to protect me.

He acted because he felt her, and didn't know that's what it was.

And the truth lands heavy and unmistakable in my bones:

She was never going to stay hidden.

Not from the pack.

Not from the forest.

And not from me.

CHAPTER 33
FEEL ME

Winter

Catherine talks the entire drive.

Not about anything important at first. Music. Traffic. Someone she knows who once threw up in the backseat of a rideshare and still tips well because guilt is her personality.

Then, without changing her tone, she gestures vaguely out the window.

"This place?" she says. "It's where people go when they don't want rules named."

I keep my eyes forward and let her keep going.

"Students who don't want to be seen by the wrong people. Locals who figured out years ago which questions get you ignored. Men who drink like they're trying to forget something specific. Women who know better and come anyway."

She shrugs, casual.

"It's not dangerous in the obvious way. No fights. No sketchy doors. That's how it gets you."

"Gets you how?" I ask.

Catherine smiles, not looking back at me.

"Everyone who goes there thinks they know the cost."

The car slows as we turn.

"And most of them are wrong."

The shack smells like smoke, alcohol, and wet wood that has soaked up too many nights like this one. The floor vibrates with bass and bodies and the scrape of chairs. I register it in fragments: noise first, then heat, then the way my chest tightens like I've crossed a line I didn't know was marked.

Catherine moves ahead of me like she belongs here, laughing already, talking too loud, throwing sparks into dry air.

I don't.

I stay just inside the door, jacket still on, fingers tucked into my sleeves. For a moment, no one looks at me long enough to make meaning.

It doesn't matter.

Something in me shifts anyway.

Orientation.

I feel him before I see him.

No cinematic pull. No rush.

Just a quiet, unmistakable there that roots into my ribs like gravity deciding where down is.

I don't have to search.

My eyes find him on their own.

Lochan stands near the back, not drinking, not talking. Still in the way that makes everything else look exaggerated by comparison. He hasn't moved since I walked in.

Neither have I.

For a second that feels longer than it should, the room rearranges itself around that fact.

Then Catherine's voice cuts bright through the air like she's breaking glass to reset the energy.

"Okay," she says, tugging my sleeve. "If we're doing this, we're doing this."

I let her pull me another step inside.

Noise swells. A laugh breaks too loud. Someone bumps my shoulder and doesn't apologize. The air presses closer, warmer, heavier.

I can feel eyes now. Not fixed. Passing. Curious.

And underneath it all, steady and impossible to ignore.

Him.

Catherine drags me toward the bar and releases me as if she's sure the room can't eat me if she's standing nearby.

"Drinks," she says. "Immediately."

She orders without looking at me. Something bright and fizzy. Something sweet. She belongs in motion, laughing at the bartender, elbow resting easy against the counter, already halfway into a story I haven't heard.

I stand half a step behind her.

That's when it hits me how visible I am.

Not stared at.

Placed.

Like the room has decided where I belong and hasn't bothered to tell me why.

Someone brushes past and pauses like they're deciding whether to apologize. Someone else pretends they weren't looking. A laugh dies halfway through itself.

Catherine turns back, drink in hand, and stops.

Her eyes flick once, quick and unreadable, past me. Then back to my face. Then past me again.

"What," she says lightly, like a joke she's still deciding whether to make, "did I miss?"

"Nothing," I say.

She exhales through her nose, dismissing it, but she shifts closer anyway, hip brushing mine, arm grazing my sleeve. Not protective. Familiar. As if she's anchoring us together without realizing she's drawing a line.

"There," she says, louder than necessary. "You're fine."

A body fills the space beside Catherine.

Jack's arm settles around Catherine's waist, casual and practiced.

Catherine leans into him without looking. "Oh, there you are," she says, distracted. "I was about to order another."

"Then I saved you the trouble," he says easily.

Only then do his eyes find me.

Not immediately. Not obviously.

A glance that takes inventory without appearing to. The kind that doesn't linger long enough to be rude but lingers long enough to be remembered.

"Hey," he says, like we've met.

Like I'm part of the math.

Catherine keeps talking, pulling him into whatever story she's telling. Jack listens with half his attention.

The other half stays open.

Waiting to see what moves next.

And the truth slides into place, clean and ugly pattern recognition.

I came because I knew he'd be here.

Not consciously. Not with a plan.

But my body has been leading me in circles for weeks, and I've been pretending I don't understand why. The text. The silence after. The way my steps keep bringing me back to places where I've seen him before.

The next time I saw him, I wasn't going to stay where I was.

I step away from the bar.

No announcement. No hesitation. Just a clean break, like crossing a line that has been there the whole time.

The room doesn't stop me.

He's still near the back, exactly where he was.

Still. Watching everything without looking like he is.

He feels me before he looks at me.

I know because his attention sharpens. Not surprise. Realization.

I stop an arm's length away.

Close enough that the noise thins. That the space between us feels intentional.

"Hi," I say.

"Hi," he answers.

My name comes quiet, familiar, like he's said it a hundred times in his head.

"Winter."

The way he says it makes my throat tighten.

He doesn't step closer. He doesn't step away.

He just holds position, the way you hold a door when you aren't sure it's safe to go through.

"I didn't think I'd see you here," I say.

He exhales, almost a laugh. Not amused. Just… human.

"Neither did I."

Something in me loosens at that.

"Are you okay?" he asks.

It isn't casual. It isn't polite. It's careful in a way that makes me feel held instead of examined.

"Yes," I say, and this time it's true. "I am."

Relief flickers across his face, small and unguarded.

"Good."

I don't look away.

I let myself take him in openly. The lines of his face. The discipline in his stillness. The way his restraint looks like it costs him something.

I don't care who notices.

I don't care what conclusions anyone draws.

Our eyes lock.

And there it is.

Not words. Not thoughts.

A sensation that moves through me so quickly it steals my breath.

Safe. Held. Protected.

The feeling hits hard enough that my knees almost give, as if my body has finally found what it recognizes.

We stand a beat too long.

Or exactly long enough.

"This isn't a good place to talk," he says finally.

Not a command. Not a dismissal.

A boundary offered with care.

"I know," I say.

Silence stretches again, thinner now and charged.

He shifts closer, not enough to touch, just enough that I feel it. The space narrows, deliberate.

"I was looking for you," I admit.

The words are out before I can weigh them.

His eyes darken, want cutting through restraint.

"I know," he says.

And in that moment I understand: he hasn't been avoiding me.

He's been holding the line.

And standing this close, feeling how hard that is for him, this becomes just as clear.

This doesn't end tonight.

It can't.

CHAPTER 34
DEMANDS

Lochan

I'm a cornered animal, and instead of snapping, I lean into her.

With everyone watching.

She could have stayed. She could have pressed harder, forced words out of me in front of the whole goddamn room. Instead she walked away with nothing, like my silence was the answer she needed.

She leaves.

The moment unravels around me, laughter reconnecting, bodies sliding back into their circles, the night pretending it didn't just hold its breath for us. Hands return to drinks. Voices return to volume. The bass keeps thudding through the walls like it never faltered.

I stay where I am.

Pulse too high. Jaw locked so tight it aches. My hands refusing to remember how to be casual.

She didn't push. She didn't ask again. She let me sit there exposed, as if she wanted to see what I'd do with it.

I move before my wolf does.

Not toward her. Away. Out through the crush of bodies and stale heat, into the sharp cold behind the bar. The air hits my face like a slap and I welcome it.

Pain is clean. Pain is simple. Pain is something I can control.

Eyes follow me as I go. Not openly. Not obviously. Just enough to register that I've been seen leaving the circle of people who are "allowed" to be loud.

Outside, the gravel lot is wet and uneven, reflecting a few hard lights. The music leaks through the siding in a muffled pulse. Exhaust hangs low in the cold. Somewhere close, someone laughs, then the sound gets swallowed by distance.

Beyond the last strip of light, the tree line starts.

When I stop at its edge, the dark presses close as if it recognizes me.

I stare into the trees without seeing them. I wait for my breathing to slow into something human.

It doesn't.

A presence slides in behind me, too smooth to be accidental, too calm to be concern.

Jack.

He stops close enough to be deliberate. Not close enough to be touched, because Jack never does anything that can be called a mistake.

He speaks.

I don't turn.

He doesn't say my name.

"You're out of control," he says, mild as weather.

An observation. A note made in the margin of my life, as if I already crossed a line and he's simply letting me know he watched the crossing.

I keep my eyes on the trees. I don't give him the satisfaction of a reaction.

Jack steps a fraction closer, stopping just short of my shoulder. Close enough that my wolf registers him as interference.

"Do you have no shame?" he asks.

I don't answer.

He breathes out, a hint of amusement riding it. Not humor. Enjoyment. Jack enjoying leverage.

"You might as well have fucked her on the bar," he adds, satisfied with the image, "for all the attention that stunt just bought you."

The words are crude on purpose. A slap meant to make me lunge. Meant to make me prove him right. Meant to turn me into a story that can be repeated with a laugh.

Heat surges behind my ribs.

I turn my head slightly, just enough to catch him in my periphery.

He isn't watching me.

He's watching the spill of light behind us, the bodies shifting inside the windows, the edges where people pretend the night is unmonitored. Hands in his pockets. Relaxed. Like nothing shifted at all.

That's when I understand it.

He isn't wondering what happens next.

He already knows.

"They won't like that," Jack says, still not looking at me.

"I did nothing," I say flatly.

Jack finally glances at me, quick, sharp, measuring. The look of a man tasting blood in water and deciding if it's worth circling.

"Careful," he says softly. "I might want a sample myself."

My pulse lurches like it's been struck.

That, that is the line. Not the bar. Not the shame. That.

Because it isn't sexual. Not really.

It's ownership language.

It's hierarchy language.

It's Jack reminding me that in this world, people don't just watch.

They take.

My hands curl at my sides before I can stop them. Nails bite skin. The wolf shoves forward, furious and ready, and for a heartbeat the dark feels too small to contain what I want to do to him.

Jack steps away before I can move.

Of course he does.

Already turning back toward the door, like he didn't just light a match and toss it at my feet. No hesitation. No urgency. Like whatever comes next won't touch him.

I stay where I am.

Counting backward in even numbers from one hundred so I don't rip Jack's head off in a place where someone could call it "unfortunate" and still make it my fault.

Ninety-eight.

Ninety-six.

Ninety-four.

Cold keeps hitting my face like it's trying to wake me up. It doesn't. It just keeps me pinned at the edge of myself, where control is a posture and not a truth.

A minute passes. Maybe two.

The trees shift.

Barry is there in the dark, near the treeline, or maybe beyond it, and I'm only now allowed to notice him. A massive shadow, still as stone, eyes too intelligent to be anything comforting.

He doesn't come closer.

He just is.

A boundary.

A reminder with teeth.

Then my phone vibrates in my pocket.

Once.

I pull it out slowly, as if speed could be interpreted as panic.

The message is brief. Courteous.

A reminder shaped like concern. A request with no instructions and no room to pretend it's optional.

Remain available.

Stay close.

Do not disappear.

Polite language wrapped around a tightening leash, as if the hand at my throat is wearing a glove.

I read it once.

Then again.

The worst part is how reasonable it sounds.

I lower the phone.

And put it away.

Barry's gaze stays on me.

The treeline stays quiet.

And I understand, with sick clarity, that Jack wasn't warning me that they would tighten the leash.

Jack was warning me that I just gave them permission to.

Not because I touched her.

Because I wanted to.

And everyone saw it.

CHAPTER 35

CHARGED

Winter

The Uber Black Catherine called can only take me as far as the campus entrance, so I start the walk back to Blackwood alone.

The road curves away almost immediately, headlights swallowed by trees, leaving me alone with the crunch of gravel under my shoes and the low hum of the night closing in.

Jack has clearance to drop her closer than I can get myself, but Catherine made it very clear she wanted alone time with Jack. She didn't say it unkindly. Just decisively, like she'd already moved on to the next part of the evening. I didn't argue. I couldn't take another minute of them pawing at each other like the world was a closed room built just for two.

Especially not when the heat of Lochan's attention is still sitting behind my eyes, dizzying and unresolved. The way he looked at me back there wasn't casual. Wasn't friendly. It was looking that lingers long after you turn away, like your body hasn't gotten the message yet.

The road beyond the gate isn't really a road anymore. It narrows quickly, asphalt giving way to packed dirt and gravel, the trees closing in like they've been waiting for it. There are no lights out here. No signs. Just the pale wash of moonlight where the canopy thins and long stretches of dark where it doesn't. My footsteps sound too loud, even when I try to soften them.

The wrongness arrives slowly.

Not fear. Not panic. Something lower. A pressure behind my ribs that makes my breathing shallow without my permission. I roll my shoulders, shake out my hands, tell myself I'm tired. The walk is longer than it looks. Two miles is nothing on paper, but out here it stretches, each bend in the road revealing more of the same quiet, more trees, more distance.

My ankle twinges again, sharper this time, then fades. I stop for half a second, testing my weight, listening.

Nothing moves.

No cars. No voices. Just wind threading through branches and the far off sound of the ocean, muted and steady. It should be calming.

It isn't.

I pull my phone out and check the time.

Then, without meaning to, I check my messages.

There's nothing there. No missed calls. No notifications. The screen feels intrusive in the dark, as if a flare I didn't mean to set off. I dim it and slide it back into my pocket, annoyed with myself for expecting… something.

I keep walking.

The path slopes gently upward now, the ground uneven in places where roots push through. I adjust without thinking, body compensating automatically. I've always been good at this, moving through spaces that aren't designed for ease.

Still, the sense of being slightly off doesn't go away. If anything, it sharpens, like my body has started listening for something my mind hasn't caught up to yet.

Lochan intrudes again, unwanted. The stillness in him when I left. The way it felt unfinished, like stepping away from a conversation that hadn't actually started. I tell myself that's just proximity. Just adrenaline. Just the echo of being looked at too closely.

But the pressure doesn't lift.

The road bends, and for a moment the trees open just enough to show the faintest suggestion of light far ahead. Not buildings yet. Just glow. Civilization, distant and unreal.

I feel a sudden, irrational need to reach it.

Not because I'm afraid of what's behind me. Because something feels delayed, as if the night missed a beat and never quite recovered.

I walk faster, breath quickening, aware of my body in a way I wasn't a few minutes ago. Every sound registers. Every shift of air feels intentional.

And underneath it all, steady and insistent, is the sense that something has already happened quietly, out of sight, and I'm only now approaching the place where that absence will start to matter.

I know I've reached campus because the dark loosens.

Not all at once. Just enough. The trees thin, the ground evens out, and the road gives way to stone paths that remember footsteps. Light bleeds out from between buildings instead of dropping cleanly from above. Sound returns in fragments. A door somewhere. A voice, distant and indistinct.

There should be more of it.

Saint William Academy never goes fully quiet, even this late. Someone cutting across the quad. A pair of students sitting too close on the steps, pretending they aren't. Laughter that carries farther than it should. Movement. Proof of life.

Tonight, the courtyard is sparse.

A few figures pass through the light and disappear again, heads down, moving with purpose. No clusters. No lingering. The benches are empty. The wide stone steps outside the main building sit untouched, as if the night forgot to place people there.

I slow without realizing it, scanning the space the way you do when you're looking for someone you haven't consciously decided to look for yet.

Catherine should be here by now.

Not in a dramatic way. Just… somewhere. Cutting through the courtyard with her bag swinging against her hip. Existing loudly enough to reassure everyone she's fine.

She isn't.

The thought lands softly, without panic, and that's what unsettles me.

There's still time. Plenty of it. Jack can drop her closer than I can get myself. She could be ten minutes behind me. Fifteen.

I check my phone again.

Still nothing.

Around me, campus continues its muted version of normal. Doors open and close. Light shifts behind curtains. But the absence doesn't fill itself in the way it should.

It lingers.

And for the first time since I left the gate, the pressure behind my ribs sharpens into something I can almost name.

By the time I reach my dorm, the pressure has dulled into something more manageable. The kind you can ignore if you want to. The building hums softly, lights glowing behind curtains, someone's music bleeding faintly through a wall.

Normal enough.

I climb the stairs, unlock my door, step inside.

The room smells like detergent and paper and the faint citrus cleaner they use on the floors. Familiar. Contained. I drop my bag, toe my shoes off without bothering to line them up. The routine steadies me more than it should.

I pull my phone out again.

This time, I don't open his thread.

I open Catherine's instead, thumb hovering over her name as if it weighs more than it should. I type, delete, type again.

You back?

It looks too simple on the screen. Too normal for how wrong the night feels. I hit send anyway, because pretending I'm not counting minutes won't stop me from counting them.

Delivered. No response.

I stare at the blank space beneath it until it starts to feel like a dare. Then I lock my phone and set it face up on Catherine's desk, like visibility could make the world behave.

Only after I do, my finger drifts, unwanted, toward the other thread. The one with no name, just digits. I open it, stare at the empty text field, and for a second the impulse rises sharp as a cough.

Made it back.

You okay?

My thumb hovers.

I delete the line before it can become proof of anything.

Then I close the thread and put the phone down harder than necessary, like that will keep my body from reaching for him again.

So why does the silence feel wrong?

Not his.

Hers.

I check the time.

Catherine should be back by now. Not because of curfews or rules or anything official, but because nights follow patterns, and this one is starting to drag its feet.

I pick my phone up again, thumb hovering over her name.

I don't press it.

Instead, I sit on the edge of the bed and tell myself to wait it out. To let the unease burn off.

It doesn't.

I wait longer than I mean to before turning the lamp on.

Catherine's side of the room is too neat. Bed made tight. Chair pushed in. Her charger wound like a display. It looks reset, like someone cleaned for her.

Roommates disappear for the night all the time. That isn't unusual. What's unusual is how accounted for everything else feels. No frantic packing. No last minute change of plans. Just... unfinished.

As if she meant to come back. And the night simply hasn't delivered her yet.

I pull my phone out again.

I don't go to him.

I go to Catherine.

Our last exchange is from earlier, throwaway logistics, a text that assumes you're coming back soon because why wouldn't you.

I type again.

You back?

I hit send, irritated with myself for the question. Of course she's not back. She said she wanted alone time. She was clear about it. Confident.

Delivered.

No response.

I set the phone down on Catherine's desk, screen facing up, like that might change the outcome. Like visibility can summon people.

Minutes pass. The room stays quiet.

From somewhere down the hall comes the sound of voices, laughter spilling and fading, a door closing gently. Normal night sounds. Proof the building is still running on its usual tracks.

I check the time again.

It's late enough that Catherine would've texted by now. Not because she owes me anything. Because Catherine narrates her life without thinking about it. A "staying out" message. A joke. Something flippant and reassuring that makes the world feel orderly.

My phone stays dark.

I try to assemble the facts the way Saint William would want me to.

Jack has clearance. Jack is visible. Jack doesn't do sloppy.

Catherine is social. Catherine is careful. Catherine doesn't vanish without a word.

The logic is clean.

The feeling isn't.

I lie back on the bed and stare at the ceiling, listening to the building breathe around me. Heat clicks on, then off. Pipes shift. The small sounds you stop noticing when you feel safe.

Tonight, I notice all of them.

The absence doesn't announce itself. It just sits there, quiet and reasonable, daring me to call it wrong.

I don't.

Not yet.

But the pressure behind my ribs tightens, slow and deliberate, and I know, without knowing how. If Catherine doesn't walk through that door soon, I'm going to have to do something.

Call Catherine again.

Call campus security.

Leave the dorm and start looking.

Anything but sit here and pretend this is normal.

CHAPTER 36
GONE

Lochan

By the time the shack empties and the compound goes quiet after midnight, I'm back in my room. Window cracked. Thoughts still full of her.

Lucky doesn't knock. He just comes in, all momentum and familiar noise, like the rules loosen when it's him.

He smells like smoke and stale beer when he comes in, like the shack after last call when the music dies and everyone pretends they're walking out normal.

My brother has always been an easy smile, light on his feet, a guy people underestimate until they're on the ground. There's a violence in him that lives right next to the humor. Always has.

Two of his flanks wait outside the door, shadows shifting in the hall.

"I've got last watch," Lucky says matter of fact, like it's written into the night the same way the patrol routes are. "Far boundary. We'll be back before first light."

He glances at me. "You all good?"

Before I can answer, he's checking anyway, pulling open the closet, peering under the bed with exaggerated care, like he expects to find something ridiculous hiding there.

"Nothing under here," he says. "You sure?"

That gets a slow smile out of me.

It's been a while since anything has.

I stand and draw him in by the back of the neck, press our foreheads together the way we always have when words get in the way.

"See you in the morning," I say.

His loyalty makes me feel bare.

When he's gone, the room goes quiet again. I crack the window and let the cold air keep me honest. The house holds its air the way it holds its secrets, dry and controlled, muffling sound until even footsteps feel like an accusation.

I lie back down.

Winter's gaze flashes behind my lids. Hazel, steady, like a dare. Like she's still there, waiting to see what I do with what she pulled out of me.

I lie down fully dressed. I don't mean to sleep, I mean to blink. The cold from the open window keeps dragging me back to the surface until it doesn't.

Then my phone pings.

And again.

And again.

I'm on my feet before I read a word.

My body already knows.

Something is wrong.

I snatch the phone off the bedside table and the screen is too bright in the dark. Lucky's name. Three messages stacked, tight and clean.

Need you.

Now.

Far boundary. Ravine cut.

No question marks. No extra words.

That's how I know it's real.

I'm moving before my mind catches up. Shirt. Boots. Knife. The door is already open when I realize I didn't answer him.

I don't need to.

Lucky didn't text to ask.

Barry rises from the corner where he'd been sleeping, silent as breath, and falls in behind me. Or beside me. I don't look. I just feel the shift of him matching my pace.

I take the back route out. The one without cameras. The one the pack pretends doesn't exist because admitting it would mean admitting we built ways to move unseen.

The trees swallow me fast.

The night is thinner here, wind cutting through branches, the ground uneven under my feet. I move by memory, by instinct, by the simple truth that I have walked this land in every season of my life and it has never once felt unfamiliar until now.

Lucky's scent hits first.

Adrenaline. Iron. Something sharper underneath, a wrongness that has nothing to do with blood and everything to do with silence.

He's waiting at the edge of the cut, one flank posted behind him, the other off to my left, both too still. Not guarding.

Listening.

Lucky doesn't come toward me.

He just holds my eyes.

And in that half second, I understand: whatever he found, he didn't touch. Whatever he found, he didn't move. He's been standing between it and the rest of the world.

"Loch," he says.

Only that. My name like a hand at the back of my neck.

I step past him.

The ravine isn't dramatic. That's the problem. It looks like nothing until you're close enough to see how the earth gives way, how the ground slants and softens and lies to you. Leaf cover hides erosion. Roots snag. One wrong step turns the world sideways.

My flashlight beam sweeps across disturbed brush first. A torn branch. A scuff in the dirt where a shoe slid instead of lifted. The kind of mark you can only read if you've spent your life reading the ground.

Then the light catches fabric.

Pale.

A sleeve.

My stomach drops without making a sound.

I take one more step and stop, because my body refuses to be careless here, not even for a second.

Lucky stays behind me. He doesn't crowd. He doesn't narrate. That's his restraint. That's his loyalty.

The beam tracks lower.

Hair. Light catching. A hand at an angle that isn't natural.

And even before I see her face, before the name forms cleanly, I know.

Because the night is too still around her. Because the air feels held.

Because Jack is nowhere.

I crouch at the edge, careful. Not touching. Not changing anything. The flashlight shakes once in my grip and I steady it like that matters.

Catherine.

Her name lands in my skull like a strike.

Barry presses close, his presence a silent weight against my leg, like he's anchoring me to the moment so I don't float away from it.

I don't speak for a long beat.

Not prayer. Not shock. Not grief.

Just the cold, clean calculation that follows.

Lucky's voice is low behind me. "I didn't move her."

"I know," I say.

And the words that come next are not the ones a human would say.

Because I don't have time to be human.

I have time to be right.

I lift the light and sweep the area again, looking for what's missing as much as what's here.

No Jack.

No frantic trail back to campus.

No attempt at help.

No obvious drag line, only the off path choice, and the quietest kind of disaster.

I stand.

The world feels narrower.

My phone is still in my hand. The screen is dark again. I don't turn it on. I already know what time it is in my body. I know how close we are to first light. I know what changes when morning arrives.

Lucky watches me, waiting for orders.

The flanks don't move. They're holding their breath with the trees.

I look at Lucky. "Who knows?"

"Just us," he says. "Me, them." He jerks his head toward the two shadows at the edge of the treeline. "No one else."

Good.

Not because this is good.

Because it means we still have a window.

I step back from the ravine and force my lungs to take a full breath.

When this becomes official, the council will take control. They will name causes before they know them. They will assign blame before they've seen the ground. They will need a story that keeps the pack stable.

And Winter is tied to this the second Catherine's name becomes public.

If the council hears this first, they'll touch her second.

Roommates. Last known. Human optics. Convenient narrative.

I look at Lucky again, really look at him this time.

"Listen to me," I say. Not loud. Not sharp. Just exact.

He straightens a fraction. The flanks do too, without being told.

"You're holding this site until I say otherwise. No movement. No cleanup. No curiosity."

Lucky nods once.

"Mark the perimeter wide," I continue. "Farther than you think you need to. If anyone stumbles onto this by accident, you redirect. No explanations. You tell them it's a land slip and send them back the way they came."

His jaw tightens. "And if they don't listen?"

"They will," I say. "Because you won't give them a reason not to."

I glance back toward the ravine once, then force myself to look away.

"Phones stay dark. If the council calls, you don't answer. If Jack calls," I stop there, just long enough for the silence to say the rest. "You don't answer."

Lucky exhales through his nose, slow. "You want me to log anything?"

"No," I say immediately. "Nothing written. Nothing time stamped. You remember it. You remember everything. You say nothing until I'm standing next to you."

That lands.

This isn't delay.

This is defiance.

"How long?" he asks.

"Until dawn," I say. "Or until I come back. Whichever happens first."

Lucky studies my face, searching for the crack. He doesn't find one. He never does when it matters.

"And the flanks?" he asks.

"They stay with you," I say. "They don't leave this stretch. If someone else comes down this way, you call me first. Not the council. Not Rowan. Me."

That's the line. The one that changes things.

Lucky holds my gaze for a beat longer than protocol allows. Brother, not subordinate.

"Loch," he says carefully. "You know what this looks like."

"Yes," I say. "I do."

He nods then. Not easy. Not happy.

But solid.

"Okay," he says. "We hold."

I reach out and grip the back of his neck, brief and grounding. Not comfort. Confirmation.

"I'll come back for you," I say.

"I know," Lucky replies.

That's all either of us needs.

I turn away before I can give myself another second to weigh it. Barry moves with me, silent and sure.

Behind us, Lucky takes position at the edge of the ravine, flanks spreading into place like the night itself made room for them.

And for the first time since my phone woke me up, I feel the full weight of what I've just done move into my bones.

I didn't notify the council.

I didn't escalate.

I chose.

The bond tightens, not like a knot, but like something clicking shut.

I shift mid-run. Barry is with me. There's no room for human pacing, no room for careful.

By the time I slow, the compound is behind me and the night has begun to pale at the edges. Not dawn yet. Just the suggestion of it. The warning.

I shift back before I reach the outer paths, breath coming fast, pulse steadying as the world sharpens into angles and stone and rules again. Barry ghosts to my side, silent, alert. He doesn't question direction. He never does.

Winter's building rises ahead, dark except for a few scattered windows. Too quiet. Too still for the hour.

I check the time once, just to confirm what my body already knows.

We're close.

This is the last clean moment before the morning starts asking questions.

I don't take the stairs slowly. I don't pretend this is a social call. The building is quiet in the way places get right before morning, when night hasn't quite released its grip but no one is fully dreaming anymore.

Her door opens under my hand.

Winter is asleep.

Not deeply. I can tell by the way her breathing shifts the second I cross the threshold, as if her body already knows it's been joined by something else. The room smells faintly of cold air and detergent and her, a familiar presence that tightens the bond another notch without asking.

I don't touch her right away.

"Winter," I say, low.

Her eyes open almost immediately. No panic. No confusion. Just alertness sliding into place, as if she's been hovering near the surface for hours.

"We need to go," I say.

Something in his face looks unfinished, like he moved too fast to put the mask fully on.

She doesn't ask where. She doesn't ask why. She glances once at the room, at the life she's been occupying up until this second, and then she's moving. Shoes. Jacket. Phone in her hand like she already knows it's about to matter.

Barry steps back to give her space. His presence steadies her without her knowing why.

As we leave, I feel it, the exact moment the night slips past its point of forgiveness.

Somewhere else, people are going to wake up and notice what didn't return.

Somewhere else, the council is going to realize I moved without permission.

They will call it reckless.

They will call it insubordination.

They will call it betrayal.

They will not call it accidental.

I don't look back at the building. I don't look back at the path. The treehouse waits beyond the reach of official light, a place outside sequence and jurisdiction, where two people can speak before the world decides what they are.

Behind us, the night finally exhales.

Ahead of us, dawn sharpens its knives.

And I know, with a clarity that runs deep and unarguable, that whatever comes next I will answer for this choice.

But Winter will not answer alone.

CHAPTER 37

TAKE ME AWAY

Winter

I open my eyes because I can feel him.

Green eyes inches from mine. Steady. Unblinking. He isn't hovering. He isn't reaching. He's holding himself so still it looks like restraint has become a physical thing.

I should be scared.

Relief hits first, sharp and almost painful in how immediate it is.

"Winter," he says quietly.

My name tightens the air between us.

The room is dark except for a thin strip of hallway light slicing across the floor. It catches the edge of my desk, the chair, the open closet door.

And it catches the other side of the room.

Empty.

Not empty like someone stepped out to pee and will be back. Empty the way a room looks after it's been reset. Catherine's bed is made too tightly. The chair is pushed all the way in. Her lamp is unplugged. No jacket tossed over the back of anything. No shoe kicked half-off beneath the frame.

Catherine never left a room clean. She always left proof she existed. A lipstick. A charger. Something loud and careless.

The air is wrong without her, no perfume braided into detergent, no soft music leaking from one earbud, no restless shifting that means another body is still nearby.

Absence registers where sound should have been.

That's when Lochan's hand closes around my wrist. Not urgent. Not gentle. Just absolute.

"How did you," I start, and stop.

His gaze flicks once toward the door. Not impatient. Alert.

"We don't have time," he says. Not sharply. Not urgently. Just a fact.

My heart stutters, then finds a faster rhythm.

I sit up, fast enough that my ankle flares before dulling to a steady throb. His eyes drop to it immediately, then lift back to my face.

"You can run," he says.

It isn't a question.

"I can," I answer, just as quietly.

He exhales slowly through his nose like he's been holding that breath for a long time.

A sound in the hallway, soft and almost nothing. More presence than noise.

Lochan shifts half a step, just enough for me to see past him.

Barry sits at the end of the corridor, massive even in the low light, body angled toward the stairwell, ears up. He isn't looking at us. He's watching everything else.

Barry has never been here before.

The thought lands clean and cold.

"What happened?" I ask.

Lochan doesn't answer.

His jaw tightens like he's clamping down on a name he refuses to say out loud in this room.

"Shoes," he says.

That's when I know. Not because he explains. Not because he says Catherine. Because he doesn't.

I swing my legs over the edge of the bed. Cold floor. Shoes where I left them, toes pointed toward the door as if they were waiting. I don't reach for my phone. I don't reach for my bag. I don't look at the other side of the room again.

Lochan steps back to give me space, but not distance.

The bond hums low and steady between us, no panic, no demand. Just presence. Like gravity deciding where down is.

When I stand, he's there immediately, a hand hovering near my elbow without touching. I don't need help. I don't pull away either.

He watches my face like he's measuring whether I'll break.

"You trust me?" he asks.

The question is quiet. Bare.

I meet his eyes.

"Yes."

He nods once.

"Then we're leaving now."

Barry rises at the end of the hall without a sound. Lochan turns toward the stairs, then pauses and glances back at me.

Something softens in his expression, something human that looks almost like reverence.

"Stay with me," he says.

"I am," I answer.

And then we move.

We don't take the obvious exit. We don't take the lit path. Lochan keeps us in the seams, shadowed corridors, a service stairwell, a door that opens without hesitation like he's used it a hundred times.

Barry ghosts ahead, silent and sure.

Outside, campus air hits like a slap, cold and wet and awake. We cut across a strip of grass, then into the dark where the trees start to swallow the light.

The campus dies behind us.

The forest takes over.

Gravel softens. Dirt gives. The air turns damp and alive, pressing close like it recognizes him.

Only when the trees fully close around us does Lochan slow. Not because the forest demands it. Because he does.

He releases my wrist carefully, like setting something down that could break if handled wrong.

"Stay close," he says. Not a command. A courtesy.

I feel it before I see it, the shift in pressure. The way the night leans inward, attentive. Barry lifts his head. The forest stills.

Lochan doesn't look at me while it happens.

That is the mercy.

There is no violence in it. No spectacle. Just surrender so complete it feels older than fear, one shape giving way to another like truth finally allowed to surface.

When I exhale, the sound shakes.

And when I look again, the wolf is already there.

I wait for the part of me that knows how to run. The part that has kept me alive through seventeen beds and seventeen schools. The part that always knew when something wasn't safe.

It doesn't come.

What comes instead is recognition. The same thing I've been feeling since the bus crossed into Bradford, since the track, since the forest, since his arms. Just this. Just him.

He doesn't wait for me to react.

He turns and moves, and my body understands without being told where my place is.

He doesn't run away from me.

He runs with me.

Barry breaks forward into the trees. Quiet. Controlled. Enough.

Lochan stays close, circling just enough to keep himself between me and whatever the dark might decide. He angles his body where the ground is softest, the slope gentlest. He places himself like a shield without ever touching me.

It takes me a second to understand. They aren't leading me. They're running with me.

A corridor forms without words. Space opens where my feet land. Roots that would have caught me are already avoided. When I stumble, it's into absence, not obstruction.

I don't have to keep up. I just have to move forward.

My ankle answers me. Not perfectly, but honestly. Dull pain. Then heat. Not relief.

Function.

My breath finds a cadence that feels borrowed but familiar, like stepping into a song I haven't heard in years but somehow know the words to. Each step lands cleaner than the last. The forest stops testing me.

Barry runs wide and returns, a living boundary I don't have to think about. Lochan stays close enough that I feel the air shift when he changes pace, the subtle correction when the ground dips or narrows.

He never touches me. He doesn't need to.

I realize they aren't watching where I am.

They're watching where I'm going.

The trees thicken. Light disappears completely. Time stretches, then compresses. My lungs burn, then adapt. Sweat slicks my spine beneath my jacket, but my stride doesn't break.

Lochan flicks an ear back once. Not to check on me. To listen.

Whatever he hears doesn't slow him. He angles left, guiding us down a slope I wouldn't have chosen. The ground gives under my feet, forgiving, and when I slide, it's into control, not chaos. I follow without question.

We cross water. Cold shocks my ankles, sharp and clarifying, and then it's gone, swallowed by forward motion. On the far bank, Lochan slows just enough for me to recalibrate.

I'm not chasing them.

They're carrying me forward.

And then I feel it.

Not arrival. Not safety.

Absence.

The forest thins ahead, opening into a pocket of space that feels deliberately untouched. The air changes, heavier with resin and damp wood, quieter somehow, as if sound knows to behave here.

The structure resolves out of the dark without announcing itself, boards and beams emerging between the trees like they've always been there.

The treehouse doesn't look hidden.

It looks… forgotten.

Lochan slows, the run ending not where it must but where he wills it to.

He scans once, listening, confirming.

Then, without spectacle, he shifts back.

The wolf folds away like a shadow along a seam. Bone reorders. Weight changes. Breath catches and steadies.

Lochan stands there again. Human. Barefoot.

The clothes are there, stacked inside the treehouse like an old habit, like planning for exactly this. He pulls them on without looking at me, fast and controlled, as if his body is still too loud and he's forcing it into human shape by will alone.

He grips the ladder and climbs. At the top, he turns back, eyes intent.

"Come."

I don't hesitate.

I climb.

My hands shake. Cold, adrenaline, the run, it doesn't matter. The wood creaks beneath me, then holds.

Inside, the air smells like old sap and smoke and rain that never fully left. The space is small. Finite. Contained in a way my chest recognizes as relief before my mind catches up.

Lochan stands with his back half turned. Bare feet on wood. Skin flushed faintly from the shift, hair damp at the nape of his neck, curls darkened by mist.

I realize I'm staring. And I don't stop. Not because he's uncovered.

Because he is unhidden.

There's nothing defensive in the way he stands. No readiness to bolt. No need to check the door. The surrounding stillness isn't vigilance.

It's certainty.

And I understand, all at once, why this place isn't guarded.

It doesn't need to be.

Nothing comes here unless it's meant to.

Lochan steps closer, stopping just short of touching me. The space between us is charged, dense with everything we haven't said, everything we don't have language for yet.

"You're safe," he says. Not a promise. A statement.

I nod even though my body already knows it. The bond hums low and steady between us, not pulling, not demanding. Just present. It feels different here. Deeper. Like it's sunk into the grain of the wood and wrapped itself around us.

Barry shifts below, a soft thump that registers more awareness than sound.

Lochan's attention flicks outward for a heartbeat, then returns to me. When it does, his expression changes. The control is still there, but it's stretched thin now, translucent.

"You shouldn't have had to see it," he says quietly.

I know what he means.

"I'm glad I did," I answer.

His jaw tightens. He doesn't argue. He lifts one hand and braces it against the wall beside my shoulder, close but not trapping. Not touching. Just near enough that I can feel his heat.

The proximity is unbearable.

Not because I'm afraid.

Because I'm not.

The bond tightens, just enough to remind us it exists. Just enough to make every inch of space between us feel deliberate.

Outside, the forest settles around the treehouse, accepting the quiet the way it always has.

Inside, everything holds.

Neither of us moves.

Not yet.

Then I feel it again, the thing that's been happening to me, the thoughts that don't arrive like my thoughts. Not words. A repetition. A discipline so tight it borders on pain.

Keep her safe.

It pulses through him, over and over, like a vow being held shut in his chest. Not desire. Not fear. Control layered on control.

Lochan hasn't moved, but he is bracing. Containing.

I don't mean to speak.

The answer is already there when my mouth opens.

"I am safe now," I say quietly.

He looks at me then. Really looks.

Whatever he sees breaks him open. Disbelief first, then recognition sharp enough to still him completely.

His breath leaves him in a single, unguarded motion.

And then he goes down.

Not collapsing.

Not falling.

Kneeling.

Forehead to the wood. Hands braced at his sides. The posture unmistakable in its meaning.

Not submission as weakness.

Submission as truth.

And the forest answers him.

AUTHOR'S NOTE

Winter spends her whole life making herself small enough to survive. Lochan spends his whole life making himself invisible enough to lead. And then they find each other in the dark and neither of them can look away.

That's not a love story.

That is an awakening.

I hope this book made you feel seen.

— A.D. Gallo

ACKNOWLEDGMENTS

To the ones who sit with me in the silence while I live in my worlds, and wait patiently for me to return.

To the works of classic romantic literature that made me fall in love with books in the first place.

You are all in every page.

WHAT COMES NEXT

Part Wolf is Book One of The Bradford Wolves series.

Book Two: Part Queen is coming October 2026

Winter knows what she is now.

The compound knows it too.

A NOTE FROM
THE AUTHOR

Some stories don't end when you reach the last page.
If this one stayed with you, you don't have to leave it here.

Connect with me

WEBSITE: adgallo.com,

Amazon Profile: https://tinyurl.com/ADGalloAmazonProfile

Facebook: A.D. Gallo

Instagram @a.d.galloauthor

TikTok @adgallo.

9 7989 9 6 4 0 9 6 0 0